UNDERWAY

Good Times in Uncle Sam's Canoe Club

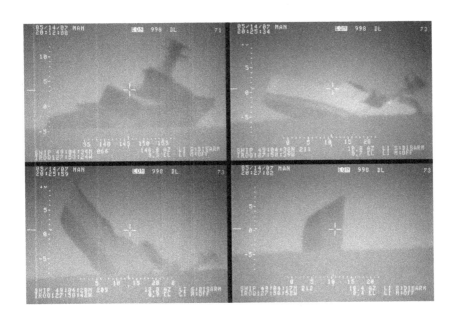

ERIC ATNO

As told by E. Dana Atwood

PAGE PUBLISHING, INC.
New York, NY

First originally published by Page Publishing, Inc. 2019

ISBN 978-1-68456-165-0 (Paperback)
ISBN 978-1-68456-166-7 (Digital)

Printed in the United States of America

Other works by ERIC ATNO

I dedicate this book to my father. He was a US Air Force pilot in the early 1950s. There was a "Police Action" happening at the time. It is known as the Korean Conflict or the Korean War. Some call it the Forgotten War. He never spoke of missions or things warfare-related. What he did was tell me stories of the crazy sons of bitches he served with. It really sounded like fun to me compared to high school. I was a horrible student; I hated school. The only thing I really cared about was surfing and, of course, girls. Going to college was not an option for me. I decided to visit the local navy recruiting office. I had to get the hell out of New Jersey. Hopefully, I would get stationed in San Diego, California, where I could do some real surfing. I liked the idea of wearing a uniform. I could get paid and eat free food. I was only seventeen years old, so my father had to sign the recruitment papers. I remember him asking me, "Are you sure this is what you want to do Ace?"

"Yeah, Dad, I think this will be fun."

"Okay," he said as he signed my young life away. "Good luck!" he said with a smile.

He told me years later that it was a very difficult moment for him and that he trusted me.

And so it began, the beginning of a twenty-six-year odyssey. With a mighty stroke of my father's pen, I was locked in to a four-year hitch in the US Navy. I guess you could say that I owe all my navy experiences and all the consequences, good and bad, to my father. I'm not sure whether to thank him or kick him in the nuts as hard as I can.

CONTENTS

TESTIMONIALS

"This book is awesome: You have tremendous perspective on your life, and the people around you. And a talent for feeling the story."

Achilles Perry, Eric's friend and lawyer.

"You write very well son. You tell a great sea story. It's just a little too raunchy"

W.J. Atno, Eric's father.

"No habla Ingles"

Esteban Reyes, Eric's gardener

AUTHOR'S NOTES

My name is E. Dana Atwood. The *E* is for Emmitt. I like the name Dana. It was my grandfather and great grandfather's name. It's been in my mother's family for many years. I don't know where the fuck Emmitt came from. My father's name is Winfield, as was his father's and his grandfather's. It was a family name that dated back to the Civil War. I guess my father figured naming a kid Winfield was just too cruel. Emmitt, however, was just cruel enough. Thank you for reading my book. I want to say a couple of things before we get underway.

This book is a novel. It is a fact that I spent twenty-six years wearing the cloth of this great nation. I was a proud member of what we wistfully refer to as "Uncle Sam's Canoe Club," or the US Navy. I took some artistic liberties with the names, timelines, and events contained herein. This was done mostly for reasons of continuity and interest to you, the reader. Therefore, this text should never be cited as anything historically valid. It is, by definition, a novel. The anecdotes and sea stories are mostly true. I couldn't make this shit up. Having said that, please accept the following waiver: If you are one of those naval or military historian assholes like me who are addicted to the History Channel, STOP! If you experience nausea watching navy-related shows or movies because of inaccurate historical content, STOP! If things such as incorrect timelines, incorrect uniforms or uniform items, and incorrect or inappropriate protocol as depicted on the screen make you want to throw something at it, *stop!* If you involuntarily cringe at the sheer stupidity of absurd Hollywood bullshit such as RADAR screens that beep and Jon Bon Jovi playing a chief petty officer, *stop reading this book now!* Most of the musings I am sharing are from my flawed and often alcohol-addled mind and memory. They are therefore subject to question. If you decide not to heed this warning/advice, I don't want to hear any bullshit from you regarding inaccurate content. It's a freakin' novel! How many times do I have to say it!

An old joke:

What's the difference between a sea story and a fairy tale?
A sea story starts with "This is a no-shitter."

An old quote:

The reason the American Navy does so well in
war is because war is chaos and the American
Navy practices chaos on a daily basis.
—Grand Admiral Karl Doenitz,
circa 1945

A definition:

Underway: a ship in motion: not at anchor or aground.

UNDERWAY 1

The Last Time Underway

The last time I got underway on a US Navy ship was horrendous. I was horribly hungover. We pulled out of Victoria, British Columbia, Canada. Actually, it was Esquimalt. They pronounce it *Es-Kwai-Malt*. We had a ton of live exercises and operations to conduct before we pulled into San Diego. The weather was brutal. Trust me on this: there is nothing worse than being hungover on a ship at sea when the weather sucks. There's no crying "Mommy." My fellow chief petty officers thought it would be fun to take me out for a last hurrah just to make sure I felt like a completely hammered dog shit in the morning. Lucky for me, I had removed myself from all responsibilities. I was a senior chief petty officer (E-8). I had two chief petty officers (E-7) and four first class petty officers (E-6) working for me in my division. With the fresh bouquet of Molsen Canadian on my breath, I told them I was done. I had anticipated this day and prepared the division leadership prior to getting underway. I was passing the torch, so to speak. I had removed myself from the watch bill. I was not to stand watch; I was not to draft any messages, evaluations, or award recommendations; I would be along for the ride; I would be a passenger. ✐

"You guys are in control." I told them that I would be easy to find if they needed guidance. At this point, I needed to drink a ton of water and sleep off this horrible illness that was manifesting between my ears and in my guts and bowels.

It was an extremely eventful couple of weeks underway. Air operations were seemingly nonstop. It was as if we were launching, recovering, or refueling a helicopter every hour or so. Small boat operations were another constant. The ship had to refuel at sea every other day. It was a tremendous amount of work. For the first time in my twenty-six-year career, I was able to step back and watch in silent awe at the way these young people went about their dangerous business. We actually sank a ship. The poor old HMCS (Her Majesty's Canadian Ship) *Huron* was rousted from mothballed slumber and towed out to the middle of the ocean and was designated a target for destruction. There were two Canadian ships and four US ships taking turns pumping whatever ordnance they had into this sad, lonely, and empty wretched, defenseless hulk. We even shot small arms and grenades into the poor thing.

The money shot was supposed to be from the submarine. The USS *Some City* (Jacksonville, Los Angeles Albuquerque, Houston, take your pick) was lurking beneath. The plan was that as soon as we "skimmers," or "targets," as the Bubble Heads (submariners) referred to the surface navy, were done punching holes in the abandoned ship, they would creep in and throw a MK-50 torpedo at the target and end the show. And what a show it would've been. The MK-50 torpedo is a horribly powerful and effective weapon. It doesn't slam in to the side of the ship like in the films *Das Boot* or *Run Silent, Run Deep*. Not even close. This modern torpedo travels directly beneath the target. Once the target is acquired by means of telemetry, SONAR, and/or magnetic sensors, the fire control system identifies the big hunk of metal above it as a target. The result is frightening. A tremendous explosion beneath the keel of the ship is powerful enough to create a vacuum that actually causes the ship to dip below sea level because of the low pressure created from the initial blast. This lasts for about a second. The ship sinks for an instant, and then the unimaginable explosion occurs. The poor hulk flies up in to the air. I pity anyone onboard. On the way down, it slams into the water and breaks in half. *Ooh! Aah! Thanks for coming folks, the show is over!*

The problem is that we skimmers put such a whoopin' on the *Huron*, the old gal just couldn't take anymore. The *HMCS Huron* sank with dignity, if there is such a thing. That's like getting kicked in the nuts with pride. I saw the whole thing. I watched a fossil from the Cold War going down to the bottom of the ocean. I couldn't help but feel that the ship and I had something in common. The submarine was so pissed at us for sinking the target, they went deep and headed west without saying a word. Fuck them. It was fun sinking a ship. My apologies and respect go out to any of our Canadian friends and allies who were connected to the HMCS *Huron.*

Now it was back to business. We had more shit to do. I had removed myself from being a senior chief, and it was time for me to witness the Grand Ballet being performed. As I watched the events unfold before me, I thought to myself, "Goddamned, these young people are good!" What I was most proud of was that they were doing this insane job with humor. They were working long and hard hours. Sure, they would bitch a little, but they could still laugh and bust each other's balls. I like to think that I had something to do with that. I had learned from the best. There will be more on that later.

At one point, another feeling or emotion slapped me in the face like I was a redheaded stepchild; it occurred to me that I, too, was obsolete. Just like the *HMCS Huron.* I realized that I wasn't needed anymore. This crew and the United States Navy are doing just fine without me. Was it because of all the sage wisdom I had shared over the years? No, it wasn't. We just had the smartest and most competitive young people in the history of our all-volunteer armed forces. It wasn't that way when my father signed those papers in 1982. Things had changed and evolved. I realized that it was for the better. It was now my time to "punch out."

There was a time when I was so delusional that I actually thought that the navy needed me. I foolishly thought that I had to be there to train, mentor, and be that amazingly smart and capable leader that the navy and this country needed to take care of any threat and keep the world safe. One look around me on this ship that day was enough for me to realize that that idea was pure folly. This big machine, the United States Navy, would keep on chugging, keep on rolling just fine without yours truly. That epiphany kind of hit me in the gut. It was a real ego-blower to realize that the vacuum created by my departure would be absorbed in mere seconds.

This was a time of retrospection. I thought about where I came from. How I got here. I analyzed the journey, the people, or the "crazy sons of bitches," as my father would say, not to mention the rare experiences among other things. I thought about and honored those who had come before me, as was our charge, according to the Chief Petty Officer's Creed. I wondered how I was still alive after all the shit I had done, seen, and gotten away with. Most of all, I felt so proud of the sailors busting their asses and laughing at the same time. My mentor would call it the "thin blue line" that ran through all of us. I think that meant that all our actions and inactions, our lessons learned, mostly the hard way, kept going down the line. Our leadership styles and experiences trickled down to the next young sailor and so on. I realized a long time ago the importance of this ethos. It's hard to explain, but it helped me through my time in the navy. I'll try to tell you about it. It was quite a journey. Now, I was having a strange feeling that I was now having that was completely alien to me. I think it was called self-pity, maybe even the verge of depression.

I looked out at the beautiful angry blue Pacific. So much salt water has passed under my keel. I went down to the chief's mess to see what was on the TV. I settled in for a few minutes, watching an old episode of *South Park*. It was one of the ones with Timmy (*Timay!*) when the word was passed over the general announcing system or 1MC. "Senior Chief Petty Officer Atwood, your presence is requested in the pilot house." Hmmm, that's interesting. "Your presence is requested" usually meant that it was not an emergency, but you should get to the bridge or pilot house as soon as you could without busting your ass because the captain would like to talk to you. On the other hand, if you hear your name followed by "Bridge" or "Lay to the bridge," that meant pinch it off, wipe it, zip it up, and run to the bridge *now!*

I figured that the captain, or "pocket captain," as some would refer to her, wanted to talk to me. We called her that because she was tiny in stature; however, she was strong and powerful in her position. It could not have been an easy assignment for a five-foot-four-inch woman to be in command of all this testosterone and just two other females. It was an interesting dynamic. I thought she merely wanted to have a departure chat with me. You know, tell me how great and important I had been. *I wish you were coming on deployment with us. The ship won't be the same without you blah, blah, blah…* I soon found out that it was not the case.

When I got to the bridge, I was greeted by a smiling captain. Pleasantries were exchanged. And then she got down to business. "I received a message from the commodore that he wants to do a maneuvering exercise this afternoon."

"Okay, let's do it. It'll be fun."

"The problem I have, Senior, is that I don't trust my junior officers."

"I don't trust them either, but you're the skipper." I was pushing my position, but I had nothing to gain or lose. "What about the Canookies?" Meaning the Canadians. "He's cutting them loose." A tactical signal came over the radio. It was the old Tango Alpha 88-tack-9—there's more to it, but it basically meant "You are detached, proceed on duties assigned."

"So it's just us? Piece of cake! Bring it on." This was the last gasp of an outdated man who thought he may be vital one last time.

"I don't remember seeing this on the SOE," I mentioned casually.

"It's not on the schedule of events, Senior, this just happened."

That's when I realized that I was the person she was relying on in this circumstance. Holy crap! Was this a gift from the my-pussy-was-just-hurting gods?

"Okay, Skip, your call."

"Bos'n assemble all junior officers not actually on watch in the pilot house please."

"Yes, ma'am!" The word was passed over the 1MC general announcing system throughout the entire ship, and in less than a minute, I was surrounded by ensigns and lieutenants junior grade. The captain knew what was going on before I did. That may be why she was the captain.

"You have to teach these people about tactical maneuvering at sea. Like, now."

"Okay, how much time do we have?"

"Well. It's 1436, he wants to kick it off at 1500."

This was when she asked to speak to me on the bridge wing. We stepped outside. The fresh air felt good. I was sure I still smelled bad.

"These kids don't know what the fuck they are doing, Senior," said the serious captain as she watched the pilot house or bridge fill with fresh-faced junior officers.

"Such language, my captain." I was once again flaunting my short-time attitude. I was smiling. The look on her face erased my smile. She rephrased, "These young naval officers of the line don't know what the fuck they are doing."

"Of course, they don't, they're JOs and they're dumb by definition." I was pushing it now. I could tell that she was not pleased. I decided to kick it down a notch. "What can I do, Captain?" We were still on the bridge wing. The sea had calmed down considerably. You could always tell by the color of the ocean. If it was a pretty blue, it should be a good ride. Dark blue or gray could be unpredictable, which was bad. Black was the worst. Anything with foam on top made it dangerous. Right now, it was a little dark but getting bluer, so that was a good thing.

"You have to give a crash course on tactical maneuvering."

"I'm guessing to…them?" I said, pointing to the absurdly young and inexperienced pale-faced and clueless officers who had assembled on the bridge when beckoned.

"That's right, Senior, *them*. Like it or not, they are our future leaders."

"Now I know why I am retiring."

Once again, my attempt at humor was met with an icy stare. But I could sense a little smile trying to emerge. She really meant business. No more smartass, which was not always easy for me. This was actually pretty serious.

"It's your basic maneuvering exercise. We've done it a million times, but they haven't." The captain nodded her head toward the pilot house where the junior officers were nervously assembled.

"Senior Chief, I need your help."

"No problem, Captain. I've got this. I'll take care of it."

Before I stepped from the bridge wing into the pilot house, the captain actually grabbed me by the shoulder and said to me, "I trust you, Senior Chief. All military protocol is out the window. Just keep my ship safe. And, oh, please do *not* make us look stupid."

"Like I said, Captain, I've got it." I immediately turned my attention to the pasty-faced knuckleheads on the bridge. They were all looking at me for guidance. Guidance they were about to get.

I was on. "Good morning—or afternoon—I guess, to you good people. We all know each other, and I'm sure we all respect each other. The captain has given me positional authority to lead a shortly upcoming maneuvering exercise from this bridge. In other words, I am in charge up here. Time is critical. Safety of the ship is paramount. You will do what I tell you. Please forgive any departure from standard military procedures and protocol. The language will be terse and most likely a bit salty. You must deal with that for the duration of the exercise. Do what I say, and we will get through this safely. Most importantly, we won't look stupid!"

"Do you understand?" I wasn't yelling at them, I was yelling near them. I wanted to make a point, and I was getting a little nervous.

"Who went to the academy?" I asked, perhaps to assuage the tension on the bridge. This interrogative was met with a meager two out of eleven. You can always tell a boat-schooler simply by yelling "Go, Navy!" Because of the catechism they received at Annapolis, they were trained to reply, "Beat Army!" Try it sometime; it's kind of fun.

"Where did you go to school?" I got a smattering of Northwestern, Cornell, and Notre Dame. I think I even heard a Brandeis. I thought that was strange. I didn't think Brandeis produced any military officers.

"Did they teach you about tactical maneuvering?"

One of them chirped up and said something inane and stupid. He was either an engineer or a lawyer because he didn't answer the question. He may have been the Brandeis guy. They didn't know shit. The clock was ticking. I now had twenty-four minutes to teach these clowns what took me two weeks in school to really understand. Twenty minutes! "Listen to me! You will do exactly as I say from now until the end of this exercise. I want you to understand that this is the REAL WORLD. You sorry sons of bitches [I sort of stole a line from General Patton] are responsible for maneuvering properly and, most of all, safely. Once again, we will NOT LOOK STUPID! Do you understand me?"

"Yes, Senior Chief!" I was eating this shit up. I glanced over to the captain as she pretended to read message traffic. I knew that she was subtly monitoring all the activity on her bridge. "All of you will be prepared to write. There will be signals in the air and everyone writes down the signal." I had a thought. I couldn't trust these knuckleheads, so I called Radio Central and made sure that the correct circuit was patched into the bridge and down in the Combat Information Center (CIC). "Where is the signal book?" I was met by blank stares. "ATP-1! Goddammit! What do they teach you idiots in school?" I was pushing my limits, but now I needed to get the job done, keep the ship safe, and not look stupid. I had my orders.

The captain didn't blink. I was on my own. I didn't have time to be nice. It was time to go old school on their asses. "Listen to me! All of you. Here is how this will go down. You will be on the scope." I pointed to Ensign Shitbag. "Your job is to keep track of all of the ships we are sailing with. There are only four of them, so it shouldn't be hard. One of them will be the guide, probably the carrier. That's where the commodore, who is running this show, is currently residing."

I looked around on the shelf where the Allied Tactical Publication governing maneuvering usually was kept. I found it. Then I asked, "Where are the call signs?" Blank stares. I was getting tired of blank stares. Holy shit, really? I got on the bitch box. That's a direct line from the bridge to CIC. "Combat, Senior Chief. Get the fucking call signs up here now!" Internally, I was basking in my power and self-importance. I still had to keep the ship safe and make sure we did not look stupid.

"Okay. *You* test the circuit. You are the radio talker. Got it?" Deer in the headlights. "You push the button and speak in to the handset. Are you really officers in *my* navy? Lieutenant Numb-nuts [I actually used his real name], you are on the maneuvering board." (Or the Mo-Board or Chart 5090, as we would call it.)

"I think I saw one of these in OCS." He sounded like such a goober.

"Yeah, well, this isn't OCS, son, this is the real world."

"It's about relative motion, people. Do you understand that?" More retarded looks. "As I said, the Carrier will probably be the guide. There will be a signal directing us to take position on the guide. Remember, it's all relative. Ensign Clueless here will plot our position relative to the guide, and we will figure out what course and speed we have to do to get to the correct position *relative* to the guide. We will also calculate the time it will take, when we will be on station, and where the guide will be when we are at 'Alpha Station,' AKA, where we are supposed to be. It's not that hard, folks. There are three factors: time, speed, and distance. Any two gets you the third. You got it?" There were more blank stares that were more distressing than the last ones.

"Holy shit! Are you people officers of the line or what? You need to nut up right now!" I made another quick glance to the captain. She was stoic as usual. She trusted me. This event was totally on me. Of course, she was ultimately responsible. But she basically gave me her ship.

"It will probably start with a line abreast. That means that we all line up next to each other. You have to pay attention to the order of our positions. That will come with the signal. We have to plot the guide's position and then the position where we are to occupy. Then we will calculate that position using this maneuvering board. Remember that it is all relative." I think the word *relative* is what screwed with their heads. I totally understood. I spent two weeks in Dam Neck, Virginia, until it finally clicked. "Listen, the guide is there, we need to go there." I said this while pointing at the Mo Board. "Remember that we are all moving across the planet, so you can't just go to that spot. It's like a quarterback in a football game. He doesn't just throw the ball to where the receiver is but where he's gonna be! Do you get it?" Allah be praised! I finally saw a light bulb or two go off. "What time is it?" It was 1500. "Shit, here we go."

Right on time, the signal was in the air. I heard the Fleet Tactical radio circuit make a crackling noise. That meant someone had pushed the transmit button and was about to speak. A signal would be in the air. "Write this shit down, all of you!"

"All stations, Charlie Five Bravo, this is Charlie Five Bravo, execute to follow." Form One (every ship's call sign in the order they were to proceed was transmitted over the radio), followed by "over." Dang, I was wrong. Instead of a line abreast, he called for a column. No problem. Adapt and overcome.

I looked at LTJG Goofball whom I assigned radio duty. "Wait your turn and roger out. Do you know how to do that, son?"

"I think so. I'll try, Senior Chief."

I gave him a look that I think genuinely scared him. "Try not. Do or do not. There is no try." My brilliant Yodaism was lost on these children, but the captain got a chuckle out of it.

When it was our turn to roger up, he pressed the Transmit button and said, "Alpha seven Papa, roger out."

"Good job. Now let's figure out where we have to go. Mark the guide! Where are we from the guide? Plot us on the reciprocal position. Where do we have to go? What is the course and speed? Okay, you morons, this is how we do it." I showed them how to figure out the basic line of relative movement to station. We knew our stationing speed (Sierra Speed), so we could calculate our relative speed to station. Figuring the time was easy.

"Any two gets you the third, folks. Time, speed, and/or distance are all we need. This isn't brain science or rocket surgery." Some more light bulbs went off during this phase of demonstration and training. Perhaps the junior officers weren't as dumb as I thought. They actually caught on. It was a challenge, but they learned how to compute course and speed to station, time to station, and the bearing and range to the guide when on station.

The radio crackled again. "All stations, Charlie Five Bravo, this is Charlie Five Bravo, Form One. Stand by, execute, over." It was time to roger up once again in turn. We did this successfully, and the stress level decreased a little bit. We maneuvered to station success-fully after a little bit of chaos. The captain seemed relieved.

Things got smoother as the exercise unfolded, and things started to click. We turned and wheeled to port and starboard. We calculated the course, speed, and time to station. Eventually we were in a line abreast with five hundred yards separating each ship. I knew the money shot was coming up. The good old Corpen Sierra or "Search Turn." The formation was in a line abreast, side by side cutting through the water at twelve knots. One by one, each ship would make a 90-degree turn, and all ships would be in another line abreast again pointing in another direction. It was a tricky and often screwed up maneuver. I knew this would be our biggest challenge. I've seen a ship or two screw this up, and they looked pretty stupid. I knew exactly what my captain meant. If you were a seagull looking down on our formation, you would see the ships slicing through the ocean side by side. Luckily, we were the outside ship or the farthest from the guide. That meant that we would go to the new course as soon as the signal was executed. We would turn toward the forma-tion, but they kept steaming until the next ship made the turn and found them next to us. But this time, they were on the other side. It went down the line until all ships were once again in a line abreast in reverse order. I told you it was difficult. It took me years to master this one. I had twenty-four minutes!

We did it correctly. We made it through the whole exercise, and I was exhausted. The ship was safe, and we didn't look stupid. The captain was very happy. She took me aside and thanked me. I took the compliment and said, "Skip, I want to thank *you*. Just when I was feeling sorry for myself, you gave me a lovely parting gift. You set me up for success. It was a challenge, but honestly, it was fun. I'm ready to go home now. I wish you the best in your career. You're a good leader, and I appreciate that." I was done. I went out on a high note. I went out on top.

That was the last day I spent underway in the US Navy. I retired from the navy a month after we pulled in to San Diego.

UNDERWAY 2

The First Underway

I will never forget the first time I got underway on a US Navy ship. It was early May of 1983. The ship was the USS *Callaghan* (DDG-994). The place was San Diego, California. That was by design. I will explain later. I arrived on pier 2 with one Seaman Recruit William M Portman Jr. He and I had competed in our trade school in Dam Neck, Virginia. I finished number one in the class; he was number three. Both of us chose this magnificent ship in San Diego. He wanted to be in the same time zone as his family. I just wanted to surf in San Diego.

We both looked at this amazing machine parked at pier 2, Naval Station, San Diego. There was an interesting story behind the ship, our new ship. She, the *Callaghan*, was originally commissioned by the Shah of Iran along with three others. There were four ships total. The idea was for Iran to be the dominant naval force in the Persian Gulf, North Arabian Sea, and Indian Ocean. It was a good plan, and it would've worked. Unfortunately, the Ayatollah Khomeini had other plans. In 1979, a force of Islamic fundamentalists and disillusioned (okay, I know that's subjective; objection sustained) students overthrew the shah and the government. They had their reasons. They took a bunch of hostages. We all know this. It was a mess. Meanwhile, down in Pascagoula, Mississippi, there were four really nice brand-new and paid-for ships. The US Navy jumped on this opportunity, and they were named *Kidd* (DDG-993), *Callaghan*

(DDG-994), *Scott* (DDG-995), and *Chandler* (DDG-996). They were all named after dead guys. The DD meant it was a Destroyer. The G meant that it had guided missile capability. It was a very cool ship. Portman and I were awestruck when we finally got to pier 2 at the Naval Station and were able to look at our new home.

Portman and I had a little bit of history. We were in the same class in Operations Specialist Class "A" school in Dam Neck, Virginia. We had also gone through boot camp together. Boot camp was a joke. You learned how to march. You learned how to fold your underwear and make your rack. If you kept your mouth shut and did exactly what you were told, you were good. Just like Forrest Gump. "Because you told me to, Drill Sargent!" After boot camp, it was time for trade school. We both, Portman and I, flew to Virginia to learn how to be operations specialists. We got to Dam Neck, which was a stinking sewer swamp-ass hellhole. The next day, we were training to be RADAR operators, or "Scope Dopes," radio operators, log keepers, navigators, and button pushers. On day one, we were told that we could choose our duty station based on class rank. That meant whoever finished first got to pick first. That was all I had to hear. For the first time in my life, I became a good student.

The competition was on. I had to beat twenty-two guys, including Portman. I was hell-bent on being stationed in San Diego. I went to night study every night. Most of my competitors would be out in town or at the club on base. Occasionally, I would bowl a few games at the bowling alley on base and enjoy a tall Old Milwaukee or five. I was too young to go out in town and drink. I shifted my focus. I was determined to finish number one. About halfway through the training, it was clear that I was the guy to beat. No one was going to surpass me. I was not going to let that happen. Portman was right behind me. So was Dave Goodson. We all wanted a California posting.

Goodson was a lot like me. He was a kid from suburban New Jersey. He had the accent and the attitude. Portman, on the other hand, was a creature I had never been exposed to. He was from Pocatello, Idaho. He loved shooting mammals such as elk and deer. He would also slaughter a wild turkey if given the chance. He was a big kid. He was at least six feet and two hundred pounds. He was pretty smart. He had a big chest, big arms, a big head, and a big mouth. He was very cocky and hated the fact that I beat him in "A" school. Hey, it's hard to beat 98.86 percent. Our adversarial relationship was just beginning. He finished number three. He was on my ass. It was a view he would have to get used to for the rest of our careers.

Operations Specialist class "A" school lasted thirteen weeks. At week ten, we were able to pick our duty stations or billets. The instructor, a first class petty operations specialist petty officer named OS1 Mitchell had a list on a clipboard. I was dying to see what was available, especially since I had first pick. He read them off. There were ships in Norfolk, Virginia; Mayport, Florida; Yokosuka, Japan; Long Beach; and, thankfully, San Diego, California.

It turned out that there were several available California billets. The Battleship New Jersey needed a young operations specialist. Dave Goodson requested a side bar with me and asked that I not take the Jersey so he could grab it. A battle wagon wasn't really my style, not that I had a style yet, but I thought I was more the Destroyer type. A "Tin Can Man." There were other options. Then I saw it. USS *Callaghan* (DDG-994), San Diego California. There were actually two billets on the *Callaghan*. I chose one of them. After Dave snapped up the New Jersey, to my amazement, Portman selected the other *Callaghan* billet.

Dave was happy with the New Jersey. After graduation, Portman and I packed our sea bags and headed out to San Diego. When we arrived at Lindberg Field, we split a cab to the Naval Station, pier two. So here we were at the 32nd Street Naval Station in San Diego looking at what would be our home for the next few years of our lives. We were met by OS3 Jamie Baier. He was very nice and friendly and relieved much of our tension. He introduced us to the guys in the division. They seemed like nice normal guys for the most part. I would soon learn that was not necessarily the case—the normal part anyway.

We three began the check in process. We actually had a paper checklist in our hands. We had to see about fifteen people. There was the security guy, the admin and money people. There was the chief of the mess decks, who was glad to see us. We met our division officer and the operations officer or department head. We had to meet the executive officer who was a bit terse but businesslike and somewhat friendly. It seemed as though he felt that he had something better to do. We were both calming down a little. We spent about two minutes with the commanding officer. That was a bit intimidating.

Of course, Portman, being the loudmouth that he was, wasted no time in talking too much. I wanted to tell him to "SHUT THE FUCK UP!" I just kept my mouth shut and moved on.

OS3 James Arthur Baier was a great guide. He was very kind and welcoming. He treated us with respect and humor. I could tell right off the bat that he was as gay as the day was long. We're talking three-dollar bill here. I didn't care. The big redneck wasn't so understanding.

"I think he's a fucking fag!" he said to me.

"Yeah, so what? He's our shipmate now. Get over yourself, you mouth-breathing moron."

"So you're a fag lover?"

"No, you idiot, I just want to get through this, and I don't need your help to fuck this up. I can do that on my own."

The next stop was the chief's mess. Now I was really nervous. The officers didn't scare me that much. The senior enlisted, the chiefs, made me a little nervous. I don't really know why. Jamie seemed to pick up on this, and in a brotherly way, he said, "Don't worry, guys. Our chief is super cool. He's a great guy. He takes good care of all of us. In case you haven't figured it out yet, you want the chief in your court. In other words, if you don't piss him off, your life on this ship will be easy."

Chief Simons was the coolest dude I had ever met. He greeted us with a big smile and a handshake. I could tell right away that he was the real deal. By that I mean that he looked you in the eye. He told us exactly was he expected from us. He also told us that he would make sure that we had the most time off while in port, and that he would do everything he could for us.

"I see that one of you was an honor grad at Dam Neck. They sent us a letter."

"That was me, Chief," I said.

Portman's face was turning red.

"How about you, Mr. Portman?"

"I finished third, Chief."

"Well, look at you, guys. It is a privilege to welcome you to our division. Now listen to me. All I ask is that you show up on time. You will be properly groomed and in the proper uniform. Do you guys understand?"

"Yes, Chief," we said in unison.

For the most part, I kept my mouth shut and only spoke when I was spoken to. Portman did not. There is an old saying in the navy: "You don't get a second chance to make a first impression." I was witnessing a big-mouthed redneck knucklehead spouting off and digging his own grave. He even went as far to say that his poker skills were superior to anyone on the ship.

"Just keep your mouth shut," I said to myself. "I'm number one, and he was number three, and they all know this."

He wouldn't shut up. "Do I have to live on the ship? How long will we be at sea? Do I get to use the phone? Am I allowed to go to Mexico? Is gambling illegal? Who does the laundry?" All reasonable questions, I guess, but this wasn't the time for them. I was just glad to be on this very cool ship.

Jamie Baier magically appeared right on time and took us out of there. While I hadn't been afraid to meet the division officer or department head or the XO or captain, I knew at that moment that I better not piss off my chief. I liked him right away. I felt that we got off to a good start. I soon learned that if he, Chief Simons, liked or respected you, he might call you "Stain." Whether it was a shit stain, mustard stain, or cum stain was unknown. Conversely, if he didn't like you at the moment, or was pissed off at you, you may be referred to as "Bag." As in shitbag, dirtbag, scumbag? It's anyone's guess. I'm was just glad that I was always a "stain." I was given a rack and a locker and prepared for my first underway by getting a good night's sleep in air-conditioned splendor. I was looking forward to going out to sea in the morning.

That was the day the first day that I really felt I was in the navy.

UNDERWAY 3

The First Underway 2

I woke up bright and early and had a nice big breakfast on the ship. I thought it was pretty good. At morning quarters, that's when the divisions all meet, muster was taken, and the plan of the day was shared. Portman and I were the new guys, so we were introduced to the division. After quarters, Chief Simons said since Portman and I weren't on the watch bill yet, we may want to go top side and "watch San Diego go by," as he put it. I took him up on that. We sailed under the Coronado Bridge. We passed downtown, made a left near the airport and another couple of lefts at Harbor and Shelter islands. Now it was a straight shot to the open ocean. I stood there in awe and amazement of the power of this machine. It truly was a spectacular unit. It was 563 feet in length and 55 feet across. It was 9,600 tons of American steel. That it could easily cut through the water at thirty-plus knots was truly impressive. Once we cleared Point Loma, we made a full power run. Holy shit! This great big ship seemed to start flying. Maybe that illusion was created because the main engines were General Electric LM-2500s. There were four of them, and it sounded like a DC-10 taking off because it was the same engine as the DC-10. I was standing on the flight deck and just taking it all in. As all four engines, both shafts and propellers, kicked in to high gear, it kicked up a ten-foot rooster tail. It was a wave big enough to surf on. I felt so proud to be in uniform aboard this beautiful, powerful ship.

Let's go on a virtual tour of the ship's deck equipment and weapons, shall we? On the main deck up forward is the forecastle or fo'c'stle (pronounced foke-sul). On the very tip of the fo'c'stle or the pointy end is the bullnose. That's where one of the mooring lines is fed to tie the ship to the pier. There are also chocks bitts and cleats that are there for the same function. There are two standard navy stockless anchors up forward at 9,600 pounds apiece. They are attached to a couple hundred feet of anchor chain with a very large and powerful motor called an anchor windlass, which will haul the two anchors up when needed. A little farther aft is the forward vertical replenishment or vertrep station. That is basically a drop zone for helicopters to deliver supplies. Then there is a five-inch .54-caliber gun referred to as Mount 51. It can fire a five-inch projectile of various applications (high explosive, proximity fuse, illumination) upwards of thirty miles. The last weapon on the fo'c'stle you will see is the MK-26 guided missile launcher. It has two rails that can launch the standard surface to air missile or SM-1, or Anti-Submarine Rockets or ASROC. The SM-1 is guided by the fire control RADAR, at Mach 2.4, and can nail a target at fifty miles or so. The ASROC is basically a MK-46 torpedo with a rocket on its ass that can deliver a weapon to a target in about a ten-mile radius.

As we head back aft, there are different kinds of deck equipment, including a motor whale boat and the captain's gig. We will pass by various bitts, cleats, and davits. As we emerge from the windbreak, there is another MK-26 missile launcher. Let's go down the ladder to the helo hangar and flight deck. All the way aft is the second gun mount or Mount 52. The other main weapons systems are a few decks up. There are two defensive systems on the 0-4 level fore and aft. These are the Phalanx Close-In Weapons System or CIWS (see-whizz). It is a self-contained tracking and engagement system with a six-barreled Gatling gun that throws three thousand rounds of 20-mm depleted uranium per minute, that's fifty rounds per second, at an incoming or threatening target. Directly amidships on the 0-3 level, there are eight Harpoon missile tubes. The Harpoon is a surface launch cruise missile (SLCM). It is programmed prior to launch by the team in CIC. It is a "fire and forget" weapon. In other words, once you hit the button and send this sub-sonic unit toward its intended target, there is no way to stop it. The ship has a very impressive array of offensive and defensive weaponry.

I was so happy to be considered a shipmate to these great American sailors aboard this fascinating machine. I felt, I felt...I felt kind of sick. Oh no! I couldn't be the new seasick guy. These guys would be merciless. But the ship was bobbing up and down and rocking gently side to side. At first, it was calm and comforting. After a few hours, the inner ear and human physiology started to make me want to puke. I fought it. I remembered all the blue-fishing trips with my dad and brother off the New Jersey coast. Now I had to not embarrass them and not be the puking guy. It's always hard. I knew that no one would feel sorry for me. I was in the big leagues now. I found Portman, and he was feeling the same thing. I could tell he was ready to barf. I didn't show my hand. He was a much better poker player, but this was real life.

It was time to join the division up in the combat information center or CIC. CIC is where all the tactical information from the ship's various sensors are gathered, processed, displayed, evaluated, and disseminated. It's where an OS makes his money. It's a large dark room full of electronic equipment. Writer Kurt Kalbfleisch calls CIC the "blue light lounge" in his hilarious, frank, and somewhat tragic verse. On this day, it was a buzz of activity. We were in the wide open ocean, nobody around for many miles. Our job was to find a submarine. Not just any submarine, but a specific US submarine pretending to be a Soviet boat. We had anti-submarine aircraft at our disposal. They would drop hundreds of sonobuoys in the water in various patterns. A P-3C Orion could cover a significant volume of the sea. Not just the ocean surface, but in all three dimensions. These devices were "spit" out of the aircraft and gently entered the ocean with the help of a small parachute. The hydrophones could be deployed at varying depths and listen to what may be lying below the surface, hopefully a submarine. Some of them could also go active or "ping," sending a noise signal into the water, hoping for a return echo. If a sonobuoy got a "sniff," the game was on. Think about a hungry pit bull and two German shepherds. Throw in a dachshund and a couple of Welsh corgis. Picture them with the scent of blood in their snouts. They are ravenous. That's what happens when we get a SONAR contact.

OS2 Harry Hancock was at the Dead Reckoning Tracer or DRT. The DRT was a true geographic plot of the ship's movement and whatever was happening in our little part of the world. It all had to be manually plotted. If done so correctly, it was a great decision-making tool for the leadership. They could look at the plot and decide where to send the aircraft, where to drop buoys, and where to go and kill the sub. By the way, this just in, we almost never killed the sub. The sub almost always won.

The air was crackling with radio traffic. The RADAR screens were spinning. There was a bunch of ASW aircraft buzzing about, fixed wing, and helicopters, or rotary wing. It was rather exciting. I was standing aside and keeping my mouth shut when I heard OS2 Hancock say, "Hey, new guy." Meaning me or Portman. I was hoping it was the latter. "Come over here and plot on the DRT." As seasick as I was, I eagerly took over the plot. "They taught you this in A school, right?"

"Yes, I've got it." It turned out I kind of had it. There was one very important little thing that was not passed down to me prior to taking the ruler and the plot. They had been plotting on the scale of five thousand yards to the inch. During training, it was always two thousand yards per inch. I never even thought that it could or would be on a different scale. I didn't know shit. My marks and plotting were way off. Hancock quickly realized this. To his credit, he took full responsibility, and thanks to the meticulous and accurate log of our position and marks/plots, he quickly unscrewed all that I had screwed up.

I felt about four inches tall after the XO had a full-blown hissy fit and summarily fired me on the spot. Portman was loving this. I had fucked up so badly on my first day on the ship. I thought I would be forever known as the DRT plot fucker-upper.

In short order, we were once again hunting the submarine. I was so involved in my personal woes that I forgot I was seasick. Portman wasn't so lucky. As he was taking joy in my failure, he was turning green with small beads of sweat on his upper lip and forehead. With all the entertainment, he, too, had forgotten that he wanted to puke. Now, the show was over, and puke he did. He blew chunks all over the DRT. Henceforth, he was Portman the Puker or, even better, Pukeman.

The crazy thing was that Portman joined the navy five days before I did. Although we had the same rank, that of an E-2 or Seaman Apprentice, he was five days senior to me. This would come in to play when the ship or division needed a body or a swinging dick to do something stupid or nasty. If it came down to the two new guys, he had me by five days. So I got stuck with some shitty jobs like hauling out wet garbage, sweeping and swabbing this or that. There was always scrubbing the head and showers. We all had to do these tasks, but I would always go before Portman. Five stupid days! That would change.

After the DRT mishap, it was time for dinner and to get some rest. I was told that I would be standing the mid-watch from midnight to 0630. After dinner, I was exhausted. I crawled in to my new digs and passed out hard.

It seemed as though five minutes passed when I was awakened by the messenger at 2300 to get ready to relieve the watch. I swear I had just put my head on the pillow.

That was the day I experienced real navy operations underway and felt like I was a part of something bigger than me.

UNDERWAY 4

The First Underway 3

We eventually settled in with the division. What a collection of lunatics. They were from all over. The Midwest, the South, the New York Tri-State Area, Alaska, you name it. There were a lot of personalities, lots of cocks and balls and body odor residing less than a foot from each other. We were underway a lot. I got over the seasick thing. We would work what's called port and starboard watches. That meant you were on watch for six hours and then off for six hours. This would go on for days on end.

So what was a watch? Well, the ship was cutting through the ocean at various courses and speeds. Our job, among other things was to avoid and stay away from other vessels and shipping. The six-hour watch consisted of endless hours of watching a RADAR screen. The name of that watch-stand position was Surface Tracker. The Surface Tracker would sit at the console and watch the SPS-55 surface search RADAR spin around and around on the scope. When a contact was detected, the Surface Tracker would watch or "track" that contact and report it to the bridge and the watch team. It was always hard to stay awake. The surface tracker would have the port, starboard, and aft lookouts on the internal sound-powered phone circuit called the 1JL and had to coordinate and confirm RADAR contacts with visual confirmation from the lookouts. To stay awake, there were endless trivia contests, name that tunes, made-up sex stories, anything to try to stay awake while tracking RADAR contacts.

We called the contacts "skunks." We would report these odoriferous units to the bridge. That's where they drove the ship. They didn't like to bump into things.

We would take turns maintaining an accurate navigation picture on the chart just to back up the bridge. "I think we are here. Where do *you* think we are?" An hour was spent on the bridge as the mouthpiece of things going on below in CIC. It could be an important job if things got a little hectic, which they often were in the 1980s. We would recommend certain tactics or behavior: "Combat recommends course 270 at present speed to avoid Skunk Charlie by five thousand yards in fourteen minutes." The Bridge Talker needed to be involved and engaged with all surroundings to keep the ship safe. We used the maneuvering board to supply this information.

Depending on what was going on, there was usually a radio circuit that needed a warm body to log all the traffic and answer, or "roger up," if called. You would usually spend an hour or so as the messenger or gofer. It was a nice break. If the watch team wanted sodas, you were the guy. We would rotate through these positions for six hours. When the watch was over, you got relieved by a bunch of guys who would then spend the next six hours of their lives in a dark, noisy, cigarette-smoke-filled room. The messenger also woke up the oncoming watch team.

There were many hours and days on end of boredom. There were endless drills and exercises. The training never ended. Every once and a while, it got interesting. If the weather got rough or something caught on fire, that would get your attention.

We were working up to the ship's (and my) first deployment to the Western Pacific. There are a series of hoops that a ship and crew must jump through in order to be able to deploy. These were mostly done underway. The guns needed to be shot, the missiles and torpedoes launched. All systems had to be fully operational. That included the engines, the generators, the air-conditioning, the water making, and of course, the sewage systems.

There were some in port items that needed to be checked off the list. For example, everyone in the crew must attend the live firefighting training on the naval base. Since Portman and I had just checked on board, we were assigned to the next available class. It was a three-day school. Most of it was basic firefighting knowledge; the different types of fires and which firefighting agents and systems were used were covered. The students would practice with all the portable equipment.

It got challenging during the actual live firefighting exercises. They had a couple of thick-walled cinder-block buildings with no windows. The instructors would heap a pile of wooden pallets in the middle of the space that was designed to resemble a berthing area. They would then douse the combustibles with JP-5 jet fuel and light it on fire. They would let it burn for a while. They'd wait until it was at the peak of lethal heat and smokiness. The students were given the very basic firefighting outerwear and ordered to grab a hose, enter the space properly, practicing something we had learned in class, and fight the fire. The heat was so intense, it rendered one almost immediately useless. It was impossible to see anything in the smoke. You felt the fire more than you could see it. There were about five to ten guys on the hose. Being the number one nozzleman was nothing short of brutal. Your job was to direct the spray of the hose at the fire that you can't see.

Breathing was another issue. It was impossible. Fortunately, there was a lot of air coming out of the nozzle that was breathable. The problem was the heat. You couldn't take a deep breath because of the intense heat. Your nostrils would burn if you took too deep a breath. I hate to think what would happen to your lungs, so the only way to survive was to stick your nose right up to the tip of the nozzle and take fast tiny, little breaths.

The problem was when you did that to breathe so you could survive, you couldn't see the fire you were trying to fight. You couldn't stay up front for very long. Every few seconds, it was time to "relieve the nozzleman!" After that phrase was announced by the instructors, it was time for the procedure we had practiced to move forward on the hose so the next poor bastard in line could take over. The nozzleman would then gladly go to the back of the line. This madness was repeated until the fire was out and overhauled. That meant breaking apart anything smoldering with a metal rake and water. You wanted to avoid a reflash.

My least favorite was the engine room or bilge fire. Again, a cement building simulating an engine space was filled with fuel and ignited. This time, we were equipped with an oxygen-breathing apparatus, or OBA, a strap-on device with a mask, airbags, and hoses. There was a disposable cartridge that changed the carbon dioxide in your breath into breathable oxygen. The OBA didn't stop or in any way abate the horrendous heat. The engine room fire was maybe the closest I had ever come to pure panic. It was not fun. I hoped I never had to fight a fire on a ship. As Mr. Mackey of South Park Elementary would say, "Fire is bad, m'kay?" I was relieved when firefighting school was over. I would rather be underway.

True to his word, Chief Simons got us as much time off as possible. When we were in port, we took full advantage of it. We would pack a cooler full of beer, go to the beach at the Naval Air Station in Coronado, and play volleyball. I would always bring a surfboard. Chief let me stow a board behind the consoles up in CIC. I just had to remove it prior to any inspections. I had some friends from my little hometown of Normandy Beach, New Jersey, who rented a garage in La Jolla. They were surfers, of course. They would let me use their shower and crash on their couch from time to time. I bought a motorcycle, so I wasn't completely dependent for a ride. I was in San Diego, according to my plan. I was happy.

Time in port was fun. I got to know the guys better, and I was fitting in nicely. One of my favorite guys was a Southern California nutcase in the division named Tom Towers AKA Double-T. He had another dubious nickname.

UNDERWAY 5

Captain Cockblock

Thomas Edward Towers was an interesting piece of work. He was a Southern California dude from Woodland Hills, California, with a car that had surfboard racks. He had many skills, and he was actually a very good operations specialist. He was becoming a bit of a legend in our circles. He actually got busted for smoking dope, and he convinced the captain that the navy was not doing enough to show him the right way. The captain agreed and sent him to rehab, earning him the moniker of "Silver-Tongued Towers" or "Double T." He also went by the more dubious name of "Captain Cockblock." I will explain the genesis of the moniker Captain Cockblock.

One night, I was sitting in the Enlisted Club with a couple of the guys. I was only eighteen years old, so I couldn't go out in town and drink legally in California. If I wanted to drink some beers, I had to go to the club, where there was always a group of fat chicks. I'm sorry, that is judgmental and a bit douchy, but it's true. Well, naturally, cock and balls being what they are, I would approach these ladies if they decided to give me the time of day. They would usually allow me to buy them a drink or two. Maybe it was three. Okay, four. Shit, now I'm almost out of money! Once I was in the middle of this silly do-si-do, and in walks Double T.

"Oh shit, here comes Captain Cockblock," says Portman. He immediately owned the room. He was the center of attention in our little group. Everybody loved this guy. I knew that he'd probably ruin whatever chances I may have had with this bevy of rotund West-Pac Widows.

Double T had this gift for creating and making up names out of the blue. We would be somewhere, and he would introduce us as Nelson Strongunit and Stargell Lowercase. Sometimes he would go the Nick at Night route and we would be Larry Tate and Darrin Stevens. There was Fielding Ambrose, Stanley Bagadonuts. It was kind of hilarious. The names went on and on. The problem for me was that I could never remember what my name was. I would have to grab him aside and say, "Who am I again?"

"You're Sheraton Whitesides, dumb-ass, now don't fuck this up."

I always fucked it up. I would spend all my money on girls who didn't know my real name. I was kicking myself in the nuts for being so lame.

He had another unique talent that led to his nickname, Captain Cockblock. He loved to sabotage any sort of progress that any of us were making with the females by saying outrageous and completely inappropriate things. But first, he would lure the unsuspecting victim in with his charms. On this particular night, when I had *my* bevy of chubby West-Pac widows, one unsuspecting young lady was totally enrapt. One might describe it as swooning. She had long since forgotten about me and shifted her attention to Tommy T. I looked over at Portman, and we all shared a knowing look. We knew the ax would be coming down soon. I might as well stick around for the show.

Captain Cockblock was working his magic. Female XYZ was smiling and laughing at all the right times. I knew we we're getting close to the money shot. He moved in a little closer. It was almost unnoticeable, but the heat was rising. In his best movie star voice, he quietly said to her, "You know what I would really like to do?"

"Ooh no, I don't, please tell me," she said with a girlish giggle.

Here it comes, folks. What would come out of his mouth this time? He waited the perfect amount of time. He took a sip of his beer. He looked left, he looked right, and leaned in even closer one last time.

"I'd really like to tongue-punch your fart-box."

There it was folks, bombs away! This was my favorite part. She and her friends had that classic look of amazed denial. Her mouth said, "What did you just say?" And her eyes said, *I know exactly what this asshole just said.*

He dutifully repeated the unusual request. "I really want to tongue-punch your fart-box." As predicted, the indignant disgust and anger kicked in with the girls, and the herd noisily departed the premises in a defiant mass snit.

This was where I tried to be pissed, but I couldn't. I started laughing uncontrollably. "I want to tongue-punch your fart-box?" I said incredulously. "Captain Cockblock strikes again."

I was out of money. My balls were bluer than a US Air Force uniform. My buzz was rapidly fading. Without missing a beat or even laughing, Double T said, "C'mon, let's get in my car and go somewhere."

Okay, sure, why not? I had no idea where we were going. We left the navy base and headed to North Park. He parked his Datsun 240Z in front of a corner sports bar named Tuba-Man's.

I said, "Tommy, I can't go in there, they'll throw me out."

"We're not going there, we're going here." He pointed to the building on his right, just over my shoulder. The neon sign said, "Asian Oriental Spa, Massage."

"Okay," I said, and we walked on in.

Of course, they knew him. "Tommy T, how you?" beamed the Mama-San.

"She knows your real name?" I asked.

He hugged the Mama-San and whispered something in her ear. She asked me, "You want massage?"

"Okay, sure" was the obvious response.

Tommy said, "Go enjoy, this one is on me."

"Thanks, I think." I was still pretty young and just a tiny bit innocent. I wasn't really sure what was going on, but I had a pretty good idea. I was led in to a dark little room. I lay down on the massage table and was stripped of my clothes. A lovely young Asian lady rubbed me down and then jacked me off. The old "rub and tug."

It was time to leave. Double T paid the bill just like he said he would. "Isn't that better than chasing hogs at the club?"

A rhetorical question indeed. I could barely stand on my wobbling knees. "Yeah, I am much better. Who am I again?"

UNDERWAY 6

Mess Cranking and West-Pac

The first few months on the *Callaghan* were mostly spent underway. We were still working up to our deployment. It was watch standing six hours on and six hours off, and manning the same positions and doing the same tasks over and over until you got relieved. It is hard to overemphasize how important relieving the watch is. Especially relieving the watch *on time*. Sailors could put up with a lot of shit, but relieving the watch late was death. You could lie, cheat, steal his money, hell, you can even fuck his wife, just don't be late for watch!

We were still the new guys. Good ole Portman would neglect to wake me for watch from time to time when it was his turn to do wake-ups. This led to me being late on more than one occasion. I was starting to get dirty looks and maybe even a little reputation as the "late guy." The fat-headed prick from Pocatello was setting me up for failure. I would tell him that he didn't wake me up. He would insist he did.

"Then why is there no problem when someone else does wake-ups? I'm telling you that you didn't wake me up!"

He lied and said he did, and I assured him that I would really enjoy pissing on his grave. Our leading petty officer or LPO had a hunch about what was going on and talked to the chief. From then on, everybody got a wake-up nudge and would initial a logbook to document that nudge. After this policy was implemented, I was never late for watch again.

The watches continued. So did the refueling and replenishment. Underway replenishment, or UNREP, happened just about every two or three days. Other than launching and recovering aircraft from the deck of a ship, it was maybe the most inherently dangerous thing that we did at sea. A giant fast combat support ship or oiler would be at a set location on a known course and speed. Our ship would then maneuver using radar, a maneuvering board and pencil, and what we called "Seaman's Eye." We would make our approach to this monster and get as close as 150 feet or so. Once we were established on station alongside the oiler, a tiny red shot line would be sent over by an M-14 rifle. That line was called the messenger. Now it was time to "heave around," which meant pulling with all of your tired might on the lines to eventually get a wire across the span and pull the refueling gear down the cable. Being so junior, I was always out there heaving around. We did this at all hours of the day and night. The sea state and the weather did not matter. It could be cold and rainy, the ocean could be nice and calm or rough as shit, it didn't matter. It was always dangerous.

We were a few days away from leaving on the first deployment when Portman and I were told at morning quarters that we would be reporting to supply and S-2 division for the next ninety days. Every new sailor had to do the ninety-day tour of the galley and mess decks. The army calls it kitchen patrol or KP duty. The navy calls it mess cooking or mess cranking. This activity made you a mess cook or a mess crank. The official term is food service assistance (FSA). That too was very hard work, especially underway. You're up before the crew to set up for breakfast. You get to serve breakfast and then clean up. Then it was time to make the salads for lunch, set up the line, serve lunch, and then clean up. After a little bit of rest, the routine was repeated for dinner. And then we cleaned up.

The galley was where they cook and serve the food. The mess decks were where the food was consumed. In the chief's mess and the officer's ward room, the food was served restaurant-style. The scullery was where the trays, plates, and silverware were cleaned. I think I pretty much made the whole tour during my ninety days. One of the good things was that you were not assigned an in-port duty section, so you didn't have to stay on board every third night and stand a watch. So when we pulled into port and our work was done, we could be gone for the night.

We were going on West-Pac. That meant lots of time underway. The pitch and roll of the ship didn't bother me now. Unless, of course, I was hungover. This happened a lot. Although I was not of legal age in the States, my shipmates were usually willing to contribute to my delinquency. That didn't matter now because our first stop was Hawaii, where the drinking age was eighteen. It would be a lovely excursion to the Western Pacific. We would now sail across the ocean and make stops so we could deposit whatever money we had and some of our semen and DNA. These places included the Philippines, South Korea, Singapore, Thailand, Japan, and a few other strange places. Hawaii was fun. I wangled a day off and rented a surfboard just to say that I surfed Hawaii. I learned where the cheap happy hours were so I wouldn't spend all my money in the first hour in port.

The other places were very different indeed. Subic Bay, Philippines / Olongapo City had been described as Adult Disneyland. If you had a brother, father, cousin, or uncle in the navy who went to the Philippines, all the stories are true. When you walked out the main gate, you were greeted by an array of strip bars, ladies' bars, shops, and restaurants that were rivalled by no other place in the uncivilized world. It was officially named Magsaysay Boulevard. There was every kind of bar entertainment that you could imagine. There were rock-and-roll clubs, country/western clubs, disco clubs, you name it. The bands in these places were scary talented. They played all kinds of American music, and they played it perfectly. The amazing thing was they didn't speak or read English or music! They did it all phonetically, the music and the vocals. Sometimes you could hear a hint of an accent, but the guitars and drums were note-for-note perfect.

Of course, there were women in just about every establishment. The place was teeming with small brown women that we ruthlessly referred to as LBFMs or Little Brown Fucking Machines. In my defense, I was, as we used to say, "young, dumb, and full of cum."

I couldn't help myself. I was an eighteen-year-old kid. I was out at sea with three hundred other swinging dicks for weeks at a time. In Subic, beers cost about a nickel. If an LBFM grabbed my joint in a bar, the game was over. It was back to an unbelievably tacky and sleazy roomlet in the rear of the bar for a quickie. Or, as they would refer to it, "short time." I would bang these little women and blow a load in about 9.765 seconds. Done! And then I would feel like the world's biggest loser.

I never splurged for the overnighter, or "long time," lest I die of self-loathing. I invented the word IPOD based on these experiences long before the Apple Company produced a product of the same name. I thought about suing Steve Jobs, but counsel advised against that action, saying something about no proof or some such legal-ese hogwash. IPOD is an acronym for Instantaneous Post Orgasmic Disgust. It's that powerful feeling that you just did something awful and needed to put your pants on and run as fast as you can in any direction. I'm not even Catholic, but the feeling of self-shame was unbearable, until my dick inevitably got hard again, and I found another LBFM.

UNDERWAY 7

Trouble in the Galley

The drudgery in the galley continued. The ubiquitous task of feeding and cleaning up after three hundred hungry douchebags could be a challenge, especially when the ship was pitching and rolling all over the surface of the ocean. The pots, pans, trays, food, and water were flying around. The deck was usually slick with cooking grease and sweat, so it could be exhausting and dangerous just to complete a simple task like gripping an empty metal food service tray, taking it to the sink for cleaning, and filling up a new one. Just doing so without slipping, falling, busting your ass, or dumping a tray of food was, to say at the least, challenging.

The galley tsar was a fiery flyweight of a senior chief mess management specialist named Bombay. He was a frail-looking, slight Filipino who looked like he could be snapped in half like a twig. Looks, as they said, could be deceiving. He was strong of body and even stronger in spirit. He may have been the hardest working man on the ship. He was in the galley before our sorry asses showed up in the morning, and he was the last to leave after the dinner was cleaned up. He ran a tight galley. Despite his small frame, he was a powerhouse and respected by all hands. He knew we were working hard. He worked as hard as we did. He was fair. As long as the work was done to his satisfaction, he would try to get us off the ship as much as possible. He knew how to manage people and manpower. This was especially welcome in port.

One day we were in Singapore, and all the chores were done. The senior chief cut us loose. We were allowed to go out on the town and do whatever we wanted. We just had to make sure we were back in the galley to set up the galley for breakfast in the morning. One of the good things about mess cranking was the social aspect of the experience. You met guys from other divisions and departments from all over the USA that you normally wouldn't come across during everyday operations. Not to mention you were all junior and going through the whole experience together at the same level.

One day in Singapore, it was me and Portman and a couple of the young guys from engineering. The four of us went out and did what we did best. We found a British pub and tried to drink all the beer in the place until we ran out of money, which, of course, was exactly what happened. We barely had enough Singapore dollars scraped together to get a cab back to the boat landing to catch a liberty boat back to the ship, which was anchored in the harbor. It was well after midnight when we got aboard our destroyer. One of us decided we were hungry and that breaking in to the galley would be a good idea. "Hey, we work there, right?" What a brilliant idea!

One of us, I can't remember who, crawled through the window of the scullery. That's where the crew dumped off their postmeal trays for cleaning. Once inside, like Tom Cruise in *Mission Impossible*, he managed to access the galley spaces and let the rest of us idiots in. As you may know, drunks are never as quiet as they think they are. We were soon slicing ham, breaking out bread, pickles, and who knew what else from the refrigerators. We were laughing and having a grand old time of it in the dark when the brutal bright fluorescent lights abruptly came on and temporarily blinded us all.

Of course standing there was Senior Chief Bombay. He was in uniform with his tiny, little brown fingers angrily grasping his twenty-six-inch hips. He did *not* look happy. "What you do in my galley?" This was answered by silence. The question was repeated as if we didn't hear it the first time. More silence followed. There may have been a few head-down shrugs and maybe a lame and barely audible "I don't know."

It was flashback time. I was thirteen years old and standing in front of my angry father after he busted me for foolishly stealing a six-pack of Gibbons beer, and my only defense was a sheepish "I don't know."

This was a real buzz-killer. We were totally busted. Our fledgling careers were over before they got started. This man could have our nuts removed, sautéed, and served to the crew in a lovely lemon and basil demi-glaze. "Why you break in my galley?" He was so angry I thought his eyes would pop out of his head. "Why? Why you break in my galley!"

One of the engineers, I think it was Miller, said, "I guess we were hungry, Senior Chief." He sounded like a beaten puppy. We were all just staring at the deck in silence.

"Who broke in?" Which one? Which one of you?" At that point in the interrogation, Portman broke. He silently looked at me and gave the angry Filipino an accusatory nod in my direction. He might as well had signed an affidavit right there. Bombay accepted the tacit clue as a virtual point of the finger. Then he lit in to me.

"Goddammit, At! You break in my galley! Goddammit, At!"

At this point of the tirade, Robby Browne nutted up with a voice that was almost manly and said, "Senior Chief, we all broke into your galley."

Bombay got quiet and seemed to calm down a little. He must have been silently contemplating what to do with our sorry dumb young asses. After what seemed an eternity, he calmly said, "You go wait on mess decks."

We did as we were told. We four nud-niks sat there contemplating how badly we were going to get hammered for this ill-thought-out stunt. I was shooting daggers at Portman. That fucker had thrown me under the Greyhound again. I could see the transmission, tires, and oil stains as I lay on my back under the bus.

It was now after three in the morning or 0300. I swore to myself again that I would piss on his grave, and I told him so. After an uncomfortable hour, Senior Chief Bombay entered the mess decks with two full trays of hot food that he had prepared. He cooked eggs, bacon, sausages. He made toast and brought out fresh fruit. There was much-needed juice as we were significantly dehydrated after the ordeal.

"You hungry? You eat! Then clean up and get ready for breakfast. You no break in my galley again."

Did that just happen? Did we four idiots just dodge a very large and lethal bullet? Did we just get an eleventh-hour stay of execution from the judge, jury, executioner, and governor? It appeared that we had. Once we realized we may be free men like Andy Dufresne escaping Shawshank, we scarfed down every bit of the food that our savior had graciously provided us. We were all amazed, humbled, and thankful.

Portman had the big brass polished balls to say to me with a big smile, "Looks like we got away with that one."

"I'm still gonna piss on your grave, you asshole."

Which he returned with the innocent "What did I do?" look.

"You know what you did. And so do the other guys," I said like a shipmate who had just been betrayed.

Senior Chief Bombay could have ruined us, but he chose not to. He chose to feed us instead. Why? Perhaps he knew that four beat-up, angry, unmotivated, and unproductive employees would not be best for his mission. Maybe he just thought that we needed and maybe even deserved a second chance. As a result, we four reborn knucklehead sailors worked our asses off. It was our way of saying thank you, our penitence, our atonement. Needless to say, we never broke into the galley again. I realized that day that sometimes the great power in power is not to use it. That was the day I got a great lesson in leadership.

UNDERWAY 8

Refugees

"Without food and water, there was no way to survive." I saw that on the cover of a *Time* magazine. There was a picture of a whole bunch of people stuffed onto small boats. The big headline on the cover read, "The plight of the Boat People."

I was on my way to the beach one day to check the Jersey surf. I didn't really care about the Boat People or any other people for that matter. All I cared about was the condition of the beach and ocean. *Are there waves or not? Is the sun shining? Which way is the wind blowing? Will there be girls on the beach?*

Fast forward one year. We were sailing all around the South China Sea. It was the summer of 1983. The sea was mercifully calm, flat even. It was a beautiful deep blue color. It was also very hot. So hot, in fact, that the uniform of the day was a clean white T-shirt and navy-issued khaki shorts. I was still mess cranking but getting close to my parole date. When I had a break from the galley, I would usually go up to CIC to see what was going on. I also liked to show my face to let my shipmates and leadership know that I was still alive and eager to rejoin the division.

I was up there one day, and there was a lot of activity on the radio. A bunch of different radio circuits were blaring. I found Chief Simons. "What's going on, Chief?"

"There have been reports of refuges in the area about thirty miles from here."

"What kind of refugees?" I asked him.

"They're Vietnamese. They were once officially South Vietnamese, but it didn't work out."

I thought about that for a second and then I remembered the Time magazine cover. "Are they Boat People?"

"That's right, Boat People."

"So what do we do if we find them, Chief?"

"We rescue them, son."

"Yeah, but then what?"

"Well, we feed them, give them clothes and water, and take them somewhere safe."

The shipboard helicopter was about to be launched to find the reported contacts of interest. The call for "Flight Quarters" was announced over the general announcing system.

"I've got some work to do, Atwood. And from my experience, you do too." He went to his air control console and began the mission.

I had no idea what he meant, but I would soon find out. I stayed in CIC for a little while. The helo confirmed contact with three small vessels packed with people. The ship then kicked it into high gear in their direction. We soon had shipboard RADAR contacts on three small vessels that were where they really shouldn't be. This was not a known fishing ground, and it was dangerously close to the international shipping lanes. We slowly approached the first of the floating hellholes. All hands were called to divisional quarters. Everybody was assigned work to do. Senior Chief Bombay immediately put us to work to help prepare chicken and rice gruel and tons of water. The deck crew deployed a system to transfer the people onto our ship. Once they were all aboard, the gunner's mates sank the piece-of-shit boats with .50-caliber machine guns and grenades.

I went topside, and what I saw astounded, scared, saddened, and humbled me all at once. The people were crying and begging for help. Of course, we had taken them all aboard. They were of all ages, but mostly either very old or very young. That struck me as strange. I realized later that men of military age were being summarily murdered in this part of the world. They were all filthy dirty. They were hungry and thirsty. These once proud people were stripped of their clothing and dignity.

They were cleaned with some concoction that the chief corpsman had brewed. Despite these humiliations, they managed to find their pride. There was a clothing drive afoot driven by the supply officer. I donated all my T-shirts and some other stuff: socks, underwear, uniform articles, whatever I could spare. All hands contributed. Hats were a big hit. These poor, humble, scared human beings were very appreciative. They were all interviewed. Most of them spoke English.

These people were not rice patty peasants or lay people; they were people of some means at one time. Some were college professors. Others were doctors, nurses, and midlevel government folks. They were the basic middle class of what was once South Vietnam. They were treated like criminals by the forces of the north. Their crime? Living in South Vietnam and being friendly to the United States of America. Most of them had spent time in prison or "re-education camps." They spoke of the exodus.

I remember watching Operation Frequent Wind on the six o'clock news with Walter Cronkite. That was required watching in our house. It seemed as if a vacuum was sucking up the desperate and, as it turned out, the lucky ones. Who could forget the footage of the helicopters landing on the roof of the US embassy, overpacked with people and taking off? Or the news footage of navy deck crews pushing aircraft overboard to make room for all the inbound helos?

The ones left behind had it rough. They did whatever they could to get the hell out of there. The vacuum was still sucking, but the US was not cleaning up anymore. There were so many people trying to escape, hundreds of thousands of them. One brave lady said, "If the streetlamps and street signs had legs, they would run away too!"

They knew they had to get out of there by whatever means. That's the part that amazed me. It was hard for me to imagine how life could be so horrible that you and whatever family was still alive could get into a piece-of-shit boat and go out into the black night on a black sea and hope that something better happens. They were boarded by pirates who stole their money and raped the women. They stole their meager supplies of food and water. As a result, many of the weakest, some of the oldest and youngest, had died during the ordeal. Their bodies were thrown overboard. I realized the horrors that they had been through, especially the little kids. It was far worse than any kid from New Jersey or anyone else on the ship had ever seen or experienced.

To put things into a little more recent perspective, I read years later that by 1985, the United Nations High Commissioner for Refugees (UNHCR) estimated that between 200,000 and 400,000 had perished at sea trying to gain their freedom. To put it in a little more recent perspective, the UNHCR has estimated that more than 30,000 Syrian, Libyan, and other refugees have tried to cross the Mediterranean Sea, with around 1,000 casualties. I'm certainly not saying that one cause or world event is more important than another; comparing tragedies is unproductive and illogical. But in that moment, when I saw these people with my limited life experience, I began to see the world differently. I guess you can call it an epiphany. I'm not nor had I ever been a religious person, but I had just discovered a new respect for humanity in myself. If these people were that desperate, then I was on their team!

We cooked, prepared and slopped out the chicken and rice gruel three times a day for a week. Of course, it was all driven by Senior Chief Bombay. We set up a make-shift living area under the aft gun mount, or mount 52, and built two port-a-type-potties. They still smiled and thanked me when they received their thrice daily swill. I was getting exhausted by the end of the week. We made it to Manila Bay. All the refugees were transferred to two Philippine Coast Guard vessels for processing. After breaking down and cleaning up the makeshift camp, I jumped in my rack for some much-needed sleep. The chaplain was talking on the 1MC or general announcing system. It sounded like your basic bunch of holy bullshit. Right before I passed out cold, I heard him say, "Blessed are those who give and expect nothing in return."

You're goddamned right, I thought.

The ship and crew were awarded the Navy Humanitarian Service Medal for our actions. That was the day I became part of the human race.

UNDERWAY 9

The Equator and Points North

After we dispatched the boat people near the Philippines, we headed south. The plan was to cross the equator. This involved the silliness of the Crossing the Line ceremony. It was a matter of very well-documented public record what went on while going from pollywog to shellback, so I will not waste any time on it.

We were independently steaming. This was a good thing, especially when you pulled into a port. You don't have a jillion guys from all the other ships competing for whatever that particular city had to offer. My mess cranking days had come to an end. I was now back with my real division. It felt good. Portman and I were back in the watch rotation, and underway business went on as normal. Six hours on and six hours off. Much of the on-time was painfully boring. Of course, there were constant drills, including but not limited to man overboard, abandon ship, general quarter or battle stations, and others. We would try to stay awake at night with trivia contests over our communications circuit.

Perhaps my father was some sort of prescient visionary because he sent me a book of trivia. It was like an almanac of useless information. It was a gold mine. I would sit at the surface RADAR console and hold court. I insisted the lookouts and bridge talker refer to me as Alex, as in Trebek. Of course, we spoke of other depraved things. We would see who could come up with the most terms for human male genitalia (cock, pecker, wang, ding-dong, purple-headed warrior of love, etc.), female genitalia (pussy, beaver, snatch, snapper, slime-socket, and what have you). And of course, the human sex act (banging, humping, pumping, laying pipe, knocking the bottom out of it, and others). Other than made-up sex stories, eating, sleeping, and refueling, this was how we passed the time.

We were on our way to South Korea by way of Japan. It was summer, and the South China Sea was flat as a pancake. At night, it looked like a shopping mall parking lot because of all the fishing boats. They shone bright white lights on the ocean to attract the fish. It looked like there were thousands of them, so we had to keep on our toes and keep a sharp eye on the scope. For some reason, there was a lot of phosphorescence or bioluminescence in the water in this part of the world. As a result, when we were steaming at night and kicking up a wake or disturbing or roiling the surface of the water, the ship's wake, which was normally white, turned a bright green like the green of those plastic Chem-lites. It was like a rave party underwater. It looked pretty cool.

Our first stop was Kagashima. Kagashima is a small city on the southernmost tip of Japan's southernmost main island of Kyushu. Kyushu is the same island that is also home to Nagasaki and Sasebo, among other cities. It's a beautiful little town. I met a girl there.

I didn't even want to go out that night. I didn't have any money. Brubaker and Coffman pretty much dragged me off the ship. We had to ride in a liberty boat because the ship was anchored out in the harbor. We wound up at a place, a dance club, called the American Club, imagine that. When you walked in, you paid a cover charge. I don't remember how much it was because Brubaker paid for me. Cover charge paid, you were awarded with a bottle of Japanese Scotch whiskey. (As Bill Murray said in the movie *Lost in Translation*, "For the good times, Suntory times.") I know that "Japanese Scotch" sounds like an oxymoron or juxtaposition, but bear with me. There were glasses and ice on a counter or bar area. If you wanted to mix your hootch, there were vending machines with every kind of mixer you could imagine. You could have whiskey and Coke, whiskey and water, whiskey and iced tea, whiskey and grape soda, whiskey and whiskey, whatever you wanted.

I saw Naoko. She was beautiful. She looked like a little doll. She had perfect skin and perfect hair. Her smile made me weak in the knees. I was in love, and I hadn't even spoken a word to her. I said to Coffman, "My god that girl is beautiful! Look how cute she is."

And then, so very uncharacteristic of Bob, a guy who could barely speak to his friends and was a mute savant around females, said to me, "Go talk to her."

I did just that. She spoke Japanese, English, Russian, and four Chinese dialects. She was eighteen years old. She was an artist and a violin and piano player. That's just overachieving, if you ask me. We danced and drank and had a fun night. I walked her home at the end of the night and gave her a kiss. At one point, I asked her what her father did for a living. Her answer was, "He sells guns." Okeydoke, let's not meet Papa-San. We traded mailing addresses. I told her I would write to her, and of course, I did. She always wrote back. After that, every time we pulled in to a Japanese port, she would take a train and meet me. It was in Nagasaki that we had sex for the first time. It was her first time and very special. Alas it was time to get underway again. The South China Sea was calling. Our job was to maintain a powerful presence and keep the shipping lanes open and free. This included some time in the Yellow Sea, the body of water between Japan and Korea. It also included a port visit to Pusan, South Korea.

UNDERWAY 10

Korea

We pulled into a nasty little port city called Pusan, Korea. Mayweather and I got off the ship and jumped into the first cab that we could find.

"Take us to beer," we said.

"I take you good place." was the driver's response.

We looked at each other and shrugged. We had no idea where we were or where we were going. We were along for the ride at this point. Our Korean cabbie pulled up in front of a seedy little building that did *not* look like it served beer.

Mayweather paid the driver in Korean won and said, "C'mon, let's go." I didn't want to be alone in South Korea, so I reluctantly followed. Naturally, the establishment was a whore-type house and a rather extensive one at that. We were greeted in the foyer by no less than a dozen young ladies; all of them would be competing for our business. Mayweather's dick wasted no time selecting an Asian lovely and quickly sequestered to a room down the hall.

"I'll be right back."

"I'll wait for you."

I sat there waiting as the buzzards began to circle. The offers were afoot. One alluring lass convinced me to wait for my friend in her room. I resisted but eventually succumbed. I followed her like a dumb lamb to slaughter. There was an Asian porno playing on a small television in the corner of the room, right next to the futon.

The room stank of perfume and incense, enough to gag an orthodox Christian congregation. It was a bit overpowering. I looked at the porn on the TV, and my dick got hard immediately. She touched my bulge, and my pants came off. I still don't know how that happened.

"I'm just waiting for my friend. I have no money for you, okay?"

"Okay, okay." I don't think she spoke many Englishes (sic).

She jumped on top of my painful erection like the pro that she was. She spit in her palm and rubbed it on her vaginal unit. Now if that's not enough to make you run for the hills, you've got a serious problem. I didn't run for the hills. I guess I've got a serious problem. It may have taken three mighty down strokes of her tiny Korean frame on top of me before I lost control. It had been so long, I swear I felt the fluid drain out of my eyes.

IPOD. "Shit. I gotta get the fuck out of here." I put on my uniform as quickly as humanly possible, and that was when she demanded money. I argued that I was merely waiting for a friend. I stated most cogently that her pornography and aggressive actions led to an unfortunate ejaculatory situation. I tried to explain that I was not responsible, nor should I pay for whatever services may or may not have been rendered. I just wanted a beer, for crying out loud! Perhaps it was the language barrier or a cultural thing, but she was not happy. She stormed out of the room right behind me and was yelling something in Korean. I'm guessing it was the equivalent of *Hey, Moose and Rocko, this American just fucked me and doesn't want to pay!*

"Mayweather, where are you? We gotta go!" Fortunately, his timing was similar to mine, and we were both ready to run. And run we did. We did get a look at Rocko on the way out. He was half our size, but he did have a revolver in his hand. We just kept running and couldn't stop laughing at the absurdity of the whole episode.

That first and last night in Pusan wasn't over yet. We eventually found the neighborhood with all the bars and bar girls. My balls were sufficiently drained, so it was time to get my drink on. Mayweather was a notorious drinkasaurus, and I was ready to do some steaming myself. We drank for many hours. There was no shortage of beer. They also had this horrible clear white rocket fuel called Soju and a sweet champagne-type cocktail called Oscar that came in peach and grape flavor. There were three ships in port this evening, and every sailor seemed to be on this particular two-square-block area. Water sought its own level.

There was one point in the night when I was superbly schnockered. That's when I foolishly thought it would be a good idea to engage a fat boatswain's mate from the USS *Bagley* in some form of tête-à-tête. I don't remember the contents or subject or any details of our disagreement. I do remember that this portly and sweaty fellow's posture was one of imminent offense. I really didn't want to get into a fight in a foreign country, or anywhere else for that matter. The more I used my words, the more he bared his fangs. This stalemate went on for a few uncomfortable minutes.

From the corner of a drunken eye, I saw a flash of white. The fat Bagley deck ape did two perfect pirouettes, fell to the floor, and started twitching. His mouth started bleeding. I glanced to my right, and there was Portman. He looked like Muhammed Ali in that famous photo standing over Sonny Liston after knocking him the fuck out. All activity in the bar stopped for 1.7689 seconds. Then all hell broke loose. Callaghan was fighting Bagley, Bagley was fighting Callaghan. Bagley and Callaghan were fighting Koreans. It was a free for all melee. Bottles started flying. I was hiding under a table.

Portman found me and said, "Come on, let's get the hell out of here!" We found the back door and ran down the alley for two blocks without stopping. We finally did stop to catch our breath, but that was almost impossible because we were laughing so hard. We peeked around the corner and saw that the fight had expanded to the street. The shore patrol and Korean officials, both military and municipal, had arrived at the scene. We had two hours to get back to the ship, so we started walking.

"Why did you do that, Portman?" I thought it was a legitimate question.

"Well, I could see you two was squared off. The Bagley guy was angry, and you were laughing and being a smart-ass as usual. I knew it would be a fight."

We walked a little more and caught our breath.

Portman was gasping for air and laughing, said, "I've been in a few scrapes, Atwood. In my experience, the guy who hits first usually wins."

There was another long pause. "I knew you weren't gonna hit first, so I did."

"Yeah, okay, I get that, but why? Why did you do it?"

"I didn't want you to lose. You're my shipmate."

"You're a strange duck, Portman, a tough man to figure out." *Maybe I won't piss on your grave after all.*

We got to the gate of the facility where the ship was moored and were met by members of the Republic of Korea (ROK) Army. They were in full battle dress with loaded M16 rifles. They were a bit intimidating and looked like they meant business. Their demeanor softened when they recognized us as American sailors. They broke into big smiles and tried to communicate as best they could in broken English. It was kind of funny, and we played along.

The whole time, there was the unmistakable sound of a party wafting through the dark and salty air. I know a party when I hear one. Portman heard the same thing. A quick look around and along the quay wall was the source of the noise. There was a great big gray ship with the number *9* painted on it. I was still relatively new to the navy, so I didn't know every hull number or even the class of ship.

I asked our new friends, "What ship?"

The response was, "Demba."

The look I gave Portman said, *What the fuck is a Demba?*

"I think he said Denver, as in USS *Denver* [LPD-9]," he said confidently.

"How the fuck did you know that?" I asked, somewhat stunned.

"That's Waybrant's ship. We've written back and forth a few times."

I remember Waybrant from A School. He did pretty well, was in the top five. We hit the beach and the club a few times. Enough times for me to be impressed with his partying prowess. Portman and I looked at each other and smiled. We were both thinking that if there was a party on Waybrant's ship, not only was he there, but he was most likely in charge or hosting it.

"Let's go check it out." We agreed it had to be done.

As we got closer, it got louder. The partying seemed to be up on about the O-4 level, or the fourth level above the main deck. The sound of the music and revelers was unmistakable. There was a rager going on aboard the USS *Denver* (LPD-9). We walked up the brow, and there was a first class OS on the quarterdeck. He would know what was going on and if Waybrant was involved. I took charge.

"Hey OS1, is Seaman Waybrant aboard tonight?"

"Did he invite you guys?" he queried as he eyed us up and down suspiciously. Time to bullshit a just a little bit.

"Yeah, we went to A School together." That part was true, but he didn't actually invite us.

He asked our names and walked to a ship phone out of earshot. After a couple of minutes, he returned and said, "He'll be right down."

Sure enough, strutting down the passageway was a tanned smiling Waybrant dressed in his finest liberty togs.

"Portman, Atwood, what the fuck!" We high-fived and bro-hugged.

"Thanks for the invite, Way-Man." I glanced over to the OS1. He kind of gave me a knowing nod.

Waybrant quickly figured it out. "No problem, man, it's great to see you guys. Come on up."

We walked up the four ladders, down a passageway, and out a door to the weather deck. It was the ship's signal bridge, where the signalmen work. Their job was to communicate with other ships using other than electronic means, such as flashing light, flags and pennants, and semaphore.

Semaphore was the person-to-person communication by way of arm signals. Yes, the old—make that *very* old—skill was still very much in use in the modern navy.

What we saw on the signal bridge that night blew our young minds. It was a full-blown fiesta bordering on orgy. There were women who could not be mistaken for anything but hookers. There was loud music, and most amazingly, there was booze! It took me a minute to process all this. It was a bit surreal. Something like this would never, I mean *never* happen on the *Callaghan*. We had a guy who got busted trying to smuggle a bottle of Jack Daniels in his sock. He went straight to captain's mast and got busted, fined, and restricted to the ship for a month. A stunt like this would lead to keel-hauling and expulsion from the navy.

"You guys want a drink?" I snapped out of it and accepted the offer. There was a plastic tub with a huge batch of Mojo sloshing around in it. Mojo was a mysterious evil Filipino concoction. I don't really know what was in it, but it fucked you up. It's evil because if made properly, it had very little or even a pleasant taste. Then it hit you, and you suddenly find it hard to stand, let alone walk.

I was sipping my Mojo. I was witnessing guys taking bar girls into fan rooms and closets that were configured for human horizontal activity. Then I saw a couple of guys snorting a white powder.

"Is that coke?" I asked Portman.

"No, man, it's crystal meth, speed. You want some?"

I was almost too amazed at what I was seeing to answer. I declined. I had no problem polluting my body with alcohol and beer, but man-made chemicals scared me.

The party raged on. The Mojo flowed. It was 2300, an hour before midnight, when Portman and I had to be back on the *Callaghan*. We reluctantly made our way down and off this crazy party vessel.

Before we left, our buddy Waybrant ladled some Mojo into a plastic military canteen, making it a de-facto flask. "Here you go, guys, a little parting gift from the *Denver*." We said our thankful goodbyes and stumbled down the brow.

Surprisingly, a small contingent of our ROK buddies were on the pier and said they would walk us to the ship that was parked a hundred yards down the pier. I started thinking and eventually conveyed my concerns to Portman who was holding the flask. He agreed that it would be really stupid to try to sneak a canteen full of illegal hootch aboard the ship. So what to do? Well, there was only one thing to do. We must drink it. Of course, we offered the libation to our hosts, who greedily accepted. We found a spot in the shadows behind a warehouse and passed the canteen around.

In minutes, the much smaller Korean soldiers were wasted. I'm pretty sure they were slurring their words, but their English was so bad, it was hard to tell. We drained the canteen and teetered to the brow of the *Callaghan*. One of the ROKs looked at me and said, "Huss-rah, huss-rah?" Then he cupped his breast and repeated the suspected request. "Huss-rah?" I was looking at him like he had two heads.

Portman said, "He saying *Hustler*. He wants a fuck-book."

I was impressed. I was beginning to think that Willie Portman could speak fluent Korenglish.

"Stay right here." I made the international signal for back off or hold on by putting my palms out toward him. "Stay right here." I urged. I boarded the ship and went down to the berthing compartment. There were a few guys up watching TV. "Who's got a fuck book? I've got a drunken ROK out on the pier who wants to see some American pussy."

"Mayweather is still out on the beach," One of the guys said. That's perfect because that perv always had reading material under his mattress. I slid my hand between the mattress and the rack, and sure enough, I could feel the shiny paper of a men's magazine. I gathered up three specimens of varying raunchiness and went back up to the brow. It was now after midnight, so I couldn't access the brow.

My heavily-armed, drunk, and horny ROK buddy was anxiously waiting on the pier. He lit up when he saw what I had in my hand. I was able to toss the media from the main deck of the ship down to the pier where it was quickly retrieved and analyzed. The ROK was ecstatic. He liked what he saw.

I went to bed. It was a long and strange day. As I lay in my rack, I recounted the events of the day: I had been raped by a Korean hooker, I was at the hub of an epic melee, I partook in a highly illegal, drug-fueled, insane party on a US Navy vessel, and I got a host nation soldier schnockered and provided him with entertainment in print. Not bad for the first day in port!

That was the day I realized that I was experiencing some crazy shit with some crazy sons-of-bitches.

We left Korea with no injuries and a monster hangover. There was a buzz on the ship that Portman and Atwood started the now legendary Green Street Brawl of 1983. There was no proof, and the XO dismissed the whole ordeal. We had to go north to Japan for ship repairs and maintenance.

UNDERWAY 11

KAL 007

We got underway and left South Korea and made our way around southern Japan. We pulled into the port of Yokosuka. It was a beautiful fall day. My sea and anchor station was up on the fo'c'stle as a line handler. I was one of the guys pulling or "heaving around" on the mooring lines and tying the ship up to the pier. I actually liked it better than being in the combat information center or "combat," especially when we were pulling into a foreign port for the first time. It was like a free harbor tour. On a clear day, you could see Mt. Fuji from Yokosuka Harbor. It was very close to my nineteenth birthday. I called Naoko, and she agreed to meet me at the Yokosuka train station. I requested and was granted three days of leave. We took the train to Tokyo and met up with three of her friends. I had never been to Tokyo, and there was no better way to see it. I've experienced the hustle and bustle of New York City many times. Tokyo could give New York a run for its money.

We celebrated my birthday. The girls sang to me. "Hoppy boss-day too yoo...." It was the cutest thing I had ever seen. Four young Japanese girls were singing happy birthday to me! I was in heaven. We had a wonderful time in Tokyo. Naoko rode the train with me to spend the last night in Yoko.

This was long before the ATM. I needed to go to the ship and grab some cash from my locker. When I did, I was told that my leave was cancelled, and the ship was getting underway in three hours.

"Are you fucking kidding me?" I couldn't go back out and tell her. This was also long before cell phones and texting. I left her standing there at the front gate of the navy base waiting for me. I wonder how long she waited. I was sick with guilt and grief. I knew I had lost her. I wrote a pitiful letter of apology. I said how there were real-world events that were out of my control. I begged for forgiveness, but I never heard from her again. I'll tell you more about that later.

So why did that happen? What was this real-world event that had ruined everything? Well, the Soviets decided to shoot a Korean Airlines Boeing 747 airliner full of humans out of the sky for allegedly flying into their sovereign airspace. KAL flight 007 most likely impacted in the water near Sakhalin Island, that's north of the main Japanese islands, just off the coast of that lovely garden spot called Siberia. We were the closest US asset and were quickly dispatched to show our might and give these Commie, Pinko, Russkie bastards the what for.

It didn't work out that way. We screamed north from Tokyo Bay. All four engines were on the line. Our destination was a search area in the North Sea of Japan, close to the Sea of Okhotsk. When we arrived, we were the only US warship in the area and were quickly surrounded by many assets of the Soviet navy. They were not happy with our presence on their back porch. They made this feeling clear with their endless intimidating behavior. Their favorite pastime was dominating our voice radio traffic and RADAR frequencies. I must hand it to Ivan, that was our "term of endearment" for the Soviets during the cold war. He was good. They could and would intrude and jam our radio and RADAR frequencies with impunity. We called it MIJI, which stood for meaconing, intrusion, jamming, and interference. It became a verb that was used daily. They were MIJI-ing the shit out of us. They had powerful transmitters that would blast electromagnetic energy on the same frequency as our RADAR and radios, rendering our equipment useless. Their specialty was without a doubt intruding on our unencrypted or "uncovered" radio circuits.

When the other US ships showed up on the scene, the radios were a buzz of activity. Ivan wasted no time with their MIJI activity and making us crazy. Of course, we had codes, protocol, and such. But he seemed to know all this and would constantly meddle in our administrative and tactical radio traffic. I actually envied him. He was so much better than us. I imagined the counterpart of our watch team on the Russian ship just laughing at the dumb Americans falling for the same shit day after day.

It got to the point where we were starting to recognize each other's voices on the radio. Ivan sometimes sounded like he just crawled out of a Louisiana bayou. He probably spoke better English than most of the *Callaghan* crew. We had an authentication system. It was a card, about the size of your basic index card. The card changed every six hours. It was a matrix of numbers and letters. The intention was that if you suspected someone of evildoing on the net, you would pose a challenge. "Charlie Four Hotel, this is Delta Three Tango, authenticate Bravo Romeo, over." The recipient would go down the left side of the card and find the letter *B*, then a glance directly to the right where the letter *R* was living. The letter directly beneath that was the authentication. "I authenticate, Charlie."

This process didn't slow down these borscht-eating bastards one bit. This went on for almost two months. We were standing watches eight hours on and eight hours off. I didn't know if it was day or night. It didn't matter. The weather was turning to shit. We were surrounded by hostile Russians. I had lost my beautiful Japanese girlfriend. There were no signs or pieces of KAL-007. My friends were all in college. I was in Siberia. I was so stressed out that I was getting nosebleeds. I was starting to feel sorry for myself.

It was a relief to have some friendlies in our midst. We now had a little more firepower. Besides more firepower, we also had "The Link." "The Link" is a Tactical Data Information Link or TADIL. In this case, it was Link-11 or TADIL-A. A tactical data link was how US and allied assets shared tactical or combat data and information. This allows on-scene commanders the ability to see a real-time tactical picture. This was vital when making important tactical decisions, such as engaging a target or turning over the control of friendly aircraft from one control unit to another. It came in handy when prosecuting submarines or any target of tactical interest.

Allow me to explain. A ship had sensors to detect, track, and gather tactical information. Among these sensors is RADAR,

SONAR, electronic, intelligence, visual, and other means. This information was fed to a suite of computers and processors known as the Combat System. AEGIS was an example of a US Navy shipboard Combat System. This system rendered a true geographic real-time dynamic display on the consoles in CIC. An air search RADAR had a reliable range of a hundred miles or so. The surface search was good for about thirty miles. Passive electronic data could be collected at a much-greater range. Under-the-water data collection depended on the sea conditions, temperature, salinity, pressure, and ambient noise. So basically, each ship had a data collection "bubble" of five to one hundred miles. Let's say there was a ship fifty miles away. If the two units could make both of their tactical pictures become as one, that greatly expanded the surveillance area. Throw in another ship, and you've tripled the coverage by several hundred miles. Add a link-capable aircraft, and you're really in the link business.

In the case of Link-11 or TADIL-A, this information was shared over an encrypted data radio circuit. There was a common reference point that all the units used as the middle of the tactical picture. The tracks from each participating unit were sent out relative to that fixed geographic data link reference point or DLRP. The data was sent via a messaging protocol in a burst of encrypted energy. The combat system talked to the link processor, which bundled the surveillance messages and sent them to the encryption and radio equipment. The data went out over the airwaves and was received, decrypted, and processed by the receiving combat system, and then appeared on all the participating units' consoles. The units transmitted and received link data at specific times so there was no electronic conflict. There was, however, a lot of management in an active link. Keeping the link up and running was a full-time job. The parameters such as DLRP, the frequencies, crypto, and track block numbers were constantly changing. Units came in and out of range and thus came and went from the link picture. The data systems administration (DSA) radio circuit was constantly buzzing with activity. It was a lot of work and was very important, especially given our current tactical environment and potential threat.

One day, the link really came in handy. A link-capable Japanese P-3 was flying around in Japanese and international airspace; out of nowhere, two Soviet Sukoyev fighter planes showed up and headed for the P-3. A P-3 was no match for any attack aircraft, so we recommended that he headed south toward Japan; he wisely did just that. So did the Reds. In fact, they followed the P-3 into Japanese airspace. We had it all on our link picture, and we were capturing data. I thought to myself, *Didn't these sons of bitches just shoot down an unarmed civilian commercial jet because it flew in to their airspace?* Meanwhile, we fired up our fire-control RADAR and got a missile ready to shoot. We had a "white bird on the rail," which meant a live guided missile was in position to fire. The Command circuits were alive.

I didn't know how high up the chain this critical and potentially deadly information went, but we had what we call a "fire control solution" on the Soviets. We also called it a "green board." That meant we could send a very fast, accurate, and lethal weapon toward the two aggressive Soviet aircraft that were right now invading Japanese airspace, with the push of a button. Keep in mind that this was the eighties and the height of the Cold War and Reagan era. Needless to say, the tension was palpable. The decision came back over the red phone to *not* engage. The instant that call came over the radio, the Sukoyevs broke off and hightailed it north and out of Japanese airspace. We had just avoided what may have been a very serious international incident with scary consequences.

It was getting to be winter, and it was getting cold, nasty, and snowy outside. I was missing the South China Sea in summer. I really missed Naoko.

I was on watch the night before we were detached. We were tracking a Soviet Kara class cruiser that was about twenty miles north of us. It was relatively calm. All of a sudden, this monster of a Cold War ship bristling with weapons systems came barreling straight for us. I plotted his progress and alerted the bridge. When the Kara was about ten thousand yards or five miles from us, the general alarm sounded, summoning all hands to their battle stations. *Dong, dong, dong,* "General quarters, general quarters, all hands, man your battle stations."

Oh shit. Had the tensions reached a boiling point? I wondered what was going on behind the scenes. Ronald Reagan was president, so who the fuck knew? This could be the real thing. The ship was suddenly alive with activity. Sleeping sailors now wide awake were desperately donning combat gear and running to their GQ stations. The door to CIC flew open, and here came the rest of the division, most of whom were sleeping except for the degenerate gamblers. My buddy Mayweather was the last one in the space before we secured the doors and prepared for battle. He was in his underwear. He had five playing cards in his hand. He was hoping that this GQ was a drill or a mistake. He was one card away from a straight flush. Unfortunately for him, the poker game was over.

It turned out that there was an electrical, or class Charlie, fire in one of the engine or machinery spaces that caused the alarm. The Kara turned away from us as if he had detected our general alarm and heard our saber rattling. We didn't know why they backed off so suddenly. Perhaps they thought and realized correctly that they were no match for us. Maybe they smelled a little blood and chickened out at the last minute. We'll never know. Ivan was enigmatic. That's what made him such a challenging adversary. God, how I miss the Cold War!

The next day we were done up there. It was cold and snowing. We would go back to Yokosuka for fuel and supplies. Then it was a straight shot to Pearl Harbor. I was looking forward to it because our chief arranged for Portman and me to take the E-4 exam. Success on this exam would lead to promotion to third class petty officer, or E-4. The chief was always looking out for us. This should be an easy transit across the vast Pacific. I was hoping to be able to call and maybe even see Naoko. Alas, once again, it didn't work out that way.

We were awarded the Meritorious Unit Citation for getting our ass kicked by Ivan. I honestly think that we earned it. It's not like getting the silver or bronze star medal; it is, perhaps, a dubious honor, but I still wear the ribbon. It was a very stressful time up there in Siberia. I don't know if it was good or bad. It just was. That was the day I realized what it felt like to get out of a potentially lethal situation with your life.

UNDERWAY 12

The Storm and the Appendicitis

Our time in Japan was once again cut short. This time there was a typhoon making its way north from the South China Sea toward the main island of Honshu. I didn't bother calling Naoko. I figured she was done with me. I didn't blame her. I would write her another letter. That should fix it, I told myself.

We bugged out of Yoko just in time. The wind was at our backs. Huge rolling storm waves were pushing us east towards Hawaii. We were about seven hundred miles into the Big Blue, as the Hawaiians call it, when we got a call from the USS *Bagley*. They had a sailor onboard with acute appendicitis. Apparently, it was about to explode and become toxic and perhaps kill him. There were no doctors on any of the ships that were sailing east. All we had were enlisted hospital corpsmen, as hard as that is to believe, it was the case. It was too rough to launch and recover aircraft on any ship. There was no way to get this poor schlub to the carrier, the USS *Constellation* (CV-64). We were way all too far away from land. The decision was made to take him aboard the *Callaghan* and go back to Yokosuka. It made sense. We were the newest and fastest ship in the group. The big problem was the raging typhoon that was between our position and the intended destination. So the *Bagley* pulled up next to us in a very large and dangerous sea-state. Lines were shot across, and we pulled this poor bastard over on a high line in a stretcher. I wondered if it was the same guy I was squared off with a few months ago in Korea.

Wouldn't that be funny? We got this sick sailor on board and made a 180-degree turn. We were sailing right into the mouth of a monster storm. The captain ordered twenty-four knots, and away we went.

The first day wasn't so bad. It was just big smooth rolling waves right on our bow. There wasn't the anger that I have seen in the past. Not yet. Day two was worse. The sky was darker. The wind was whipping the surface of the ocean into a foam. The waves were huge. The ship maintained a speed of twenty-four knots. The third day was brutal. We were in the middle of the storm and all of its fury. We were slamming into thirty- to forty-foot waves at twenty-four knots. The ship was flying out of the water and then smashing back down to the black sea with a violence that made the whole ship shimmy and shake in ways that it really wasn't designed to do. Imagine 9,600 tons of American steel and equipment, not to mention some three hundred American young males, being airborne one minute and then submerged the next. The ship was going as fast as possible through the tempest. We burned a lot of gas. I'd been asked if I was seasick during this operation. The answer is no. I was too scared to be seasick.

The ship started breaking and cracking in uncomfortable places, but we still kept our speed at twenty-four knots. We lost a bunch of life rails. A few radio antennae became part of the Pacific Ocean floor. Our forward missile launcher took too many waves and was knocked out of commission. The worst part, for me anyway, was when we developed a crack in the superstructure of the ship right outside CIC. That's the third level above the main deck. It's perhaps thirty or forty feet above the water. I could see daylight, and water was pouring in.

Okay. That's enough. Let this Bagley guy die. Let's throw his sorry ass overboard and save ourselves. This is getting ugly. That's what we were all thinking to ourselves.

Negative. It was full speed ahead. Our skipper, the captain, was determined to save this guy.

Battered and bruised, after four days of misery, we made it back to Yokosuka. There was a team of Japanese welders on the pier waiting for us. We quickly off-loaded the broke-dick *Bagley* asshole. I realize that is a bit harsh. I didn't know this guy. He may've been very cool. We just wanted to cross the ocean and go home. There was a lot of spouting off. But I know when, and if, it got really ugly, we would've done anything to save this guy. We were venting like the little bitchy, catty sailors cunts that we were.

We quickly got ready to head right back out in to the very same storm that just about killed us. Eight hours later, we were heading east again. Fortunately, the wind and sea-state had abated a bit, and we headed in a safe direction. It was still uncomfortably rough, though. I guess it's all relative. One had to strap a seat belt on while sitting at a RADAR console. I even strapped on the rarely-used belt that hid under the mattress, or "fart-sack," of every navy rack. It was rough as shit. I got so used to being tossed around that it became natural. Eating was a challenge. But like any challenge, you adapt and overcome. To successfully eat a meal in these conditions, you had to spread your legs out for balance as you sat in front of your tray of food. One arm went around your tray on the table lest it went flying. The other hand shoveled food in to your face. There were always drink glasses flying about. Try to imagine what it was like to take a dump (a bowel movement, a number two, poop—we're talking caca-doodie), when all the forces of nature were working against you. It was very difficult when the laws of gravity were fighting you on all three axes.

We eventually made it to Pearl Harbor and then San Diego. The sea was rough the whole time. I knew I had a problem when I was watching an episode of *Cheers* on the shipboard cable TV. Norm took a sip of his beer and put it on the bar. My first thought was *He better hold on to that beer or it will go flying*. I had been underway for way too long.

San Diego looked good. I planned on taking some leave and fly home to New Jersey to see my family. My first deployment was done. That was the day the navy selected me to be a third class petty officer (E-4). We tied the ship up at the Naval Air Station, North Island. That was the day I completed my first deployment without dying. There would be more.

UNDERWAY 13

In Between Deployments

Portman was selected for advancement as well. *But*, and this is a big *but*, I was selected for the first increment of pay. Portman made the third increment. What did that mean? We both were advanced on the same day. However, my date of rank and pay began immediately. Portman's pay kicked in three months later. That meant that I was now three months senior to Mr. Portman. I might really have to watch my ass now. He no longer outranked me by five stupid days. I was out ahead. I would never look back. There's an old saying, "If you're not the lead dog, the view is always the same."

There was no excuse for Navy Numb-Nuts to *not* kill every exam. A simple query to the Navy Education and Training Command in Pensacola, Florida, would give you the answers to the advancement exam. It's called a bibliography. They listed all the documents where all the questions on the exam came from. It's a freaking no-brainer. I spent my downtime going over these Naval Warfare Publications or NWPs. I tested in the in the ninety-ninth percentile. It was easy. Portman mistakenly thought he was smarter than me. Perhaps he was, but his evaluations weren't as high as mine. This was probably because of his cocky attitude. To his credit, he could not be beat in poker or pool. He must've had a casino or gin mill in his barn growing up in Bum-Fuck Wherever. His problem was that he was a shitty winner. When you took money from the guys who write your evals and have some control over your destiny, you should be more humble.

Back in San Diego, life was as normal as it could be. The ship spent some time in the shipyard for some badly needed repairs. Once again, our chief got us off the ship as much as possible. There were lots of beer and beach volleyball. It was fun. This was new to me. I really didn't know what it was like to be in the navy and *not* underway.

I tried to go surfing every chance I got. There were a lot of chances. My friends Barry and Stewie lived in La Jolla and would let me crash on the couch when I was in port. I kept a wetsuit and a surfboard at their meager, comical little apartment. I loved surfing at Windandsea. It was a heavily local reef break right at the end of Nautilus Street. If you knew someone who lived around there, you may be accepted in the lineup. Woe be it for the dude who showed up out of nowhere and tried to catch a wave with all the locals. I saw a lot of fights out in the water and on the beach.

Meanwhile, back in the navy. We went to countless Anti-Submarine Warfare (ASW) classes and team trainers. In the mid-1980s, there was a very powerful focus on the Soviet submarine fleet. It's pretty much all we did.

There were other things too. Tommy T, Louis, Portman, and I went to Naval Gun Fire Support (NGFS) School. That was fun. Our job was to fix our position. Then we would talk to the Marine on the beach who would radio in the grid or position of a target on the beach. We would plot that position and work with the gunnery fire control guys and put a five-inch round on or close to the target. Mr. Jarhead would adjust fire, and we would pound the shit out of the target. We were the best team in the business. We actually scored the highest score on record in training and absolutely killed it in live firing. This all happened after a night of beer guzzling and methamphetamine abuse. We were young.

It was time to start getting underway again and preparing for the next deployment. There were lots of watches, lots of UNREPS (underway replenishment), and lots of time underway. That was our job. That's what we did. We were getting ready to head out again. We would be heading to the Indian Ocean / Persian Gulf.

It was a Monday at morning quarters. All of OI (operations and intelligence) Division was assembled, and the leading petty officer and chief were putting out the orders of the day. Chief Simons posed a question, "Is there anyone, E-4 or above, who has a place to stay at no cost to the government and would like to go to Anti-Submarine Air Control [ASAC] School?" In a Pavlovian reflex, my hand shot up immediately. This was an amazing opportunity. I had a motorcycle. I was pretty sure I could crash on the couch in La Jolla. This was very exciting. The chief took my offer right away. We went to the ship's office, and thirty-day orders to ASAC School were cut.

OS2 Wojo, he had a huge Polish name like the guy from Barney Miller, so we called him Wojo. He was scheduled and billeted for the school, but he was on the outs with his wife and decided to decline the orders to ASAC School. At the last minute, he decided to get underway with the ship instead.

My chief took me aside and said, "We usually don't send someone so junior, but I have faith in you. Don't fuck this up." That was the last thing I wanted to do. It was another navy school. I was getting the hang of this shit.

That was the day I got another great lesson in leadership: if you take a chance on someone and let them know that you trust them, they will break their balls for you. And that's exactly what I did.

UNDERWAY 14

Anti-Submarine Air Control

Anti-Submarine Air Control School was right up on the hill in Point Loma, San Diego, California, a beautiful multimillion-dollar location. I loved it. I would ride my motorcycle around the neighborhoods of Point Loma and made a promise to myself that I would live there someday. I was determined to take full advantage of this opportunity. I could just imagine Portman's face turning red in anger. I was now the Secretariat to his Beetle-Bomb. I didn't care. I would still piss on his grave. I had thirty-day orders to Air Control School in San Diego. Point Loma to be more specific. This was a very good thing!

ASAC School taught me how to control and maneuver US Navy anti-submarine aircraft with the intention of searching for, localizing, and attacking Soviet submarines. I had to learn the characteristics, capabilities, and limitations of the ASW aircraft in our arsenal and, of course, those of the enemy. I was trained on the tactics of search, localize, and attack. I took to it like a duck to water. Like a pig in shit. Like a Filipina hooker to a stack of pesos. Okay, that's a bit much, you get the picture. It was challenging, but I loved it. I ate it up. I graduated and was now a real live Anti-Submarine Air Controller. I knew enough and had enough experience to be very dangerous in the real world. In other words, I didn't know shit. But I was about to learn.

I was on the pier when the ship pulled in and tied up. Before the brow was in place, Chief Simons was visible on the quarterdeck area.

He just looked at me intently. I gave him my best poker face at first, then with a big smile, I gave him two thumbs-up. He just pursed his lips and sent me a deep and respectful nod. He turned around and walked into the ship. I knew he was happy, maybe even proud. I was just so happy that I didn't fuck up. I didn't let my chief down. That was the day I became a stellar stain in my chief's eyes. I couldn't have been any happier!

UNDERWAY 15

Deployment Preps

We were getting ready for another deployment to the Western Pacific and Indian Ocean. I was no longer standing the conventional watches. My job was now controlling the shipboard helicopter in accordance with their schedule. I was spending a lot of time at the Air Control console. It could be somewhat stressful at times. During ASW operations, whether it be exercise or real world, there was a lot going on. I would sit at my console, in front of my RADAR screen. On my head was a headset with the radio in my left ear and four or five internal circuits in my right ear. I would have to flip a L/R (left/ right) switch in order to communicate with the watch team or the aircraft. In the midst of a hot and heavy ASW event, this could be challenging. Of course, this irked Portman.

The principal means aircraft use to detect a submarine is by deploying sonobuoys. Here's some more on sonobuoys. Sonobuoys are high-tech cylindrical units that are about five feet long and maybe ten inches wide that contain a listening device or hydrophone. They are launched by the hundreds from the aircraft and perform various functions. They can be set to various depths. Some just listen. Some of them make noise. Some do both. When a sonobuoy hears something, it is "hot." The data that the buoy is receiving is electronically linked through the aircraft and down to the shipboard SONAR squad for analysis. Some aircraft will go out and spit a thousand buoys. If one of them goes hot, the game is on.

There were times when I would have a P-3C Orion operating at high altitude dropping or "spitting" buoys and linking back the tactical data information to the ship. Meanwhile, my shipboard SH-2 helicopter would be down low, standing by for localizing data and direction, should one of the many P-3 buoys got a sniff. If it got really juicy, an SH-3 might show up on scene asking for guidance during the localize and attack phase. The SH-3 had a SONAR array in its underbelly. I would tell it where to "dip" its SONAR, and they would lower the unit into the ocean and listen for or sonically reach out and touch an area where there may be an enemy submarine. It was all very exciting. A five- or six-hour flight with me at the console would elapse in what seemed like mere minutes.

One night, as we were working up for deployment, we were in charge of guarding the High Value Unit (HVU) in the Southern California Operations Area, or SOCAL. It was a large amphibious ship full of Marines getting ready to land troops on the beach at Camp Pendleton. I was tasked to take control of an SH-3 "dipper." My orders were to make sure that no submarines would molest the landing force. I was to conduct random dips near the amphibious landing area. Pretty loose orders indeed. The aircraft checked in with me. I said, "You are to conduct random dips in the vicinity of…such and such…" I really didn't know what the fuck I was doing. The pilot did everything I said. Holy shit! I was a twenty-year-old kid in charge of a US Navy aircraft and its crew.

I saw the tactical link picture on my scope. I had positive control of the helicopter. I thought to myself, *If I were an enemy submarine, where would I be?* It wasn't that hard to figure out. By the third dip, we had contact on a US sub pretending to be a bad guy. It didn't take long before every ASW aircraft in the area was in the sky and hitting me up for direction. They didn't get to mess with a real sub very often, so they were like ravenous rottweillers. I was quickly getting overwhelmed by all the aircraft on my radio frequency looking for blood. Thankfully, Chief Simons, who always knew what was going on, picked up on this. All he had to do was look at me. I looked at him, and he sat down in at the other Air Control console right next to me. He dialed in the control frequency, which was our land / launch circuit.

"You're doing great. Just try to relax a little bit. Have fun with this. This is fun, right?"

Actually, it was exceedingly stressful for me, but it was getting better now that the chief was with me.

"I'll take everything above two thousand feet. You take all the low guys. Just keep the lateral separation. You're in charge, Mr. Atwood. I'm from the government. I'm here to help!" He laughed like only he could. He had done this shit before. I was shitting in my pants.

"Come on, Atwood, there's a reason I sent you to ASAC School. It's moments like this, son! This is what it's all about. Now stop looking at me like a half-gay deer in the headlights and do your fucking job! Woo-hoo, this is fun!"

My chief would say to me, "This is what this Cold War is all about, Petty Officer Atwood. Those Air Intercept weenies turn a fighter at a target, and the aircraft systems take over. They get to kill one, maybe two, enemy. When *we* are successful, it's much more severe. We're talking a hundred or more enemy killed. We become instant mass murderers! That's pretty fucking cool, right?"

That's when I knew he was a lunatic. It's also when I knew that I wanted to be the same kind of lunatic. We conducted the movement of these aircraft like a fine symphony or Russian ballet. I felt so professional and vital for the first time in my life. I looked over at the plot and could see that Portman wanted to kill me. He was so horribly jealous. Soon, all the aircraft were running out of fuel and had to go home. That was fine with me. I was exhausted. That was the day I realized I was a career navy man.

UNDERWAY 16

Losing Doug

After a year of workups and time in the shipyard, it was time to get ready for deployment. Chief Simons had groomed me to be a competent and confidant Air Controller. My air control log was filling up with hours of control time and all kinds of US and NATO aircraft. We were scheduled to go on a six-week "shakedown" mini cruise that would take us to Anchorage, Alaska, Vancouver, British Columbia, San Francisco, California, and then home. We would have a month of slow time and then six months at sea, or underway.

The day we were set to get underway, the Chief wasn't at morning quarters. Our leading petty officer (LPO) was running the show. When he was asked about the Chief, he didn't have much of a concise answer. He said that the Chief had to go see Doc Hanson, the Chief Corpsman on the ship. There was some strange lump on his neck, and he had to go to Balboa Naval Hospital for some tests. Blah, blah, blah. I didn't give it much thought.

It was a busy underway period. I logged a lot of air control hours. I missed my safety net, my chief. The liberty ports were fun as always. It was June, and Anchorage, Alaska, never got dark. Vancouver had great beer and the hottest naked strippers in the world. San Francisco was always a blast. If a straight and single man couldn't get laid in SF, he wasn't trying. I guess that's true for the gay guys too.

We pulled out of San Fran, and I was severely hungover as usual and had just passed under the Golden Gate Bridge when we got the bad news. Chief Simons had gone in to surgery to take care of a cancerous tumor that was correctly diagnosed by our shipboard Corpsman. By the time he got under the knife, it was too late; cancer had spread to his organs, and he didn't make it through the procedure.

My hero and mentor was dead. I felt like I was kicked in the nuts and guts at the same time. I was overwhelmed with denial, sadness, and most of all, anger. I had lost a father figure, a friend, and a shipmate. He left behind a wife and two teenage boys. We would all go fishing out of Point Loma. We had so much fun. I was profoundly sad. I wanted to get off the ship, but that wasn't going to happen. We all had to nut up and get underway for deployment again.

And that's exactly what we did. It was time to head west again. In show business, they say, "The show must go on." The navy says, "Time and tide wait for no man." That was the day I realized that the mission was far bigger than any one of us.

UNDERWAY 17

Deployed Again

Once again, we were underway on the high seas. Our helo was flying ten hours a day. That meant my ass was in front of a RADAR screen for half the time. OS2 Stu Rather was the other Air Controller. He took the other half of the flights. There were the usual two or three days in Hawaii. Mass quantities of alcohol were consumed. Brain cells were summarily and mercilessly slaughtered. In the Philippines, brown women were compensated for their services. There was much DNA left behind. Portman and I had grown distant. It helped that we were the same rank and now getting paid equally for it. That lasted about three months. I was selected for E-5 or second class petty officer. Once again, I made the first increment. Portman was selected, but yet again, he was in the third increment, so he wouldn't see the pay for three months. History repeats itself for sure. I was one step ahead of him, and he hated it.

Portman was a strange hillbilly. While I was missing the Jersey Shore and going surfing every day, he was whining about missing elk-hunting season in Idaho. I had pictures of young women in my rack; he had pictures of murdered and skinned elk hanging from a tree next to the barn in his back forty. He was hanging out with Woody more and more. Brian Wood was a very quiet and extremely strange backwoods country boy from somewhere in Missouri. Some of the strangest guys were from Missouri. I don't know why. The two of them would practice wild turkey calls as they assembled muzzle-loader rifle kits for their exhaustively planned big post-deployment turkey and elk hunting trip.

One night, Woody walked off the ship late on a night before we got underway with a gym bag in his hand. I was on watch on the quarterdeck when he asked for permission to go ashore. He didn't show up for quarters in the morning and missed the ship's movement. When we got underway and pulled in a week later, he was standing on the pier. He turned himself in and was prepared to face his punishment. He just didn't want to go to sea that week. I never asked him why. He went directly to captain's mast for NJP or non-judicial punishment. He was reduced in rank, fined, and sent to the brig for three days with nothing but bread and water. Holy shit! Now we all know that the navy, unlike the other services, is still deeply steeped and influenced to this day by the traditions and customs of the British navy. But three days of bread and water was downright Captain Bligh–esque! I couldn't believe we still did this type of Machiavellian madness. Woody still didn't say a word. He went off in cuffs to the brig. He returned to the ship and our division in four days.

"Holy shit, Woody! Three days bread and water! What was that like, man?" His expression didn't change. He was as stoic as ever. "The bread was pretty good" was all he said. Did I mention this guy was a little off?

The other weirdo from Missouri was Marvis Wigman. We called him either Weird Marv, Wiggie, or Wigwam. He had this strange and unsettling habit of staring at you and smiling. One time, I had had enough and asked him what the fuck he was smiling at. He had a strange cadence and affectation to his voice. He sounded a bit touched, perhaps inbred. "I was just wondering what you would look like in a Batman suit." He gave me his creepy smile that you would rather see from behind bars or bulletproof glass with one of those freaky masks, like Hannibal Lecter. These were just two of the lunatics that I was deploying with for six months. We would all be sleeping and working inches from each other. Nevertheless, we were well prepared to head out to our ultimate destination, the Indian Ocean.

UNDERWAY 18

Hong Kong and Portman's Bullshit

Heading west from the Philippines, we made a stop in Hong Kong just after a typhoon had passed through. We experienced a bit of it at sea, but the worst was over. The weather was nice and warm. I had duty the first night in port, but I didn't mind. I learned that it is actually a good thing sometimes. All the nonduty crew would hit the beach as a de-facto RECON squad. They would scout out where to go and, more importantly, where not to go. The next day at quarters, you got the 411 and made a plan based on their experiences. I did just that. I stood a bridge watch cutting RADAR fixes every fifteen minutes to make sure we were not dragging anchor. It was easy and even relaxing. The view from the ship was pretty cool. In Hong Kong, there were steep green hills behind a skyline of modern buildings. Merchant ships were constantly coming and going from this very busy international hub.

The next day, I got some good guidance from the guys and had a plan in mind. I was ready to go and so was Portman. He didn't have duty the last night or on this day, which meant that he would have duty on the next day. He approached me with a proposition. Of course, I was leery at first. He was the king of the fine art of Buddy-Fuckery. Why should I trust this guy? He was out to get me, right? He secretly hated me. He was jealous. He always tossed me beneath the Greyhound. Oh, I couldn't wait to piss on his grave, but as soon as he mentioned English females, I was all ears. He told me that he had met two girls in a British pub, and they agreed to go on a lunch date if he brought a friend. A friend? Okay, call me crazy or stupid, but I had been underway for quite a while, so I agreed. I thought maybe there was a chance that Shipmate Portman really needed a so-called Wing-Man in me. I had no other solid tactical plan for Hong Kong, so I reluctantly agreed to double date with the elk-hunting hayseed from Idaho.

I immediately began to question my judgment. I harkened back to the pepper incident in Thailand. We were in Pattaya Beach, Thailand. We had to take a liberty launch to get to the beach. These boats held about thirty people. They had an automobile engine bolted to the stern. Protruding from where the drive shaft would be in a car was a straight eight-foot shaft with a propeller at the end. This was not your basic Mercury outboard engine with a proper outdrive. There was no rudder or steering system. To turn the boat, the operator would lift the shaft and prop out of the water and pivot the whole unit, engine and all, to one side or the other. I thought it was funny. These liberty boats got you close to shore, but you still had to jump in the water and wade to the beach in knee deep water.

It was a great liberty port. There were lots of bars and restaurants with really good and cheap seafood. There were also plenty of women. I was walking down the main drag and ran into Portman, who was eating some barbequed stuff on a stick. "What's that? Is it any good? Where did you get it?" I asked innocently enough.

Portman started gushing. "Oh man, this is the greatest. You gotta get one. That little stand right over there. Here, try this." As usual, his poker face gave nothing away. I foolishly took a bite of something I didn't recognize. It turned out that it was some kind of pepper. Let me rephrase that. It was the hottest fucking pepper probably on the planet. I've had some hot ones before. My father once grew some Hungarian peppers in our garden that were inedible. I think they were only used medicinally. These Thai bastards were hotter. It wasn't like, "Whoa, that's hot!" It was, "Holy shit! My mouth is in agony! I will never taste food again! Portman, you motherfucker, I'm gonna piss on your grave!" My mouth was on fire for an hour. It truly was brutal. Of course, he was laughing his ass off at my expense. You'd think I had learned my lesson.

Back in Hong Kong, we took the liberty launch from the anchored-out ship to the shore landing. I followed Portman around the streets of this interesting city. It's a very cool place. Hong Kong is a cultural mixture of Chinese, British, Indian, and other things in between. It reminded me of Chinatown in New York or San Francisco. There were plenty of wares being peddled on the store fronts and curbside. We arrived at a very nice hotel that was obviously built to cater to Anglo guests. There was a restaurant on the top floor. I started counting the cash that I had on hand in my head. I looked at Portman. He strangely knew what I was thinking.

"Don't worry, Atwood, I've got lunch. I've been saving. You're gonna like this girl. I told her all about you."

You'd think sirens would be going off in my head, but he was brilliantly playing the ego card. I was balls deep in this operation. As the elevator went up floor by floor, I kept thinking, *Okay, how has this asshole set me up for failure this time?* Perhaps curiosity got the better of me. I thought, *What the hell? I can have some other-than-ship food with white women. Portman is paying.*" It seemed worth the risk. I could always just punch out if I really wanted to.

Ding. Twenty-first floor.

We were a little late. The girls had already been seated. The waiter saw us to the table. I couldn't believe what I saw. There were two young and very attractive English girls sitting there waiting for us. I whispered to Portman, "I may rethink the whole pissing on your grave thing." They had pale/pink skin and bright-red lips with blue eyes and gorgeous smiles. Their names were Daphne and Veronica.

The alpha one, Daphne, whom I immediately and correctly assumed was Portman's target, laid into him. "You're ten minutes late, Yank!"

"Sorry, it was his fault," he said, pointing at me. "He had to do his nails." Under the bus I went again. I didn't care. I was smitten with this lovely creature who was smiling at me. I was also horny. There was a vacant seat next to her. I quietly sat down and introduced myself. I couldn't stop looking at her face. Her skin was positively glowing. Her feminine pheromones were driving me caveman crazy.

I don't remember what we ordered for lunch. I know there was rice. There was also tea and Chinese beer. Veronica stuck to the tea and water. She seemed very hungry. It was an absolutely lovely lunch experience. Daphne was a bit raunchier than her friend. She actually asked us how we released ourselves sexually while out at sea. Her words were, "What do you do when you lads want to have a wank? You know, toss one off?" These words I still use today. She made the international hand gesture for human male masturbation. Veronica just took it all in and smiled. Of course, Portman and I were laughing. "Seriously, what do you blokes do?"

"Tell her about Spankin' Rankin Willie," I said.

"You tell her, you're a better storyteller."

"Yeah, but you're a better liar."

I acquiesced and reluctantly told the disturbing story of Spankin' Rankin. I was hoping that Veronica wouldn't think less of me. "There's an Irishman from Boston named Kevin Rankin. He's a signalman or 'skivvy waiver,' as we call them. He had interesting masturbation practices and philosophies. He knows that we all, including him, need to 'toss one off' or 'have a wank,' as you would say." I pointed at Daphne. "He is of a mind that since we all do it, why try to hide it? The problem is he takes it to the next level. Actually, it's probably several levels. He will announce his intentions to anyone in the berthing space. 'Okay, guys, I'm feeling kind of horny, I think I'll go to the rack, bust out my *Penthouse* and rub one out.' All of the guys roll their eyes. They were getting used to this and turn up the volume on the telly [I was speaking to English people].

"Believe it or not, this became normal! This is the insane world that we live in. It gets worse. He would do exactly as he intended. Then he would broadcast a blow-by-blow or, in this case, a stroke-by-stroke accounting of the activities behind the curtain of his six-by-three-foot rack.

"Yep, getting hard, stroking it, feeling good...

"You see where this is going, right? Let's just say that he announces the events of the entire episode from disturbing start to disgusting finish. And he does this with absolutely no frigging shame."

The lovely British girls were silent. This was an understandable silence. "So that's the story of Spankin' Rankin." I thought for a second that I had shared way too much ribald adult information with the ladies. But they both burst out in uncontrollable laughter, and their faces turned bright red.

"There's no fucking way that is true!" challenged Daphne.

I responded with a very calm "I can't make this shit up."

The conversation returned to more civil topics. We told each other where we were from and about our families. Things were going great. It was even fun spending time with Portman, who dutifully paid the bill. It was time to leave. The unspoken question was "where do we go now?" The gentlemen rose from the table first, followed, of course, by the ladies. That's when I noticed the condition of Veronica. I'm no OB/GYN, but I think I know a pregnant lady when I see one. It appeared she was well into her nine-month term. I'm guessing maybe seven? But what do I know? The look on Portman's face was one of supreme victorious cockiness. It was a look that said, *Aha, I got you! Good luck, asshole!* Although I had vowed long ago never to play cards with the man, I maintained my best poker face. I swear I did not blink.

I kept my smile and asked them, "Where do you two plan on going this evening?" He was still grinning like a retarded monkey and told about his plans. I said, "That sounds nice. You two go enjoy that. Veronica, how about we go for a nice walk in Hong Kong? Please don't worry about your friend, Daphne, I will make sure she gets home safely." My smile never broke. This action deflated Portman's cockiness a little bit. That made me happy. We let them leave first.

Before getting on the elevator, he looked back at me with a cocky look seeming to say, *I'm getting laid tonight. Have fun with the preggo!*

I made a lame attempt at a British accent and said to her, "Perhaps we should adjourn to a location in closer proximity to your temporary domicile?" She was impressed. I didn't tell her that my father was a fighter pilot *and* an English teacher.

"Okay, let's go. But I have to go to the loo first. It's one of the benefits of my condition." We were alone in the elevator going down when she finally addressed the three-hundred-pound gorilla.

"I guess I ate too much," she said, touching her protruding belly. That was enough. It broke the ice, and we both laughed all the way down to the first floor.

The question now was what to do and where to go. "I don't know my way around here. Where would you like to go? How does ice cream sound?"

"Let's just walk a bit and enjoy this lovely weather," she said.

"That sounds great. I love walking in a new city, I really do. I'm following you."

"He didn't tell you I was pregnant, did he?"

"No, he did not. But it's okay. It's more than okay. I am enjoying spending time with you regardless of your…er, uh…condition. I'm enjoying this more than you can imagine."

"I can imagine many things."

"Can you imagine being stuck on a ship with over three hundred smelly men? That's three hundred dicks and at least six hundred testicles. Not to mention three-hundred-plus assholes. I am loving this time with you, and I thank you for spending your time with me."

We locked arms and slowly strolled down the big, busy avenues of downtown Hong Kong. We talked about many things. I didn't ask about the kid's dad or her plans or anything personal like that. I thought that might be rude. We stopped for ice cream and decaf coffee and talked some more. I was having a great time. I couldn't give half a shit what Portman was doing. After she paid for the ice cream and coffee (so far, this episode had cost me exactly zero dollars, US or Hong Kong), she asked if I would walk her home to her hotel. What do you think I said?

"Of course, I just hope you know where it is."

"It's this way, c'mon." We spoke of music and both agreed that Billy Joel was one of the best artists ever.

"So what's your favorite?"

"Theme from an Italian restaurant," I replied in an "everybody knows that" lilt.

She started right in. Not from the beginning but from the lively part. "Brenda and Eddie were the popular steady, and the King and the Queen of the prom, dah, dah. Riding around with the car top down and the radio on dah, dah, dah, dah."

My turn. "Nobody looked any finer, or was more of a hit at the Parkway Diner…"

Between the two of us, we got about 90 percent of the lyrics. We were arm in arm and singing at the top of our lungs. We could've been on the moon, but we were in Hong Kong, so a lot of people were looking at us. At one point, when she was singing, I looked at the passersby on the sidewalk, and most of them were smiling. They could tell that we weren't a couple of drunken Anglo loudmouths. Rather, we were a happy, excited young couple who were expecting a baby. Another person, or me, at another time, may have found this uncomfortable, but I embraced it. I was walking and singing with a lovely pregnant lady. Most of all, I was away from the ship, the crew, and all the navy environs. I was the envy of Hong Kong. Could it get any better? Well, it did.

"Please, come up. It's a nice room with a great view of the harbor."

"Are you sure? What if Willie and Daphne are up there?" I heard an evil little chuckle. My innate (Spidey) senses told me that this was a good thing. "She's not up there. She will drain every dollar he has. American and Hong Kong and then send him on his way."

I thought, *Uh-oh, this isn't good.* A blue-balled angry redneck could be trouble. "She may be in danger," I said, "I don't like this. I'm concerned for her safety."

She chuckled again. "My friend can handle the Idaho Potato Head," she said very confidently. Now I was laughing so hard, I could barely stand. "Come up, and I'll make us some nice tea. We may even have even have a cold beer if you fancy that. Come on up, and we can talk about how we will never see each other again." How could I refuse? Up to the room we went. It was number 1611. I will always remember that for some reason. She boiled some water and made tea and cracked a beer for me. There was an uncomfortable silence. I'm sure it was just me. I didn't know what to say or do next. She finally broke the silence.

"You've been very nice today, kind even, thank you."

"The pleasure was all mine. You are a lovely young lady. Thank you for the date. I wish you luck." I immediately realized how dumb that must have sounded. Now I was really at a lack for words.

I searched my brain for something, and she said, "What would Billy Joel say?"

"Only the good die young? Vienna waits for you? I love you just the way you are?" I threw it out there.

She didn't miss a beat and sang, "They got a divorce as a matter of course and departed the greatest of friends."

"Are we the greatest of friends?" I asked her.

"Tonight we are. Look, I know I am huge and ugly, and my life is a mess. I don't know how I am going to handle this little person inside of me, but that has nothing to do with you. You're a good guy. You've been so very nice to me. Please sit back and take your shorts off."

That knocked me a little off balance, but I rolled with it. Once again, I did not question or argue. She took very good care of me in very short order. I think she actually enjoyed blowing me. I had no complaints. We both fell asleep on the couch. Her friend Daphne came in late and confirmed Veronica's earlier prediction. I had to get back to the ship before liberty expired, so we said our goodbyes.

"You're my greatest of friends in Hong Kong." It was the best I could come up with in this awkward situation. We kissed, and I made my way to the ship.

I saw Portman at quarters. He didn't look so cocky. He had a bit of a defeated look on his big round face. He didn't know that I knew that he got played by a white chick. He also didn't know that I had received the best blow job that a horny pregnant chick can give to a sorry young penniless American swab-jockey. I felt as if I had a full body massage. I was tingling. Perhaps it was because of the sexual release. Maybe it was because I knew Portman tried to screw me over and only managed to screw himself...again. He's not a dumb guy, but I wondered if and when he would ever learn!

I stayed aboard and rested up the next day. I was done with Hong Kong. I couldn't do any better than the previous night. We were soon underway for a transit to the Indian Ocean. It was kind of nice not feeling like semisolidified hammered hamster dung on the way out of the harbor. The next few months would be mostly boring.

UNDERWAY 19

Heading to the Indian Ocean

We hoisted or weighed the anchor, departed Hong Kong Harbor, and turned right or to the south. The sea was rough, and my stomach wasn't digging it. It's always tough when the sea was lumpy right off the bat. If you're at sea for a few days or a week, and it turned nasty, it's not a problem. The galley chose this day to serve steak and lobster. I could barely keep it down. Others weren't so lucky. Fortunately, I wasn't hungover, so I didn't have my head buried in a plastic bag returning the steak, lobster, and pineapple upside down cake. We headed south and passed the island country of Singapore without stopping for a port visit.

Now we were in the Straits of Malacca. That is the narrow body of water between the Malaysian peninsula to the north and the large Indonesian island of Sumatra to the south. It is a super highway of shipping. It's like a California freeway in the sea. There is what is called a "Traffic Separation Scheme," which is tantamount to the lanes on a highway. It is a major global trade artery that is constantly full of shipping laden with millions of tons of cargo coming and going from the Far East every day. It is a dangerous thoroughfare, so watch-standers have to be on their toes. Contact avoidance is the most obvious and constant challenge. If you adhere to the traffic scheme on the navigational chart, you should be okay. Because the strait is so narrow (that's why we call it a strait), there are lots of tidal currents and unpredictable eddies that can affect the navigation of the ship. RADAR fixes were taken every two minutes. The lookouts, surface tracker, CIC team, and bridge are super busy trying to coordinate and trying not to occupy the same space as another vessel. Then there is the unpredictable tropical weather.

On this day, as we transited the Malacca straits, we were almost at the western terminus. The Andaman Sea and Indian Ocean, as well as a whole bunch of island clusters, lay before us. There was also a massive wall of purple and black boiling clouds greeting us to this part of the world. The temperature dropped, and the wind picked up. Suddenly, a thousand-foot-high water spout developed a few miles ahead of the ship. It started on the surface of the ocean and spun all the way up to the base of the clouds. The base was a violent torrent of whipped-up seawater flying up in a mist as the body of the sea-borne tornado twisted and writhed skyward. It was frightening yet beautiful. There was nothing we could do but hope this monster wouldn't run into us. It would be like an Arkansas trailer park episode at sea. We couldn't go around it to the right lest we run aground. To the left would put us head on to oncoming shipping.

It was at that exact decision-making moment that the ship lost all power. The term "deafening silence" is appropriate here. All the ambient shipboard noise, the engines, ventilation, auxiliary machinery, the generators, and even the lights, all shit the bed at once. Now the only option was to float around like a cork or drop an anchor and maybe cause a maritime pileup like a foggy day on I-5 in Fresno. Both were bad choices. Luckily, the engineers unfucked the problem, and all power was restored in a few seconds. It seemed longer than that. The storm had broken up as well. It seemed to be an eerie harbinger. It was as if the Indian Ocean or IO was welcoming us and warning us at the same time. Maybe I think too much, but this marked the beginning of a very long and tedious deployment in this very strange, volatile, and dangerous part of the world.

We made it around India and the island country of Sri Lanka, whose navy consists of two cabin cruisers and five wind surfers. They made a silly declaration that their territorial waters extended twelve miles from their coastline. The recognized standard for international nautical boundaries is three nautical miles. We were tasked to sail to exactly three and a half miles off the coast of the capital of Colombo and just sit there and look cool. It was a big "fuck you" to Sri Lanka. That's an example of how the US Navy kept the sea lanes and the oceans free. By the way, Colombo, the capital city of Sri Lanka, actually looked like a pretty cool place through the binoculars.

After our little political statement, we made our way to the Indian Ocean proper. There was no shortage of drills as we headed north toward the coast of Iran and the North Arabian Sea. The focus was on rules of engagement, or ROE. We ran practice scenarios wherein a potentially hostile aircraft would approach the ship in a threatening way. We would practice the canned radio transmissions known as "deconfliction" reports."

"Unknown aircraft at XYZ location, heading XYZ, at XYZ altitude, this is a US Navy warship operating in international waters requesting your identity and intentions, over." We did the same thing for small craft. This would go on for months.

There was no real known Soviet submarine threat in this part of the world, so my ASW skills were not needed. The watch rotation was not all that aggressive for me. I was still one of two air controllers, and we would share the time evenly. Often, the helo would be down for maintenance. I found myself with actual time on my hands underway. So I decided to use that time to my advantage. I started working on my Enlisted Surface Warfare Specialist (ESWS) qualification. In order to qualify to wear the ESWS pin, a sailor had to learn everything about the ship. It started with all the basic stats and specs. You must understand the combat systems and its capabilities and limitations. Engineering included propulsion, electricity generation, water making, air-conditioning, ventilation. Firefighting and damage control was a big one. You really had to know all that shit to qualify. Let's not forget the mind-numbing supply and maintenance systems. It took quite an effort to qualify. There were a few hundred signatures, and you had to spend a lot of time in spaces all over the ship and learn about all the equipment. It was a great way to pass the time in the IO.

Once the book was signed off, it was time for the oral boards. The first round was usually in front of a panel of Chiefs from each department. Their job was to probe the depth of your knowledge on each subject. If they detected weakness, which they always did, they would tell you what topic you needed to work on. Then you came back for another "Murder Board." If they thought that you were ready, a full-blown ESWS board was scheduled. The board usually consisted of a few chiefs, some division officers, and a department head or two. It can be pretty intimidating, but I was ready.

They stared with the basic stuff, then dug deeper. A lot of it was open-ended situational stuff. There were virtual tours through various spaces as we sat there in the Wardroom. At one point, the Chief Engineer said to me, "You are a molecule of air. Take me on a trip from the outside air, through the engineering plant, and off of the ship." I took him through the intakes of the gas turbine engines where I was mercilessly compressed through a series of turbines or fans. Then I decided that this molecule (me) would be what we call "bleed air" instead of part of the combustion process and made my way through the shaft and out of one of the 119 small air holes in each of the five propeller blades as part of our Prairie/Masker Air System on both shafts, and in a belt surrounding the ship just below the waterline. These tiny bubbles acted to mask the sound of the ship and the propellers spinning through the water. I did pretty well and was awarded my ESWS pin. Unfortunately, we still had over two months of deployment left.

The Indian Ocean and Kristofferson

The Indian Ocean is a vast place, to say the least. The ship was assigned to the North Arabian Sea, very close to the mouth of the Straits of Hormuz, which leads to the Persian Gulf, right off the southern coast of Iran. We were to maintain a presence in case firepower was needed in the region, and we would also monitor the shipping coming and going from the gulf. Much of this monitoring was done with the helo. That also meant me. We would fly two missions during the day and two at night. We called it the DDA and NDA for Day Dick Around and Night Dick Around. I would keep an eye on them as they flew around identifying the endless stream of commercial shipping. They would radio the details of each vessel to me: the type of ship, the deck equipment, the number of cranes and smoke stacks, and, of course, the name and nationality of the ship. This data was forwarded to the watch team, where a message called a "Rainform" was generated and sent to some Coast Guard database someplace in Florida where I'm sure it was thrown in the shitcan. We did this day after day.

Every once in a while, it would get interesting if the weather got nasty or the aircraft had an issue. The most common issue was a "chip light." A chip light is the result of an errant piece of metal being detected in one of the aircraft's gear boxes. Helicopters are extremely complex beasts. Transferring the power from the engines to the main and tail rotors requires a complex network of gears, cables, hydraulic systems, and lots of oil. These gear boxes were working hard, making a horizontal power source become a vertical one. Maybe it's the other way around. I'm not sure. Anyway, there were a lot of metal gears grinding against each other at high RPM. Every once in a while, a little piece of a gear may get tired and shear off, then go for a swim in the oil bath of the gear box. There were magnetic sensors inside the gear boxes that lured these errant shards, and when they did, it sent an alarm to the cockpit.

More than ten times when we were on a DDA or a NDA, the pilot would report a chip light. It always woke me up a little bit. The ship would go to emergency flight quarters. We would point into the wind. I would talk the helo down to the flight deck. Most of the time, it was almost nothing. Usually, a little piece of metal. Every once in a while, however, it was a problem, and the aircraft would be down for maintenance. I was always glad that the crew was safe, but I did enjoy the down time.

We also trained constantly on emergency procedures. The Emergency Low Visibility Approach or ELVA was the air crew's favorite. My job was to bring the aircraft to the ship in zero or simulated zero visibility. I had a little yellow book called a TACAID that had the sequence of procedures.

Me: "Sea Snake one seven this is Freddie. This will be a RADAR assisted approach. I hold your contact on the two-five-zero radial at seven miles from the ship. Altimeter setting is two-nine-nine-three. Maximum pitch and roll is two. Read back altimeter setting."

Pilot: "Two-niner-niner-three."

Next, I would establish the lost communications and missed approach procedures. Now it was time to line up the aircraft at four miles from the ship and four hundred feet of altitude to conduct a gradual rate of descent to arrive at fifty feet of altitude and half a mile from the ship. This was the short strokes and heavy breathing part. I would alter the heading to adjust for wind direction and speed as well as ocean current with my face inches away from the screen. Every half mile, the helo should be fifty feet lower.

"Three miles, three hundred feet." If I was a little off, I would call an adjustment. The helo slowly got closer, 250 feet off the deck at two and a half miles. Two miles out and 200 feet. Small heading corrections now.

"One Seven, you are left of centerline. Turn right five degrees assigned heading is two-six-five." Then they got so close, I would lose them on RADAR. "One Seven, Freddie, half a mile, altitude should be fifty feet. If ship or wake not in sight, execute missed approach." I got pretty good at the ELVA. I soon learned that the quality of your ELVA determined the level of respect you got from the air crew.

We did this for months. It was hot and dusty. It was time for some scheduled repairs and maintenance for the ship aircraft and crew. At the time, there was no friendly port to pull into in this part of the world. Back then, we had repair ships called Tenders. They specialized in fixing deployed ships. We needed a bunch of fixing. A repair ship or Tender did just that. It repaired and even manufactured things. There were machine shops, electrical shops, even a printing shop. Just about anything you needed to keep a ship afloat. They also had pussy. I mean females. Holy shit! You could almost hear the boners a-poppin' and the smell of testosterone boiling.

We were in the Gulf of Oman in a relatively safe bay tied up next to the USS *Jason*, the tender. The *Jason* was the oldest ship in the navy at the time. It was about as old as my dad. That was a really old ship. On the Jackstaff flew the old "Don't Tread on Me" flag. Yellow, with the snake emblazoned. There were females aboard. The presence of women really brought out the Cro-Magnon in the crew. I admit I probably would've escorted a *Jason* chick on a tour and thrown down a bone in a fan room, but I had to work. Even though we were riding majestically at anchor, there were a lot of air operations going on. That meant I was at my console quite a bit despite the fact that our shipboard helicopter was in the hangar during the repair availability. Most of it was routine stuff. I would provide flight following for mail and logistic aircraft. This was a crazy part of the world, so if a US air asset was out flying around, it was wise to have someone watching.

It was axiomatic that if the SPS-48C air search RADAR was spinning, either me or Stu Rather were sitting at the scope with a headset on. One day while we were tied to the *Jason*, I was controlling a mail hop and one "special use" helicopter that was intending to land on the very ship we were tied to. Both ships went to Flight Quarters, and a CH-46 landed on the *Jason* and sat there for a while. I found out that they were offloading a bunch of civilians and a ton of equipment. What kind of equipment? I did not know at the time. It took so long, they needed gas to fly home to their base somewhere in Oman or Kuwait. They fueled up and split. I watched them as long as my RADAR and UHF radio would let me. "Pony two five, you are in the dark. RADAR services terminated." That meant "I don't see you anymore, you're on your own." The pilot was very cool and professional, as they all were.

He was gone—or "off my RADAR," so to speak—but there were other things going on. There were other aircrafts checking in. It seemed like every five minutes, my left ear would crackle with another aircraft wanting to talk. It passed the time. I had nothing better to do. I actually enjoyed it. I could be down in berthing playing cards and losing money to Portman or I could be up here padding my logbook. An H-3 carrying mail, spare parts, and humans to a ship in the Gulf checked in with me for flight following. I saw his RADAR contact and verified his Identification Friend or Foe (IFF) codes on my screen. I had him make a turn for positive identification. I saw him turn. I had him. I knew where he was going. I followed his flight, and then there was another one. That's okay, I was cool. I learned from the best. And then a third H-3 checked in followed by a fourth. *What am I, LA Central here? Chief Simons, I need you!* But there was no one around but me, the dummy at the scope.

I kind of heard the door to CIC open and the sound of a bunch of feet and voices. It looked to be a tour of some sort. I had aircraft going places that were relying on me to point them in the right direction and make sure they safely avoided other aircraft. I could hear my department head, the ops boss, explaining the contents and purpose of the space. Then I heard a voice right behind my right ear. A gravelly, deep American voice with no discernable accent was speaking.

"What type of aircraft is that?" There was maybe a hint of a Southern accent.

"It's a US Navy SH-3."

"How much fuel does it hold?"

"Enough for about three hours of safe flight, sir, fully loaded."

I was balls deep in safety of flight for numerous air crews, and this unidentified civilian was chirping in my ear. Where was my ops boss? Where's my chief? The distinctive basso voice continued with the interrogatives. "What is their ceiling? What's the max load? Do they have any weapons?"

I answered these questions as best I could as I watched my computer-generated symbols move across the screen from right to left and from north to south. He still kept asking questions. "How much fuel? How many in the crew?" Holy shit! Enough! I had been nice long enough.

I finally took my eyes off the screen and turned around for a brief second. I saw a bunch of civilian men with facial hair in black T-shirts. What the fuck were they doing at my air control console? The guy asking the questions looked familiar. He had sparkling eyes. I think they were blue. It's hard to tell in the dim blue lighting of CIC. He was sporting a salt-and-pepper beard. "I'm sorry, son. I just love helicopters. I know you're busy. My name is Kris." He held out his hand, and of course, I shook it.

The operations officer or ops boss stepped in and said, "Petty Officer Atwood, this is Mr. Kris Kristofferson and his band."

"Nice to meet you, Kris. I hope you enjoy whatever the fuck you are doing out here," I said.

He laughed and said, "We've got a gig on the ship next door young, Mr. Atwood. I hope you can make it."

Just then, one of the helos called me and requested a safe vector home. Small talk was over. He seemed to know this and didn't take it personally. Not that I cared. I went back to work. Kris K. patted me on the back, then he and the gang turned around and tromped out of the space.

I thought, *Shit, that's the guy who wrote that piece of shit song "Me and Bobbie McGee!"* I hated that song. I should've kicked him in the nuts!

Things eventually calmed down a little bit. I had a little break. The Ops Boss came over and sat down next to me. "Hey, Ops, What the fuck is Kris fucking Kristofferson and a bunch of fucking civilians doing at my fucking console when I'm trying to do my fucking job asking me a bunch of fucking questions?"

"He told you, Atwood. There's a real live concert, music type, one each on the *Jason* flight deck tonight."

"Why was he so curious about flight ops?"

"Well, he actually flew helicopters in the army and later as a commercial pilot. I don't think he was in Vietnam. I guess he was curious about our current capabilities. You know he wrote the song 'Me and Bobby McGee?'"

"Don't we shoot Chinese spies for asking about our current capabilities? And I hate that fucking song! I'm glad Janice Joplin is still dead." I may have been a little cranky; it happens.

He chuckled, knew I was a little spun up from the air controlling. "Lighten up, Atwood. Get done here and go relax and enjoy some live music. Oh, and by the way, if there's some friggin' in the riggin', I will look the other way."

He was referring to the unauthorized engaging of sexual activities with a human of the opposite sex somewhere in the ship. Well, that never happened, but I appreciated the support.

The concert was great. My buddy Kris and his band put on one hell of a show. It was such a nice break from business as usual in the Indian Ocean. He was very humble and respectful. I don't know why. We didn't pay for tickets or buy any T-shirts. We were mostly a bunch of non-college-going dummies who decided for some reason to serve our country in the navy. Right after they finished a song named "Three Hundred Pounds of Hungry," Kris said, "I hope that young air controller is out there tonight."

I stood up and yelled, "I'm right here, Kris." I was maybe twenty-five feet away.

"All right! You're doing a great job, son! You're all doing a great job! It's an honor to be here playing for y'all! God bless you! We love you!"

Then he started playing Bobby fucking McGee. I hate that fucking song!

UNDERWAY 21

Beer Day and Australia

We spent months in the IO / North Arabian Sea. There were plenty of drills. We spent a lot of time on plane guard station. In an aircraft carrier battle group environment, there was always a ship a thousand yards directly astern of the carrier during flight operations. Many times, that was us. On this deployment, it was the USS *Constellation* (CV-64). One thousand yards is roughly a half of a mile. For some reason, when you were one thousand yards behind a gigantic ship that was launching and recovering aircraft, it seemed a whole lot closer. It was an impressive thing to witness. My love of aviation and aircraft had me out on the bridge wing watching the carrier crew, and their air crew performed the ballet of flight deck operations for hours.

There seemed to always be some kind of hostage situation or terrorist hijacking or bombing in the region. That precluded us from going anywhere. We were just sailing around in circles, waiting for orders. We were maintaining our presence with a show of force. Once again, the link picture had to be solid. The DDAs and NDAs continued. Many hundreds of ELVAs were completed. Some were more precise than others. We were underway for well over forty-five days when we finally got detached to head south for Australia.

More than forty-five days at sea meant one very important thing to an American sailor. It meant Beer Day. It was a navy regulation that if a ship was at sea for more than forty-five days, was more than five days away from port, and if the commanding officer authorized it, each sailor should receive two twelve-ounce "beverments" of the beer-type variety.

Beer Day was fun. I knew a couple of guys who didn't drink, so I made deals with them for their allotment. I paid one guy cash and took an in-port duty day for another. I wound up with eight beers in total, which I finished in record time. It was very relaxing and very much unauthorized. The supplemental beers I mean. I actually had a nice little semi-authorized buzz going on. Our next stop was Australia. I had heard many stories about the beer in Australia, and I heard about the women.

The ship pulled in pier side to a quaint little southwest Australian port named Bunbury. It is more of a town than a city. I guess I could compare it to someplace like Erie, Pennsylvania, or Port Angeles, Washington. We had to wear our dress uniforms in port for the first day, as if the locals didn't know exactly who we were. It was a very friendly place. The old folks actually stopped us on the street to thank us. They were referring to World War Two, of course, specifically the Battle of the Coral Sea. The Japanese were very close to spreading their influence to the continent of Australia, and there wasn't much the Australians could do to stop them. Luckily for them, the US Navy won the day at Coral Sea, and the Japanese threat was forced northward to regroup. They never made it that far south again.

It was hard to buy a beer in Australia. Not because we couldn't, but because they truly liked Americans. A couple of us and Portman found a nice little hotel with a pub and started drinking the delicious Australian beer. I struck up a conversation with a nice woman named Maggie, who was about ten or twelve years older than me. I wasn't actively hitting on her; I was just being my version of what I thought was charming. Portman, on the other hand, was relentless with his Neanderthal approach. She was with a friend, an even older lady named Sue, who was mostly quiet and only chimed in when asked a question. Portman was telling the ladies how great he was. I mostly kept my mouth shut, except, of course, for the occasional sarcasm usually directed at Portman, whose grave I had sworn to piss on. I let him dig his own grave. The bar banter went on for a while until it was time for us to leave.

"Okay, it was nice talking to you. We're in town for a few days. Stop by the ship and ask for me, and I'll give you a tour. If something interesting or fun is going on, please come and get me." I wrote my name on a bar napkin, the oldest trick in the book.

We decided we were hungry and time to test the Bunbury cuisine. The three of us American sailors left the ladies behind and started walking down Main Street, Bunbury, foraging for food. A car abruptly stopped next to us, and it was Maggie and Sue, my new Australian friends. "Let's go for another drink somewhere else," she said.

"Can my friends come?" I was always looking out for my shipmates!

"Of course, get in, boys." She got out of the car and moved the seat forward so we could all pile in the back.

We did as ordered. She drove us to another cool hotel and pub on the edge of town. Once again, the beer was great, and the locals were extremely friendly.

"So it's kind of funny how you randomly bumped in to us on the street," I said innocently.

"It wasn't random. When you walked out, Sue said to me, 'You go find that boy and don't let him get away.' Luckily, you weren't that hard to find."

My little brain started to process this. I thought she might be hitting on me. This was a totally new experience for me. No woman had ever been so bold around me. Now I was really beginning to like Australia. "Okay, so you found me. I'm not getting away. What happens now?" I realized that I could get a little bold here.

"Well, we could get some food and drink and go to my place." Are you kidding me? Was this really happening? This was easier than shooting fish in a barrel.

"Your big friend over there told us that you were gay," she said, nodding toward you-know-who.

"Is that right? Well, what do you think about that?" I asked with a big grin on my face.

"I think that it's rubbish, and I'm determined to find out."

"All right, sounds good. Let's go." I turned to my shipmates. "See ya, fellas!"

The look on Portman's face was classic. He tried to cock-block me, and it bit him in the ass once again. This was even better than pissing on his grave.

We went to a little market, and she bought beer, wine, olives, cheese, crackers, and some other stuff including Vegemite (*yuck*!). This night just kept getting better. We went to her house, which was a former schoolhouse. She and her husband—oops, that's right, I said husband—bought it with the intention of making it a health retreat. The spousal unit, which I had just found out about, was in Europe and, according to her, "fucking everyone in Belgium." *Okay, I think I know where this is going*. It went exactly there. She was a sexual animal. It was a good thing I was barely twenty years old, or I never could've kept up with her in the sack.

The next morning, I had duty and needed to get back to the ship, so she said, "Here, take my van," handing me the keys to a VW van that was parked out front.

"Are you sure?" I was a bit nervous about this.

"Of course, you know how to drive, right?" I thought about that for a second and thought yes, of course I knew how to drive. But then a thought hit me.

"You guys drive on the wrong side of the road, from the wrong seat, and you shift gears with the wrong hand."

"Just take your time. You'll be fine." She gave me her phone number and told me to call her with a good time for a visit on the ship. I did just that. She came to the ship after my watch, and I gave her a very special tour, which included a quickie on the commodore's chair in CIC. I was feeling defiant, so I didn't even wipe up the wet spot.

I realized that there were two of us and two vehicles. "How do you get your van back?"

"Why don't you bring it back tomorrow? I can show you around a bit." I was pretty sure how to get there.

"Okay, I get off in the morning. I can be there around nine or ten."

"Great. See you then." I walked her off the ship and went to bed.

The next day after quarters and a quick cleaning of the spaces, it was liberty call. "Hey guys, I've got a car. Anyone need a ride?" I had about eight guys in the van heading into town. I almost killed us all about ten times. It was hard getting used to cars coming at you from a different direction. Traffic circles were especially challenging.

I managed to drop the guys off alive and found Maggie's compound. She took me for a nice tour of southwest Australia. It was another sex-filled day. In the bed, in the car, no place was safe. I spent another night in her bed, and she took me to the ship in the morning. It was a little awkward saying goodbye to a married woman. On the other hand, there wasn't any bullshit about staying in touch and seeing each other someday. It was a fun romp, and it was over. It was time to head east. Next stop Hawaii and then home. That was the day I learned that married women like to fuck too.

USS Callaghan, DDG-994 was a Kidd class guided missile destroyer honoring Admiral Daniel Judson Callaghan. He was posthumously awarded the Congressional Medal of Honor for his actions at the battle of Guadalcanal during WWII. Built in Pascagoula, MS, Callaghan was commissioned on August 29th, 1981. The ship was decommissioned in 1998 and is now an important part of the Taiwan Navy.

A full speed run, looking aft over the flight deck and aft MK-26 missile launcher. With all four engines on line, she could cut through the water at over 30 knots or about 36 MPH.

One of the three Vietnamese refugee ("Boat People") boats we rescued in the summer of 1983 in the South China Sea.

The makeshift shelter that was fashioned beneath the aft gun mount, (mount 52). There were 263 survivors who made it safely to the Philippines.

The American Club in Kagoshima, Japan. Kagoshima is on the southernmost main Japanese Island of Kyushu, the island that is home to Hiroshima and Nagasaki. This is where I met Naoko.

This is what an SPS-48C RADAR display looks like when it is being actively jammed. When an adversary, in this case the Soviets, transmits electromagnetic energy on the same frequencies as the RADAR array, the RADAR, as you can see, is rendered useless.

One of the many soviet warships flexing their muscles near Sakhalin Island during the KAL007 search and salvage mission. We were surrounded by ships of the Kara, Kirov, Krivak and Kashin classes, as well as many others. They were not pleased with our presence.

A glimpse at the evening adult activities in Subic Bay, Philippines. I'm going straight to hell!

OI Division circa 1985. Me and Tommy T (far right, first row, squatting) in sunglasses. OS1 Frank (first row, far left, squatting) literally pulled us out of our racks to take this photo. We were hurting. Pearl Harbor, HI on the fo'c'stle of the USS Callaghan.

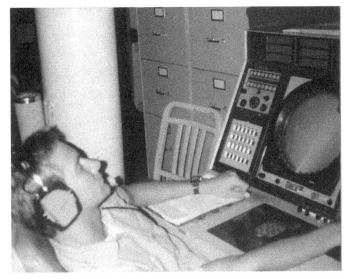

Working very hard at my air control console. Nobody messed with me until an aircraft came up on frequency. Then I was all awake and all business.

Catching a ride on our shipboard LAMPS (Light Airborne Multi-Purpose System) helicopter. As an Anti-Submarine Air Controller (ASAC) I was able to tag along with the aircrew on a few missions.

This is the Mobile Inshore Underwater Warfare (MIUW) surveillance van being hoisted for transfer to the operating site. Ad Dammam Harbor, Saudi Arabia, September, 1991.

The MIUW under SCUD missile attack. We had to don our chemical gear and hope for the best. It was a bit stressful.

PATRIOT missile batteries stationed in a field near our barracks.
This US Army system may very well have saved my bacon.

Here's a look at GI Joe-Ker with his M-16. Note that there is
no ammunition clip. It was basically a 7 pound paper weight
that I had to carry everywhere and was responsible for.

The USS Tisdale, FFG-27, transiting the Panama Canal in 1994 at the Gatun Locks during counter narcotics operations.

The infamous Guatemalan lounge chair on the flight deck of the Tisdale.

Andrea and me doing our best "Officer and a Gentleman" impression. Of course I am neither officer nor gentleman.

UNDERWAY 22

Across the Ocean and Home

We left Bunbury and headed east with one simple mission, get this ship and crew home. Of course, there was a stop in the Philippines and the three days in Hawaii. As an E-5, I had a little more scratch in my pocket and could enjoy the nightlife in Waikiki a little bit more than I had before. I could even afford a cab to get back to the ship.

My older brother, Steve, and my best childhood friend, Achilles, met the ship in Pearl Harbor for what the navy calls a "Tiger Cruise." That was when a family member or friend rode the ship with you from Hawaii to California. There were dads and uncles, nephews and friends, all were experiencing the joy of sailing on a US Navy Destroyer and crossing a very large ocean.

When I say "met the ship," I should qualify that. They "met the ship" all right. We were out in town raging the night before we got underway. I warned them not to get too fucked up. Being underway and hungover was a very bad thing. Of course, they didn't listen to me and decided to party all night. This was not a hard thing to do in Hawaii. I had to leave Waikiki and get to Pearl Harbor because I had to report for duty in the morning.

"Listen to me, you two assholes, your balls better be on that ship at 0800. That means eight o'clock in the morning. We are going out to sea, do you understand? You know how to get there, right? I'm serious. We won't wait for you." I was hoping that I made my point.

They laughed that drunken laugh, which I had heard too many times. I had to get back to the ship. I had duty in the morning. I was worried about those two knuckleheads, but not worried enough that I didn't want to go back to the ship and get some sleep.

I got up early the next morning, and there was no sign of my brother or Achilles. I had issued them orders. They knew when and where they were supposed to be.

The ship had been going through the seventy-two-, forty-eight-, twenty-four-, and twelve-hour checklists. None of these included the two drunken dumbass shit-birds from New Jersey. The sun was up, and there was no sign of my brother and friend. This was the still eighties, so there were no cell phones or ATMs. They were on their own. There was nothing I could do.

I was in the berthing space changing from my white uniform to my dungarees. The brow, the temporary walkway that connects the ship to the pier, was maybe five minutes from being lifted from the ship by a crane, and we would be underway. There was still no sign of the two errant passengers.

It was three minutes before the brow was to be lifted, and I heard my name on the 1-MC.

"OS2 Atwood, quarterdeck."

Oh shit. What did these stupid asshole motherfucking retards do? I thought to myself. I knew it was them. Why else would I be called to the quarterdeck when we were minutes from being underway?

Sure enough, here was Shitbag and Shitstain Junior in a yellow cab in front of the brow with a surfboard strapped to the roof! The brow, by the way, was attached to a crane and was ready to be lifted up so the ship could put to sea.

I wish you could've seen these two. They did everything I told them not to do. I thought to myself—no, I giggled to myself. The next few days would be rough for these guys.

"C'mon, assholes, we're leaving in a few minutes. Get your asses up here! Now!"

Achilles gave me a strange look. My brother, Steve, got out of the cab with a similar look.

"Come on, guys. We have to go. Now!" I screamed at them.

My brother sheepishly said, "We don't have any money. Can you pay the cab…"

"Please? We ran out of money," said a lame Achilles.

"You don't have any money? What do you mean you don't have any money? You ran out of money? You are definitely dumber than you look." I was a bit incredulous, but it was hard to be mad. After all, they did make it on time, albeit by the skin of their balls.

"We spent it all. We put all of our money together, and we have thirty-seven cents. The cabbie needs twelve dollars. But hey, we had fun." That was my brother, with a big dumb look on his face. The two of them stank like two breweries.

They both smiled at me. I guess it was like a smile that a parent couldn't be angry with. The crane was about to disconnect the brow from our ship.

I wanted to be angry, but in the strangest and most perverse way, I was proud. I didn't have the money. The officer of the deck was a chief quartermaster that I knew very well, so I asked him if I could borrow twenty dollars. He reached in to his pocket and peeled off a twinkie without saying a word. He had seen the whole ordeal unfold and took it all in. He was laughing. Navy chiefs are the best.

I paid the cabbie and took those two dummies aboard and then down to where they would be sleeping. They were a mess. I think they slept for two days straight. It didn't matter because there were plenty more days to be bored at sea. We had a couple thousand miles to go. These mutants made it in just under the wire. I was pissed off on one hand, but I was cracking up on the other. These two goofballs showed up at a navy ship with zero dollars in their pockets. I felt like they got a taste of what it's like to be a real US Navy sailor.

I had to stand watch and control aircraft on the way home. My two guests accompanied me. They ate navy food three times a day and were supremely bored, but there were a few highlights. The *Connie* put on an airshow in the middle of the Pacific, which was very cool, especially when two F-14 Tomcats came blasting by the ship at supersonic speed and two hundred feet off the deck. That was impressive. Another interesting episode was when we got a SOSUS sniff of a Soviet Yankee class boat (submarine) about eight hundred miles off San Francisco.

Let me back up. SOSUS is a network of listening devices or hydrophones installed on the ocean floor. Their job is to listen for submarines. We got a "sniff." That means there would be a P-3 or two out here spitting sonobuoys for days. A Yankee boat is a ballistic missile submarine with enough nuclear weapons on board to destroy half of the US West Coast.

This was another what we called a "real-world" situation. It also meant that I would be busy for a while. I had to brief the captain and commodore. The funny part was that my brother and Achilles were standing right next to me as I was delivering this extremely sensitive and classified brief. I guess I should've thought about that.

The captain whispered into the ops boss's ear, and LCDR Cunningham sidled up to me and whispered, "Atwood, your guests have to leave the space."

"Of course, sir, I'm sorry, I wasn't thinking." I pulled the guys away. "Sorry, but you can't stay in here right now. Go and play some checkers. I'll tell you all about it later." They quietly did as they were told.

We chased the Yankee boat for a day and a half. We knew where he (Ivan) was, and we let him know it. That was a big part of the game back then. There were about 120 Soviet submarines in the Pacific. At any given time, we knew where a hundred of them were. It was that elusive twenty "boats" that kept us on our toes. It was important to find them. It was more important to let them know we found them. This was done by actively pinging the shit out of them with active hull-mounted SONAR. It was always a victory to find them and bust their balls.

We headed toward San Diego, and the Tiger Cruise continued. One of the twelve nights on the way to San Diego, I got off watch at midnight. It was my custom to go topside for some fresh air and look at the sky before going to bed. It cleared my mind and lungs and relaxed me quite a bit. This night was special. There was no moon, no clouds, and no lights or humans for a thousand miles. It is impossible to explain how amazing the night sky jumps out at you and visually yells at you with its beauty on a night like this. I felt that I had to get the guys up here. I went down to berthing and got their lazy asses out of their racks. They were like two kids getting up for kindergarten.

"What are you doing? I was asleep. I don't want to go…"

"Just shut up and come with me. All you did was play checkers all day, you lazy bastards. You won't regret this. Trust me."

They dutifully did as they were told as I led them up to CIC. I wanted to get their eyes used to the dark, so we hung out in the "Blue Light Lounge" for a few minutes to adjust their eyes for night vision. Then we walked up to the bridge and then out to the bridge wing and up to the signal bridge. I said, "Look up and tell me what you see."

You would've thought they saw the real Santa Claus. Their eyes were saucers as they gazed at a night sky that neither of them had ever seen before. It can be and was truly was spectacular. The middle of the ocean on a moonless night is the only time and place you can see this many stars and planets. It's beyond description.

My brother mumbled in awe, "This is amazing. I've never seen anything like this before."

"Of course you haven't. That's why I dragged your sorry asses up here." Achilles was speechless. "Okay, guys, I'm tired, I'm going to bed," I said.

"Is it okay if I hang out here for a while?" Achilles finally spoke.

"Me too," added Steve.

"Sure, guys. We can hang out as long as you want. Enjoy it while you can." We three stayed up there for a few more hours just looking up at the night sky and talking.

Three days later, we were tying up the ship at Naval Air Station North Island in San Diego, California. I took some leave and enjoyed some downtime in the United States for a while.

UNDERWAY 23

The Next Chapter

I enjoyed a good long postdeployment leave. It was summertime, and I went back to the Jersey Shore to see my family and friends and do some surfing at my favorite spot. My old childhood friend, Donald, and I used to dominate the break at First Avenue in Normandy Beach. We did so again, just like old times. At night, it was the clubs and boardwalk in Seaside Heights and the local watering holes, The Sandpiper and Used To Be's. The Jersey Shore was a lot of fun in the summertime. Eventually, I had to return to San Diego for duty aboard the ship. My leave was expiring soon, like it always did.

My time on my current enlistment was getting short. I decided to reenlist. I had to weigh my options, and I didn't really have any. I still had another year on DDG-994 on this enlistment. It was spent in the shipyard and underway. More watches. More air control. More team trainers and more schools. The crew was preparing for another deployment. A deployment that neither Portman nor I would be a part of. To my surprise, Portman had reenlisted as well. I think he was on the outs with his father and didn't want to go back home, lest he appear to be a failure to his father. Who the fuck knew?

Six months later, it was time for shore duty. Five years flies by when you're having fun. Portman and I took orders to attend operations specialist class "C" school in San Diego along with a bunch of other schools. Here we go again, the two reluctant amigos thrown into another competitive arena like so many gladiators. Once again, just like "A" school, the top student got to pick first. History was repeating itself. I was once again determined to land a sweet billet in San Diego, but this time it was shore duty. Willie Portman actually backed off. He didn't actively challenge me. Perhaps the big lummox was learning. He would never admit that he probably wouldn't win this round. It's not in his DNA. I still wanted to piss on his grave.

"C" School was easy, fun even. It was a lot more comfortable living in the barracks at the ASW base in Point Loma than being underway. The expected competition between me and Portman was anticlimactic and apparently over. In fact, it never really continued at "C" School. I finished first in the class. Once again, that's because I had to work and study very hard every day. Portman kind of surfed through the curriculum doing the bare minimum. He assumed an attitude of "I just want to get through this." Instead of the usual "I am a winner and will defeat all in my path!" type of attitude that I was used to from him. He finished a distant sixth in the class, but he didn't seem to care.

There were some sweet shore duty billets all over the world available to the class. I chose my shore duty with the staff of the commander, third fleet, in my beloved Point Loma, California. That was the command Chester Nimitz had during the big one, WWII. Portman took a brainless gig with the manpower command in Millington, Tennessee, of all places. Something about having cousins in Tennessee and deer hunting or some such redneck-ass shit. We parted ways with a handshake and several beers and began the second chapter of our careers. I thought I was done with William J. Portman. I was wrong.

Shore duty was an insane joke. Compared to being constantly underway, shore duty was laughable. Instead of three or four duty sections, Third Fleet had twenty. It was like a regular job. This was all new to me. My adult life so far had been spent underway on a ship being thrown about by the sea with very little sleep. It was a life of endless watch standing and controlling aircraft. Shore duty at Third Fleet was mostly a 0700–1600 type of gig. The "Duty Day" consisted of wearing a pager and/or being at the headquarters overnight once a month! I'd never made such easy money.

Even though I had it made for now, I would occasionally stand on the cliffs of Point Loma, right off Catalina Boulevard and watch the ships sail in and out of San Diego Bay. I would get a twinge of envy. Where were they going? Where were they coming from? I would wonder. Were those clowns qualified? I knew that I could do it better than they could. Alas, I was stuck on shore duty.

I received a letter from my old shipmate Louis from Colorado. He, Double T, and I killed many brain cells together overseas. The letter was a wedding invitation. He was getting married in Denver in a month and a half. That would make it August of 1990. I gladly accepted the invitation. I requested and was granted a few days of leave.

The day before I left, there was a lot of chatter in the message traffic about Iraq and Kuwait flying around. I didn't pay much attention to it. Shit, I was on shore duty in San Diego. What the fuck did I care about the Middle East? I was waiting for my flight at the airport bar. CNN was on the television with the sound turned off. They were showing the Eighty-Second Airborne Division getting on planes. The crawler at the bottom of the screen was scrolling *Hussein...Kuwait...Iraq...Deploying.* Blah, blah, blah. I didn't pay much attention.

I made it to Denver, and Louis picked me up at the airport, and we went out for a beer in his neighborhood. The only thing on the TV was this shit in the Middle East. Wasn't there a ball game on? How about some women's lacrosse or the senior bowling tour? Anything! Come on! I didn't care about this shit, I was on shore duty!

We went out and partied like the crazy old swab-jockey rock stars that we were once. The next day, there was a two-and-a-half-hour Catholic mass Mexican wedding with holy communion and all the bells, whistles, and incense. I sat in the last pew and slept through most of it. I was told my mouth was agape as if catching flies, and I may have drooled and snored a little. I was hurting. The reception was fun, though. Louis had a great and very close Mexican American family. It was a good time.

I woke up on someone's couch. It turned to be the one in Louis's basement. It was Sunday, and I had to catch a flight. I had to work on Monday morning. Tommy T was there, and he took me to the airport.

I got to work on time Monday morning, and the place was a beehive of activity. As we would say, "assholes and elbows flying everywhere." I felt like I had just emerged from a tomb when I was informed that forces from Iraq had overrun and overthrown the sovereign government and country of neighboring Kuwait. I had kind of picked up on that part. "And we give a shit, why?" That was my attitude at the time. It was a dumb statement. The answer of course was oil. I'm sure there were more global decision-making issues involved, but that was way above my pay scale. Besides that, our president, George H. W. Bush, decided to make a stand. We were in business. Only this wasn't the business I was trained for. I could care less about the land mass known as the Middle East or the Arabian Peninsula. I am a blue-water sailor who specialized in finding enemy submarines and blowing them up. I harkened back to my old Chief's contention that we were instant mass murderers. I really missed the Cold War. Ah, the good old days. Nostalgia, it just ain't what it used to be.

The next few weeks were a bit hectic, but it was just paperwork. In the operations department, the messages were flying around like confetti at a New York Yankee ticker tape parade on Broadway. Okay, so I guess this may be a little serious. I still didn't really give a shit. I was on shore duty!

It was tense at the headquarters, but I didn't have to spend any extra time at work. It was business as usual. I could surf my new favorite spot every day, Sunset Cliffs. I was sharing a three-bedroom place in Ocean Beach with two other guys from Third Fleet. I was enjoying my life.

I came home from work one day in late August 1990, and there was a registered mail item in the mailbox. Actually, it was one of those sticky yellow "Post-it" type tickets you get from the mail carrier telling you to pick something up at the post office. *What the fuck could this be?* I thought to myself. It said that the sender was US Navy Manpower, Personnel, something, something, something. At lunch the next day, I went to the local post office on Santa Monica Avenue in Ocean Beach and stood in line waiting to retrieve my registered correspondence from whomever. I didn't open it until I got home after work. I cracked a beer and sat down to see what Uncle Sam wanted from me.

What I saw on official navy letterhead stunned me to say the least. I read it three times and still couldn't believe what I was looking at. I needed every bit of my inherited genetic denial to stop me from having a stroke. This couldn't be real. This was the day when I thought I may have made a big mistake with this navy business.

UNDERWAY 24

TPFDD and the MIUW

Flabbergasted? Is that a word? It certainly isn't a sentence. I was more than stunned. What I saw in front of me, the document I had pulled out from the government envelope, put me in a state of complete disbelief, shock, and anger. I couldn't help but ironically chuckle a little at the absurdity of its content. The letter contained official orders to report to a navy unit in Long Beach, California. That's about 120 miles north of San Diego. I was ordered to report in three days. Okay, where was Alan Funt? Point out the camera and end this! Who was fucking with me? This couldn't be real! I was on shore duty for crying out loud! I thought I was safe from all things operational. I was driving a desk. I was wrong.

I hopped on my motorcycle and rode back to HQ. I knew some guys at Third Fleet in manpower/logistics. I showed them my alleged orders (I still thought that it may be a sick and cruel joke) and asked incredulously if this was real. They said that I should go and talk to Captain Art Goodwin. That was when I learned about the TPFDD.

Art Goodwin was a most respected navy captain, with almost thirty years of service in the Navy Supply Corps. He was a walking encyclopedia of navy supply and logistics. I liked and respected him very much. I showed him my orders, and he immediately verified their validity. My denial flew out the window, shit!

"How can this possibly happen, Captain?"

He said, "Do you know about OP-Plans, OS1?"

"Yes, sir, we studied that at C School. And it's OS2, sir."

"No, young man, the results just came out. You were selected for E-6, you're a first class petty officer. First increment as usual. Congratulations! I guess this is one of those kiss/kick type of things." He chuckled a little bit. I did not. I thought about the OP-Plan.

From what I had learned, an OP-Plan is a "Big Picture" outline of how the ongoing operation will be carried out. It is a broad-brush concept of how we will deploy our assets to meet and defeat the threat. There are OP-Plans for every contingency you can imagine. The defense of the Korean Peninsula (OP-Plan 5027), there were hundreds more involving Africa and the Middle East and everywhere else on the globe. The OP-Plan is a strategic document. It doesn't get in to the nuts and bolts and tiny details of fighting a war. Admiral Chester Nimitz had an OP-Plan for the Pacific theater in World War Two. "All units are to put to sea. Seek engage and destroy enemy shipping," or words to that effect. It's not that simple these days. There are specialized units all over the country and the world that are part of the plan. It is a complicated mosaic of planning and timely execution. It is a formidable task to arrange all the pieces of the puzzle to support the mission. Ships, aircraft, supplies, water, fuel, people, and the people's stuff are all pieces of the puzzle.

Enter the TPFDD or Time Phased Force Deployment Data. The "Tip Fid" is a database that runs the whole OP-Plan. It contains a schedule for all the units that will be involved in a particular operation. It knows which air force aircraft, contract, or MSC cargo ship will take whatever unit, all of their equipment, and, of course, personnel to their planned destination of operations and on what day. It goes even further than that. Captain Goodwin told me that the "Managers" of the TPFDD had to ensure that each deploying asset was complete to what he called "Level Four Readiness."

"What the fuck does that mean?" I asked. I was having difficult time breathing. He explained that level 4 readiness was not only knowing which unit was shipping out and when (that's level 1), but how much equipment: vehicles, generators, tanks (fuel/water), boxes of spare parts, personal weapons, and ammunition, etc. (level 2). Humans: every unit had a billet structure. Every billet had a unique number. Each number was a human being with a particular rating or skill set (three). Level 4 was the amount of personal baggage that each number, excuse me, person, would be taking with them, usually an allotment of two sea bags.

"So who decides when or who has to ship out, fly, or whatever?" I asked.

"The TPFDD does, son." Apparently, this TPFDD was a living thing and a powerful document.

"So why do I have these orders in my hand, Captain?"

"Well, I'm guessing there was a hole in the good ole TPFDD." He was grinning, and I was ready to puke.

"What does that mean, sir?" I was getting exasperated. Not to mention my tiny, little beer buzz had long since worn off.

"This unit of yours, let me see your orders, MIUW 105, they must've been short of an OS1 and two sea bags," quipped the sage and calm Captain Goodwin.

"Yeah, so, I still don't get it!"

"My guess is that the good folks on watch at CINCPACFLT in Pearl Harbor identified this hole. I'll call it your hole." He laughed at his little joke. "They saw the hole and made a call."

"A call? What does that mean?"

"It means they needed a body with two sea bags in the form of an OS1. Congratulations again, by the way." It still wasn't clicking that I had been advanced to first class petty officer. I was now OS1 Atwood, big fucking deal!

"Well, who did they call for shit-sakes?" I was trying not to yell at or near this fatherly navy captain.

"Millington, Tennessee, navy manpower," He stated confidently.

"Who makes the decision over there? How do they know who and how to 'fill the hole?'"

I was learning too much too fast. "In a situation like this, they have a lot of power," said a serious Captain Goodwin. The levity had left the room.

"Who are 'they,' Captain? And what kind of power do they have and why do they have it?"

Captain Goodwin calmly looked down at the paper orders that were being squeezed and crumpled unconsciously in my right hand. "That kind of power," he said, pointing to the paper pulp forming in my palm.

"Hang on, who gets to make these types of decisions?" I asked.

"I'm guessing it would be whoever was on watch at the time. Whoever answered the phone. It may be that simple. Look around this place, Emmitt." I took a little pause when he used my real first name. Maybe it was his way of trying to calm me down. It worked. He continued, "There is no time to run things up the chain sometimes. A situation comes up, and it gets handled at the lowest level."

"And no one questions it?"

"Not right now they don't. It's about getting the right amount of qualified humans and their sea bags on that plane at Norton AFB at that date and time."

"So you're telling me that some dummy answering a phone call in Tennessee from Hawaii can send my dumb young ass to who-knows-where?

"That's pretty much it, son. You nailed it."

"Is there anything I can do?"

"Of course there is. You can pack two sea bags and report to your new unit up in Long Beach." He snapped his fingers in front of my glazed over eyes and said very kindly, "You do remember that part when you raised your right hand and said something like 'I, state your name…?'"

"Yes, sir, of course I remember that. I guess I wasn't ready for this. I've got a place and a motorcycle, a car, and a girlfriend—well, a chick I was banging. I've got bills and family, they're all in New Jersey, but SHIT!" I think I may have been whining.

"Okay, Em [I prefer Dana, but I didn't correct him], I'll go and talk to the admiral right now. Go take care of your personal business. Call your banks. Mortgage, car loan, credit cards, and tell them you are being involuntarily mobilized. You can send them a copy of those orders. That should be enough. The law is on your side on this one. We will support you on this side. Listen to me, kiddo, this may not be a bad thing. I'm guessing you are a career man. You'll come back with enough decorations to snap a Christmas tree. This experience could put you way ahead of your peers, assuming you survive."

"Very funny, Captain." I couldn't help but chuckle. His calm down-to-earth, fatherly demeanor relaxed me a bit. I still couldn't get past the "Why me?" part of the whole ordeal. Then I started thinking. And then I thought some more. CINCPACFLT saw a hole in the TPFDD. They made a call to Tennessee. Some asshole answered the phone. Then it hit me like every stale metaphor: a ton of bricks. A bolt out of the blue. A light bulb going off in my head. One name came to my insanely angry mind, and that name was Portman.

"Portman." I spoke his name out loud through clenched teeth. That podunk-ass son of a bitch answered the phone in Millington and plugged my sorry carcass into the CINCPACFLT TPFDD hole. This time he may have succeeded in screwing me over. I could picture him sitting at a desk in Tennessee taking the phone call, tittering and giggling to himself like he just farted and someone else got the blame. He's sitting there thinking that he got the last laugh of our strange relationship. I was now hell-bent on making sure that would not happen.

I was probably two heartbeats away from a massive stroke. I was beyond angry. I was in a place I didn't know existed. I silently vowed to not just piss on his grave. I hatched an evil plan: drink twenty-four beers, eat four carne asada burritos from Santana's on Rosecrans, drink more beer and a bottle of bourbon, go to Willie Portman's grave, and piss all over it. I was not done. Act two: I pull down my pants and deposit a gigantic turd right next to the headstone. Wait, I was still not done. I bring a feather just like the Romans. I am now puking on Willie Portman's grave. And for dessert, I ejaculate on the very flowers I just pissed on. That may be kind of gay, but I would want to release every bodily excretion and secretion on this bastard's grave. *Shit!* I guess I was shipping out in three days.

That was the day I most humbly realized that I was merely an instrument of the Department of the Navy and a deployable and expendable asset.

UNDERWAY 25

The MIUW and the Gulf

The guys I lived with were cool and were able to get someone else in my room without anyone losing any money. I put most of my stuff and my car and motorcycle in storage and kept few things in the closet. I contacted all my banks and sent them a copy of my orders, and they all agreed to hold all my loan balances with no interest until or if I returned.

I packed my two seabags and got a ride to Long Beach. I rode in the admiral's car. He insisted. It was a nice gesture. I sat in the back seat. I checked in with the MIUW determined to be an angry asshole with a bad attitude. The Mobile Inshore Undersea Warfare unit is a Reserve unit with a handful of active duty staff or crew. I initially deemed them as weekend warrior knuckleheads who didn't know shit. I was active duty and considered myself superior. That attitude would soon change. Once I got over myself and my anger. I realized that it took too much energy to be a dick and stay angry. I also realized these guys were smart, capable, and professional. The commanding officer, a navy reserve captain, was an engineer who owned a small manufacturing company, something to do with hydraulics and rubber seals. The executive officer was a lawyer. The Ops Boss was a big wig executive at Hughes Aircraft. One of the Lieutenants was a former Naval Academy running back. There were mail carriers, UPS drivers, and teachers. There was an amazing array of diverse talent.

I was appointed the lead operations specialist petty officer. I had another First Class, a Second Class, and two Third Classes in the division. The other OS1 was an Arizona Highway Patrolman. This was a man who had vast weapons knowledge and experience. The OS2 was a registered ER nurse. One OS3 worked for Disney in Los Angeles. My favorite was OS3 Parker. He was an angry black man "straight out of Compton." "Homie from the 'hood," as I used to refer to him. He was incredibly smart and studious. He was going to school and studying political science. We would spend endless hours on watch arguing politics and current affairs. He loved to argue as much as I did. In fact, there were times when I agreed with him but would assume an opposite position just to have an argument. Sometimes the other guys would be visibly nervous thinking that a race riot was about to start, but we knew what we were doing. It never got ugly. It was fun.

Our chief was a friggin' Special Agent with the DEA! Rodney Amos was the real deal and a total real-life badass. He was also an amicable, fair, and coolheaded leader. There were times when I didn't know how to handle things. I had to go to the chief. He always knew what to do. I would follow that man to the ends of the earth. He was a great chief.

I was impressed. I was no longer feeling sorry for myself. I was a full-time sailor. I should actually be prepared and expect to get screwed. These guys were professionals and citizen sailors with families and real jobs and careers. They were the ones getting the royal screw job. I was issued a full set of woodland and desert camouflage uniforms. I wasn't really crazy about that. Now I looked like some army dude or marine. The worst was, I was also issued an M16 rifle, a gas mask, and a helmet. The rifle had a serial number, and I had to sign for it. Now I was responsible for a weapon. The thing is, I really didn't know how to fire it. But don't you know, I got a crash course in taking it apart, cleaning it, and reassembling it from a marine staff sergeant.

This was happening very fast. One day, I was a blue-water sailor on staff duty, the next I was a GI Joker with a rifle about to ship out to who the hell knows where. My little brain was spinning. Did I mention I had a little brain? It's true.

The good old TPFDD determined that it was time to meet our planes at Norton AFB, so off we went. Our destination would be the major harbor facility of Ad-Dammam, Saudi Arabia. All of the unit's equipment and vehicles were loaded onto two C-5 Galaxies and five C-141 Starlifters. All of us rode in one of the C-5s. It was a long trip from Riverside, California, to Dhahran, Saudi Arabia. We stopped somewhere in Maine, and again in Spain. We refueled three times in the air. We were all pretty spent by the time we got to Saudi. When the ass end of the aircraft opened up and the ramp went down to let us all deplane, we all walked on the tarmac. I thought of every Vietnam movie I'd ever seen. The black surface was still radiating the heat of the day. It was brutal even at night. That was the first "Toto, I have a feeling we're not in Kansas anymore" moment. There would be a few more of these moments.

After a few days, we had all our equipment and vehicles in place for the mission, which was to protect and defend the harbor facility. The mission statement made sense. The problem was we had no idea how this plan would be implemented. There was zero infrastructure for us. We, the MIUW Command, had to get very creative. Even the simplest of things such as eating, shitting, and sleeping had not been prearranged. We had to improvise. We set up a sleeping area in the coolest part of a parking lot with camouflage netting and lumber scrounged from somewhere. For food, we had a several-week supply of Meals, Ready to Eat or MREs. We called them Meals Regurgitated by Everyone. They weren't horrible, but they weren't all that exciting, either. We ate them mostly out of boredom rather than hunger. The main issue with the MRE, other than its fine international cuisine, was that they were extremely binding. Talk about shitting a brick. As Minnesota Senator Al Franken said of the MRE, "They go down and deploy successfully, but they don't have an exit strategy."

We lived like a band of gypsies, sleeping on cots, eating MREs, and drinking hot water. There was no air-conditioning or refrigeration. The September Saudi heat was brutal. It was hard to do anything during the day. So we did most of our work at night. Eventually we gained access to a closed Saudi Coast Guard administrative build-ing on the pier. We had to get the US Navy Construction Battalion or Seabees and their army counterpart involved to get electrical, water, and sewer going. One of our chiefs purloined, or creatively acquired—Okay, stole—a couple of air conditioners. We were slowly getting civilized. Almost every day, I had a *M*A*S*H* (the television show) flashback. "*M* stands for 'mobile,' and mobile you shall be!" The Command was making plans with the nearby Army supply and logistics units, as well as the Coast Guard.

Eventually, we all moved off our cots on the pier to a worker's compound outside the gate of the harbor facility. It was starting to get normal, and we were ready to become operational. The MIUW van was a mobile CIC, or a CIC in a box. It was equipped with RADAR and radios. It also had a sonobuoy processing capability. The plan was to move the van to various places in the harbor with the help of the US Army and set up shop. We would monitor the harbor with RADAR and lookouts. We also had the Coast Guard Reserve unit from Wisconsin. They had five twenty-five-foot Boston Whalers running with twin Mercury 150 HP engines and two .50-caliber machine guns. I would watch the RADAR for endless hours along with the other OSs, and if an errant contact was spotted, I would give the Coast Guard vessel or "Raider Boat" a vector or heading to intercept. The contacts were mostly fishing boats and sometimes just some junk floating on the surface. Meanwhile, we had no clue what our enemy was doing. Were they preparing an attack on our facil-ity? That's what kept us on our toes. Army Intelligence was no help. Everything they told us was wrong. We were on our own. Saddam was inexplicably sitting still, letting us build up infrastructure and offensive power. It made no sense.

This went on for months, and then one day, it got a little interesting. Again, we were in Saudi Arabia, well south of Kuwait. Our position was considered a major strategic target. A tremendous amount of war material was arriving to the port. Huge ships full of weapons, ammunition, and supplies were unloading daily. There were ships loaded with tanks and helicopters. There was even a ship loaded with aluminum caskets. That was a little unsettling. We had a daily manifest of the ships that were coming and going, and we would validate it with the Raider boats and/or our lookout. It would make sense if the enemy tried to do some damage here. The main perceived threat was the SCUD missile, especially one with a lethal chemical payload. In preparation for this, we were equipped with chemical suits and gas masks. It was very heavy hot, difficult, and cumbersome to don these uniform items and be functional.

On this day, President Hussein thought it would be wise to test one of his SCUD missiles. Apparently, he had a shitload of them. That decision was both a tactical and strategic blunder. We received a warning, and it was a total Chinese fire drill. Everybody had to dress out in the chemical gear. It was pure and utter chaos. I saw grown men crying in fear. I thought about the old wartime adage: "There are no atheists in the foxhole." In my case, that turned out to be bullshit. I wasn't the least bit afraid. If anything, I was angry. It wasn't until years later that I realized I was simply in a very deep state of denial. It turned out that Saddam was merely fueling up a SCUD and warming the engines (according to the satellite reports), so the SCUD attack that wasn't only served to reveal the weaknesses in our early warning and reaction time. These items were addressed by leadership so when the missiles really started to fly, we were much better prepared.

The real missiles started flying on the nineteenth of January 1990. I was not out in the field on watch in the van, but on watch in the barracks facility that we borrowed from our host nation. It was built to house migrant workers who would most likely be from Pakistan or India. The Saudis didn't work. They hired people to do the heavy lifting. That included us. It was a brand-new compound, complete with tennis courts, a chow hall, and of course, a mosque. It was not a dump.

We would work three days out in the field and had six days in the compound. I didn't know this at the time, but the navy had sent letters to all our families containing instructions about what *not* to send to us. High Command was so worried about the cultural differences between us and afraid that we may act like real Americans, embarrassing ourselves and insulting our hosts. I'm sure they were right. I was told that my family was instructed not to send any pictures of women showing skin. No catalogs or racy magazines were authorized. Certainly any sort of pornography was strictly prohibited. However, my brother didn't like being told what to do or not to do. So I started getting regular shipments of bottled water. Of course, he would empty out the nasty natural water and fill the bottle with eighty-proof vodka for shipment to Saudi. The "family videos" he shipped over were the XXX (triple-X) variety. As a result, I usually had a little stash of unauthorized hooch and would partake nightly while in the barracks.

January 19 was one of those nights. I was sleeping in air-conditioned comfort when I heard the sirens. This was a new sound. I should've known something was sure to happen. Just hours earlier, we were all issued a pill to take because of the threat of chemical warfare. It was as if someone had a clipboard with a checklist on it and was hitting the items in sequence. I wasn't really surprised when the shit started hitting the fan. Alarms and sirens that we had never heard to date started blaring. I threw on some clothes and walked down to our watch station, which had a television always tuned to the CNN feed out of Bahrain. Wolf Blitzer was announcing the commencement of hostilities in the region. *This is how I find out that we are at war?* I thought to myself. Then I heard a *boom! Whoosh!* And another *boom!* It was very loud. Finally there was a far-off *bang!* This was a sequence of noises that would become a daily occurrence. There was a Phased Array Tracking RADAR to Intercept on Target, or PATRIOT, missile battery in a parking lot adjacent to our position. Their job was to detect, track, engage, and destroy an incoming ballistic missile threat, which they did this with impressive accuracy. They weren't perfect, though. One SCUD made it past our position and hit a target south of us in the town of Al Khobar. I guess we were lucky on that one. It was a strange feeling to think that someone was actually trying to kill me. I couldn't help but think that I was just a goofy surfer dude from the Jersey Shore, why would you want to hurt me? Once again, my denial kicked in, and I handled the situation moment to moment in complete denial.

Back to the PATRIOT.

So the first boom was the defensive missile leaving the launch tube. The whoosh was the missile in flight. The second boom happened when the weapon becomes supersonic. Then, hopefully, there was a final far-off crack or bang. That would be the PATRIOT successfully intercepting and eliminating a target. During the attacks, we would listen for the sequence of sounds while the action unfolded. After a *boom, whoosh, boom, bang*, there was always some high-fives and a sigh of relief. One day, there was fifth noise what was new to us. It was a metallic *tinkle, tinkle, tinkle*. It was the sound of pieces of the destroyed SCUD coming down to Earth. After the "all clear" was sounded, I went out to get me some of that shit. I found a chunk of metal about the size of a piece of legal paper. The SCUD was an old Soviet weapon system, and Iraq was a client. The chunk had Russian or Cyrillic printing stamped on it. Those PATRIOT batteries did a great job. That was the day I qualified for membership at my father's VFW post in Manasquan, New Jersey.

The Coalition air campaign did an impressive job of removing the enemy threat from the air. After about three weeks, it got back to being boring, but we had to stay vigilant. Then it got really boring. It was obvious that things were wrapping up over here. Even General Norman Schwarzkopf was running out of sound bites at the daily news conferences, which, of course, were aired on CNN. The ground campaign began, and by mid-February, it was pretty much over. General Powell and the president decided that it was time to punch out. Saddam was still in power. We drove them out of Kuwait and put one hell of a whooping on them during "the mother of all battles." The original mission statement had been realized. It was time to go home. I know that sounded easy, but it was not.

In military speak, it's called retrograde. That meant cleaning all of your shit, packing, and packaging it *all* up. You couldn't leave anything behind unless it had been officially purchased by the host nation—in this case, Saudi Arabia. Then, everything had to get loaded on planes for the flight home. The cleaning part was important. Every bit of sand, dirt, and mud had to be scrubbed off all the equipment. All weapons had to be cleaned, inspected, and accounted for. Then they would be packed up and shipped out. The army had a unit tantamount to TSA or Customs. They inspected everything, the vehicles, the equipment, our bags, and us. They even had dogs! Apparently, these canines were especially trained in detecting explosive residue. The bastards found my chunk of SCUD and confiscated it. The days of bringing your kid brother a Kraut Luger or a Jap sword are over. I really didn't care all that much about that; I just wanted to go home. After what seemed like an eternal wait, we boarded a chartered Evergreen 747 and flew out of there. We partied like maniacs and drank every drop of booze on the plane in less than three hours.

Once I had safely returned to California, I took two weeks of leave and went back to New Jersey. My father met me at the airport with a twelve-pack of cheap beer, and we wasted no time celebrating. We went to a great old hangout in Newark called Nicks. Right around the corner was McGovern's. My brother and my cousin Danny showed up, and we had a blast. I spent the rest of my leave just decompressing and visiting family and friends in New Jersey and New York City. I knew that when I got back to California, it would take a few days to separate from the MIUW, and that soon, I would be back in San Diego with Third Fleet and living in my old place.

I was more than ready to get back to my business as usual on shore duty. My time with the MIUW was interesting, to say the least. It certainly changed my attitude toward the Reserves. These citizen sailors were professional and dedicated. They left behind good jobs and families simply because they were ordered to. That's what they had all agreed to do. I'm not saying it was a fabulous experience, but it all worked out, and not one of us was hurt. I went from angry asshole to a grateful and respectful shipmate to these folks. I don't regret the experience. Captain Goodwin was right. The unit received many awards. I got a Navy Achievement medal as a consolation prize, signed by a three-star admiral. I would be a force to reckon with come advancement time. Maybe I wouldn't piss on Portman's grave after all. On second thought… Now I was going home. Most importantly, I hadn't been laid in over six months. No nookie in Saudi for me. I was ready to get home and remedy that situation. That was the day I came home from war.

UNDERWAY 26

Back on Shore Duty

I separated from the MIUW on very good terms and returned to San Diego and Third Fleet Headquarters to a hero's welcome. As I mentioned, my time the in Gulf had earned me several unit commendations and citations, as well as the Navy and Marine Corps Achievement Medal (NAM). I don't know how they did it, but Captain Goodwin and the admiral managed to wangle me an additional eighteen months at the command. I guess a captain and an admiral could get a few "outside the box"—or in this case, completely unheard of—things done. I was very humbled and appreciative that they would do that for me. I decided to take full advantage of this time ashore. I was pretty sure I wouldn't be deploying again anytime soon.

I enrolled at San Diego Mesa College and studied aviation operations. I worked during the day and went to school at night. I had my cool pad in Ocean Beach. After school, I would stop at a little dump on Newport Avenue called Shanty Hogan's. Hogan, the owner/operator, was a quirky former marine helicopter pilot. He flew a CH-53 during Operation Frequent Wind and helped evacuate Saigon during those infamous final days in 1975. I told him about my refugee experience with the boat people. He told me about landing on the embassy roof and pushing a perfectly good aircraft over the side of the ship to make room on the flight deck. We also talked aviation. He had a Beechcraft Bonanza. I had just completed my private pilot training and successfully passed my check ride and received my pilot's license. Crazy old Hogan and I would spend a lot of hours flying the Baja Peninsula. If I had an off weekend, we would blast down to San Felipe, Punta Chivato, Mulege, and a hundred other dirt strips in Mexico. It was a ton of fun.

He bought a karaoke machine for the bar and planned to have what he called a "Dingaling Sing-along" night twice weekly on Tuesdays and Thursdays. We had spent more than a few nights singing by the campfire under the stars, so he knew that I could carry a tune without a paper bag, so he asked me if I would be the host. We agreed on fifty dollars a night and five beers for four hours. Those were some crazy times.

The strangely unique sea side community of Ocean Beach in San Diego had a municipal fishing pier jutting out into the ocean at the foot of Niagara Avenue. There was a rustic, folksy little greasy spoon café out at the end of the pier. My friend James Michaels was part of an amateur improvisational comedy group that would perform in the café for free every once in a while. One night, I had nothing to do, so I went to see the show. They really weren't all that funny. Kind of lame actually, but they had their moments. But I didn't become a regular participant and patron of their art because of their comedy prowess; I came because of a girl.

When I first saw her, I was instantly smitten. It was as if she was lit with her own spotlight in this dingy dump. She was all I could look at. She had straight jet-black hair with bangs. Her creamy skin seemed to glow. I begged James to introduce us. She did not seem the least bit interested in, or the least bit impressed, with me. I did manage to get her phone number though. I called her on three occasions. Once, I actually spoke to her, but she pretty much blew me off, so I figured I was done. There are other gorgeous chicks out there, right?

Fast forward a few weeks. I was running the goofy karaoke in Shanty Hogan's. In walked the improv comedy weenies and the lovely Miss Andrea. I was pretty sure my friend James Michaels set the whole thing up. The comedy/drama geeks wasted no time taking over the microphone and sang up a storm. This was great for me. It kept me busy, and I didn't have to sing any songs to get things going.

It was a great night. I ignored Andrea for most of the night because I was actually pretty busy.

I decided to put my highly trained and razor-sharp air controllers brain to work. I remembered her phone number, so when I had her ear for a fleeting second, I said, "Hi. Is your number still 574-8508?"

"Yeah, it is," she answered somewhat dazed. "You actually remember that?"

"Yeah, but now I'll forget it. You obviously don't want to talk to me. Oh, sorry gotta go."

It was a brilliant play. She told me later that her friend Melanie gave her the what-for. Andrea used her as a go-between to broker a call from me. It was all very junior high, but I told her that, sure, I would give it another try.

I gave it a week and punched in the digits. Of course, she didn't answer. But she did call me back. We agreed to meet at a bar in Ocean Beach, and the courtship began. We went on many dates over the next six months or so. She came with Hogan and me to Mexico a few times. We still maintained separate domiciles. At one point, her relationship with her roommate became troublesome, and my lease was running out. Besides that, I would be leaving Third Fleet HQ for sea duty soon. This is what is called a paradigm shift. After careful analysis, we decided to get a place together. We found a nice little condo up in Mission Hills, just north of the San Diego airport. It was near downtown and the trolley tracks, and the rent was within budget. We've been together ever since.

Back at Third Fleet, my time was running out. Captain Goodwin was right as far as my career and advancement was concerned. I actually was, as he said, far ahead of my peers. I had taken the advancement exam for chief petty officer (CPO or E-7) and was selected on my first attempt. That's almost unheard of. I was soon to be wearing the uniform of a chief. Portman was still a first class. It was time for another reenlistment. Naturally, I did. I heard through the navy grapevine that Portman had not done so. He had enough. I win again. Nice try, you big oaf! I will still piss on your grave.

That was the day I realized that I was indeed a career navy man. I felt confident in my chosen path. I also realized that I was very much in love with Andrea.

UNDERWAY 27

Underway Again and CPO Initiation

I spoke to my detailer and was pleased to hear that there were plenty of billets for a First Class, soon to be Chief, in San Diego. I went to a two-week ASAC refresher course up on the hill in Point Loma to get my air control currency restored. I was told by the detailer that USS *Tisdale* (FFG-27) was in need of a senior OS. He also said that because it was a Reserve Frigate, they wouldn't be going on any deployments. Really? That sounded too good to be true. Which of course was the case here. I should've gone with the old navy axiom of never trusting a recruiter or a detailer (you could probably add lawyer to the list).

I chose the *Tisdale*. It turned out that they didn't go on any major deployments, but they were scheduled to conduct a few Law Enforcement Operations, or LEOPS. I found that out when I checked aboard. The chief's Mess was happy to see me. I was another Chief Selectee, fresh meat, and was immediately treated as such. I was issued a checklist and a timeline for the whole initiation season. I use the word "initiation" with a little bit of pride. CPO initiations do not happen anymore, which is probably a good thing. The process of going from E-6 to E-7 and becoming a "genuine chief" is now called "transition." In 1992, the rite of passage had degraded to focus on humiliation and discomfort. In the current transition environment, the focus is on physical fitness, teamwork, all kinds of training, and fund raising. The idea of both systems was to prepare the sailor to take on the rigors and responsibility of wearing the khaki uniform with the fouled anchors and handling all the constant decisions that come with it.

For the next two months, I would be serving the Chiefs their meals and shining their boots. There were three other selectees on board, so at least I wasn't alone. We had to carry a big, heavy log-book or "charge book" on a chain on our shoulders at all times. If a selectee was cited with an infraction, such as not completing a train-ing requirement on time or improperly addressing a "genuine chief," an entry would be made in the book and would be used as evidence against the selectee at the trial which culminates at the end of the process. Needless to say, we were always set up for failure. It was part of the whole intention. Accepting failure, making a decision, and making the wrong decision were a daily occurrence. It was all part of the game.

The end of the game happens every year starting September 15. It is an all-nighter filled with fun and games. One of the games for us was a "Truth Serum" guzzling competition. "Truth Serum" was a concoction of nastiness supplied by none other than the selectees. We were issued a shopping list with things like Limburger cheese, anchovy paste, garlic and onion juice, eggs, raw fish. It was all edible. It was all disgusting. Naturally, I won the first round of the guz-zling contest. For the finals, I was given a choice to drink more truth serum or eat a *balut*, which is a Filipino delicacy, or so they say. It is an unhatched fertilized chicken or duck egg that has been aged while steeping in all of its foul fowl bodily fluids. I couldn't handle any more truth serum. I was not going to puke in front of these guys, so I opted for the egg. One of the initiators used a spoon and tapped the top of the eggshell to remove the lid. I closed my eyes and downed it. I could feel feathers and a beak going down my throat. It was all I could do to not reflexively regurgitate. I was then locked in a box, soaked with water, smeared with Limburger and other gross things. The whole time, I had a bull penis around my neck, like a meat scarf. I think I was sufficiently humbled. We were all found guilty in the kangaroo court despite the arguments of my "attorney." Fines were issued and paid with the money we were instructed to bring.

Eventually, it was time to clean up and put on a fresh new uniform for the pinning ceremony.

Needless to say, I was exhausted but excited at the same time. I've been to a bunch of pinning ceremonies. I always wondered what it would feel like to be *that* guy. It felt very good. A form letter from the master chief petty officer of the navy was read. The commanding officer said some encouraging words, and the CPO creed was read. As it was read, I could feel the hair on the back of my neck bristle and a lump in my throat. I still have the same reaction to this day. I can't read the CPO creed or hear it read without choking back a tear. That's how important being a chief is to me. I realized at that moment that this was the most important event of my life. Everything would be different from now on. Andrea pinned my anchors on. All the chiefs who, mere hours ago, were tormenting us mercilessly, were now shaking our hands and embracing us as brothers. I was twenty-seven years old. That's very young for a Chief. I felt confident. I thought about Doug. What would he think? Better yet, what would he say? Something dry, funny, and meaningful, I'm sure. It's interesting that I thought about Doug before I thought about my dad.

That was the first day that I actually felt like a grown-up.

Chief Petty Officer Creed

During the course of this day you have been caused to humbly accept challenge and face adversity. This you have accomplished with rare good grace. Pointless as some of these challenges may have seemed, there are valid, time-honored reasons behind each pointed barb. It was necessary to meet these hurdles with blind faith in the fellowship of Chief Petty Officers. The goal was to instill in you that trust is inherent with the donning of the uniform of a chief. It was our intent to impress upon you that challenge is good; a great and necessary reality which cannot mar you—which, in fact, strengthens you. In your future as a Chief Petty Officer, you will be forced to endure adversity far beyond that imposed upon you today. You must face each challenge and adversity with the same dignity and good grace you demonstrated today. By experience, by performance, and by testing, you have been this day advanced to Chief Petty Officer. In the United States Navy—and only in the United States Navy—the rank of E7 carries with its unique responsibilities. No other armed force in the world grants the responsibilities, nor the privileges to enlisted personnel comparable to the those you are now bound to observe and are expected to fulfill. Your entire way of life is now changed. More will be expected of you; more will be demanded of you. Not because you are an E7 but because you are now a Chief Petty Officer. You have not merely been promoted one paygrade, you have joined an exclusive fellowship and, as in all fellowships, you have a special responsibility to your comrades, even as they have a special responsibility to you. This is why we in the United States Navy may maintain with pride our feelings of accomplishment once we have attained the position of Chief Petty Officer. Your new responsibilities and privileges do not appear in print. They have no official standing; they cannot be referred to by name, number, nor file. But because they have existed for over one hundred years, Chiefs before you have freely accepted responsibility beyond the call of printed assignment. Their actions and their performance demanded the respect of their seniors as well as their juniors. It is now required that you be the fountain of wisdom, the ambassador of good will, the authority in personal relations, as well as in technical applications. "Ask the Chief" is a household phrase in and out of the Navy. You are now the Chief. The exalted position you have now achieved—and the word "exalted" is used advisedly—exists because of the attitude and performance of the Chiefs before you. It shall exist only as long as you, and your fellow Chiefs maintain these standards. It was our intention that you never forget this day. It was our intention to test you, to try you, and to accept you. Your performance has assured us that you will wear "the hat" with the same pride as your comrades in arms before you.

UNDERWAY 28

LEOPS

I spent the next year mostly underway in the Southern California Operations Area. SOCAL is a huge area of Pacific Ocean off the San Diego coast. It is cordoned off in various areas in different shapes and sizes tailored for various kinds of operations. The main area is called FLEETAHOT, where most of the surface operations happen. The shore bombardment area, or SHOBA, covers the southern tip of San Clemente Island and a piece of the ocean surrounding it. It is used to practice shore bombardment or Naval Gunfire Support (NGFS). The ASW or SOCAL ASW Range is called SOAR. There is a bunch more OPAREAS depending on what you are doing. There's a mine training area (ARPA), an electronic warfare area (SESEF), and a whole bunch more. Even most of the airspace above had areas dedicated to different kinds of air operations and training. The big one was Warning Area 291 (W291). We frequented all the areas depending on what the focus of training was on that particular underway period. We were completing all the compulsory tasks necessary to deploy. The big checklist of inspections and weapons and systems qualification needed to be completed before we embarked on a Law Enforcement Operations (LEOPS) deployment. We were underway a lot. It felt strangely good to be back at sea, underway. I guess it's a comfort zone thing. I felt right at home being on a ship at sea. I was good at it. Life at sea was tough. It could be arduous and uncomfortable. Life at sea was a little less tough as a Chief.

LEOPS represented the open ocean front of our war against drugs. Alas, the grand old Cold War had sadly disappeared with the demise of the Soviet Union. All the rhetoric I had grown up with and all the training I had received to this point was to fight the big blue-water battle with the Commies. It was time to reinvent ourselves as a fighting force. Counter Narcotics Operations presented itself as a convenient opportunity to justify the navy budget. We were to sail south to the coast of Central and South America and were assigned a box the size of about ten thousand square miles to patrol.

Our job was to report any vessels or aircraft of interest, which could be several things. The obvious one was the slick speed boat with two or more outboard engines flying across the water. We called them "go-fast boats." They were hard to detect and keep up with, and, as we would find out, hard to stop. Another vessel of interest would be a fishing boat that was not engaged in fishing and nowhere near the known productive fishing grounds. These were the support vessels. They would be stationed at a known position and loaded with fuel and supplies for the go-fasts. They served as a remote convenience store, AM/PM or 7-Eleven in the sea. An air contact of interest was any contact on our SPS-49 RADAR that wasn't flying in an established airway or at unusually low altitudes. There was a painful process of reporting these contacts to our bosses in Florida. Between the bad communications and the multilayered and confusing political process, many intervention opportunities were missed. We were new to all this, so the learning curve was steep.

We had a United States Coast Guard detachment on board to do the heavy work. They would be the ones boarding and inspecting the vessels of interest. These Coasties were the best in the business. They were 100 percent professional. I was so impressed by their focus and knowledge while stopping a vessel; whether the ship was from Panama, Venezuela, or Columbia, these guys knew exactly what paperwork to ask for and how to properly analyze it. They would match the crew listing with the people onboard. They especially were hip to many of the tricks of their adversary's trade. They knew where to look and what to look for. They were very well trained.

We also had a shipboard helicopter that we would send out to search an area. We had just enough tools, training, knowledge, and weapons to be dangerous, but we seldom got the opportunity to use them. We basically had no authority out there. We would locate what we called a "dirty contact." The idea was to stop, board, and search the vessel.

The problem was that of politics and procedure. We would identify the vessel's origin and report it to a USCG command center in Florida. Then, there would be a petition to the vessel's registered government to allow a legal stop at sea, which could take days. Meanwhile, as the painful process was chugging along, the vessel would keep going on about its business unmolested. They knew the game. Nine times out of ten, they would get to a point where they knew we couldn't touch them and slip away from the ship, the crew, the Coast Guard, the helicopter, everything.

There was one time, though, when we came upon a "fishing boat" several hundred miles off the coast of Venezuela. He had no business being this far out in such a piece-of-shit boat. It was riding low in the water, which meant it was heavy. All the fishing gear was on the deck and obviously hadn't been used in a long time. The nets were rotting, and the deck equipment was not suitable for commercial fishing. We could see through binoculars that the davits and motors were rusted and most likely seized. We began the political process. The captain decided to wait this one out. The piece of shit in our sights was so slow that they wouldn't be able to make it to safety before we got permission to board. It was a gamble, but a good one. Naturally, the Venezuelans started heading east toward the coast, but speed, time, and distance were on our side. It was time to see how crooked these governments were down here.

Two days went by, and we were still a hundred miles off the Venezuelan coast. We got word from Radio Central that diplomatic permission was granted. Our ship was given a temporary proxy to act on behalf of Venezuela and do our thing. I had no idea what manner of behind-the-scenes bullshit went on during those two and a half days. I'm guessing Senor Venezuela got pressured by someone to throw us a bone and relent to our dogged pursuit.

It was time for our first real intervention and boarding. Our Spanish speaker got on the radio and ordered the boat to heave to and prepare to be boarded. Meanwhile, the Coast Guard was suiting up in body armor, weapons, and search tools. These guys were ready to go. They lived for this shit. I was so very impressed by their professionalism.

They fearlessly boarded and took control of the boat. The crew was assembled in the aft fishing area of the boat. The first thing they meticulously analyzed was the vessel's paperwork, which included the vessel registration and crew list, including their nationality. There was a captain, a first mate, an engineer, a fisherman, and a deck hand. A quick inspection of the fishing and deck equipment confirmed our suspicions. This gear had not been operated in a very long time. None of the hoisting motors were functional. The fishing nets were twisted in a disorganized and rotting in pile on the deck. These clowns were not fishing. Then the Coasties started with the questions. Keep in mind that they hadn't even started searching anything yet.

"What are you doing this far out in the ocean, Captain?"

"*Estamos pescando.*" (We are fishing). I don't know how he said this with a straight face.

"May we see your fish, Captain?" A reasonable question from the coast guard officer in charge, Lieutenant Junior Grade Ernesto Zampa from Corpus Christi, Texas. He spoke perfect Spanish. It would be very hard to bullshit this guy.

"*No estamos sacando mucho pescado.*" No kidding, Skipper, of course, you haven't caught any fish. The last time I checked, your gear should be in the water to catch fish.

"What are you using for bait, Captain?" This should be a good one.

"We were just going to fish for bait now." All this was being relayed to the bridge by a Coast Guard translator.

"So you don't have any bait, and you haven't caught any fish. Is that correct, Captain?" I thought it was kind of cool that LTJG Zampa was treating the captain with respect. He reminded me of LT Colombo from the old Peter Falk TV show. Mr. Zampa knew he had this guy.

"*Si, Senor.*"

"It doesn't look like this equipment is working. How do you get the nets back on the boat?"

"*El pescador y el ayudante esta del otro lado.*" He pointed to the two scrawniest members of this motley crew. I think everybody at this point knew it was over. Twenty-seven of these guys could not possibly haul up a load of fish in these nets by hand. The CG still wanted more evidence, so the searching began. These guys were so good.

There was no sign of any narcotics in any of the obvious and not-so-obvious places. They did find some interesting things though. The boat ran on a single-diesel engine for propulsion, yet there were ten fifty-gallon drums of gasoline lashed to the gunwales. When questioned why there was so much gas on a diesel boat, the captain's answer was deadpan as he pointed to a tiny, little gas Honda generator. I think this guy could give Portman a good poker game. He asserted that he was carrying over five hundred gallons of gasoline for a seven-horsepower two-stroke engine.

It got better. The boarding crew now smelled blood. They found that some of the voids and tanks below decks had false bottoms and false sight tubes and were filled with, you guessed it, gasoline. That was enough. This was obviously a remote logistics support station for the go-fasts. Just out of curiosity, they checked the reefer holds and dry supply areas. As expected, there was enough food and water to feed ten guys for a month. All this data was forwarded to the area commander in Florida, and it was decided to put the crew in custody and seize the vessel.

We sailed back to the Venezuela coast and were met by our South American counterparts. *Los cinco hombres* were turned over to the authorities, as was the vessel of interest. We never found out what happened to them. We got underway and headed back out to our box in the sea.

We got about halfway to the box when we were ordered to turn around, transit the Panama Canal, go to a place in the western Caribbean Sea off the coast of Nicaragua, and await further orders. We went through the canal or "the Ditch" at night. The sun was just rising when we got through. It was pretty impressive, even at night. The lock systems, the Culebra Cut, Gatun Lake. It is amazing that this feat of engineering was accomplished with early-1900s technology and equipment. I couldn't believe that there's not a pump in the whole thing. All the water was transferred by gravity, and it all still worked perfectly!

We were ordered to rendezvous with an unknown vessel at a particular latitude and longitude. Right on time and on location, we met up with the mystery vessel as appointed. It turned out that it was two deep-cover DEA agents driving a Hatteras 45 sport fisherman yacht with about 1,200 pounds of pure cocaine onboard. We were to transfer the booty to our ship for further transfer to the DEA in Panama. I'm sure there was a lot more to the story, but it was all very sensitive and secret. It begged so many questions: Who were these guys? Who had they infiltrated? How did they do it? Where did the coke come from? Where was it supposed to be going? Were the Jefes going to know about their loss of product and revenue? All these questions went unanswered. The DEA guys were wearing ski masks and didn't say a word. The only people allowed outside the skin of the ship were those actively transferring the illicit goods. That was the Coast Guard Det and five of our crew. I watched it unfold from the bridge. When the transfer was complete, the Hatteras 45 Sportfisher silently went one way, and we went the other, toward the ditch. It was daylight this time. What a lush, beautiful, and historic ride. If you ever get the chance to cruise the ditch, do it.

We were back in our standard routine in our box officially known as AAW-1. It was warm and boring. The ocean was calm and blue. The only thing close to excitement was a minor liberty incident in a dirt street-lined cesspool town called Puerto Quetzal, Guatemala. After we tied up the ship, an advanced party set out to find the nicest hotel and set up the "admin room" for the CPO mess. This turned out to be a midlevel Motel 6 by our standards, but it did have a pool. The pool was adorned with your basic Home Depot PVC lounge chairs. The admin room was stocked with tons of local beer, and we wasted no time throwing down some kind of beer that had a chicken head drawing on the label. We were getting a little light-headed. It must've been the heat. Okay, it was the beer.

I was relaxing and reclining on the plastic furniture when the electronics technician chief (ETC) thought it would be fun to upend the unit from the feet end and dump me over backwards in to the pool. The plan worked. However, in so doing, a loud crack could be heard, and a physical crack became visible in the plastic leg of the chair. The hotel manager must have had surveillance equipment, because he was poolside and in our faces in 4.248 seconds with a pistol in his waistband.

"You broke my fucking chair! I let you guys stay here and drink, and you break my fucking chair!" That part was in perfect English. There was also a boisterous tirade in Spanish. It was true; there was a small crack, but the chair was still 100 percent mission capable. This didn't stop the Spanglish ranting. We had to do something to hopefully avoid an embarrassing international incident.

ETC very calmly offered to pay for the chair. Senor Albergo (that's Spanish for hotel) cooled off a bit and led us to his office. It was surprisingly large and nicely appointed with mahogany furniture and tasteful décor. It didn't really fit in this dump of a city. I thought it was strange that this guy was making good money here, hmmm.

So we agreed on a price. It was something like eighty thousand quetzales, I don't remember. Quetzales in Guatemala were what we called "funny money" or "Bongo Bucks." I preferred "multicolored beer chits." Let's face it, the bellwether of any nation and its economy was the price of a beer on the beach.

"How much for the round? 2,306 Bongoids? Okay, that's two blue ones, three green ones, one yellow one, and a coin. Ah shit, two yellow ones, keep the change." The amount of Quetzales that we agreed upon turned out to be about 250 US dollars. That was probably enough for a new table set, five more chairs, and an umbrella, at least.

Tim, the ETC, paid with a credit card. El Jefe put the gun back in the top drawer as the funds were electronically transferred. Just then, an idea hit me. "Excuse me, sir, since we have paid for the chair, it is now ours. We should be able to take it with us, *sí*?"

He couldn't argue the logic so he shrugged and said, "Okay, sure. *Si, si no mas problemas,* okay?"

I didn't need an interpreter for that. I assured him, "*Si Senor, no mas problemas, yo prometo.*" I made a promise.

"Where'd you learn that shit, dude?" asked the humbled and slightly poorer ETC.

"San Diego Mesa College, GI Bill, man. Your tax dollars at work" was my smug answer.

Take the chair with us, we did, to all six of the nasty little dirt floor cantinas in Puerto Quetzal. We would carry it through the dirt streets where chickens and pigs roamed freely. We would plunk it down in the middle of the cantina floor and took turns on the throne. The infamous chair made it back to the ship and was stored in the helo hangar. We used it for flight deck BBQs and relaxation for the rest of the deployment.

Our time in AAW-1 was winding down. The helo was flying almost every day, so I accrued plenty of control hours. It was all flight following and surface surveillance. The SH-60 had a cool data link called Hawk Link. That allowed the helo to beam back a signal with their radar picture in real time. I could dial them in and see what they were seeing on their scope eighty miles away. It was a valuable tactical tool when tracking down drug runners. The problem was that the drug runners weren't stupid. We would pull into Panama every few days. Every time we did this, the supply officer would be on the phone announcing exactly when we would be there and for how long, along with how much food and supplies we needed. He may as well have been talking directly to Don Pablo Escobar himself. They knew where we were and where we were going most of the time. It was a joke.

We made the obligatory trip south to dip below the equator. By the third or fourth time, the silly rite of passage was getting a bit tiresome. It was soon our time to head north and go home. We were relieved on station by the USS *McClusky* (FFG41) with little fanfare. In less than a week, we were tied up to pier 5 at the Naval Station. It was a relatively quick three-month deployment, but it felt longer.

Andrea was on the pier when we arrived, and we went back to our cozy condo. The place looked great. It had a women's touch, but it wasn't too faggy. There were no castles, dreamcatchers, tchotchkes, or bad art. Everything looked pretty classy. It was good to be home.

I had saved a few shekels while underway, so I took some time off, and we took a road trip north along the coast. We stopped at Monterey, Half Moon Bay, Morro Bay, and San Francisco, California. We visited Andrea's family in San Jose. She came from a large Palestinian clan who settled in the Bay Area. The patriarch, Grandpa Bajis, fled the Middle East before the war—WWII, that is. He was a great man, and we hit it off right away. I was amazed by his story. That's a book in itself. It was, and still is, difficult to be a Christian in the Middle East. Her family was accepting and loving. Her female cousins were exceptionally hot. We drove back down the coast road at an easy pace and had a great time. That was the day I knew I wanted to spend the rest of my life with this girl.

UNDERWAY 29

The Yards, More Underway, and Neutral Duty

Every ship or vessel requires a lot of maintenance. It's just not natural to have all this metal and machinery floating around in salt water, which is very corrosive. There is also electrolysis in salt water that rots any metal that isn't properly bonded. And all the time, the ship and systems are battered by the sea and weather and the relentless vibrations of life underway. It's really not a normal existence for humans, machines, and large metal things. As a result, the ship must go to the shipyard before during and after deployments. The length of time and scope of the work to be done in the yard depends on the life cycle of the ship. Some yard periods are longer and more extensive than others. Yard periods suck. It's true that you are technically in port and not underway. On the other hand, shipyards are nasty places. They are loud, dirty, smelly, and dangerous. They are never in a desirable part of town, and things like parking and getting to and from the ship and accessing the spaces on the ship is a total pain in the ass. The spaces and equipment tend to be torn apart. There are wires, pneumatic hoses, and temporary ventilation ducts running on the decks and overheads. There is a constant grinding noise. Painting and piping and lagging repairs create nasty chemical vapors and odors. It's a mess. If you haven't guessed, I'm not a fan of the shipyard. This is when it is good to be an OS. An OS in port is almost useless. An OS in the shipyard is completely useless. As a result, we scheduled a lot of schools and team trainers during these availability periods.

It was the normal regimen of ASW training. We practiced the art of Target Motion Analysis. TMA is the process of localizing a submarine strictly by passive means. The plot lays down the ship's motion over the planet as well as the raw SONAR data. The process requires the ship to maneuver across what is known as the "Line of Sound." Meanwhile, more lines of sonic bearing are drawn on the plot. There are a few other plotting tools and techniques employed to eventually calculate an area of probability, or AOP, one of which is called the Ekelund Range, named after the mathematical genius of an admiral who came up with this stuff. The idea is to send a helo to the AOP and spit some passive buoys. If all goes right, one of the buoys comes up hot. You go in to attack mode, drop a MK-46 torpedo, and get a kill. When you hear the instructors say the words "SONAR reports a loud underwater explosion," it was time to go to Pacers, the nearest topless gentlemen's club. We got so good at the process that we were often getting lap dances by lunch.

There was more firefighting training, of course. That never stopped. I also had to keep up my air control hours by attending the air control school "up on the hill" at Point Loma's Fleet Combat Training Center, Pacific to log live air control hours. We used to call it Big Brother School. I don't know why. Maybe it was Big Dipper. Too many brain cells have been lost. I had fallen in love with Point Loma. I would ride my motorcycle around the neighborhoods up on the hill. It would be a dream come true for me/us to live somewhere in the Fleetridge or Wooded Area of Point Loma, San Diego, California. It was pretty easy to pass the months of shipyard activity.

If we were stuck on the ship during a yard period, I would get a space on the ship with a DVD player. I'd get the OI Division guys together and show the Spielberg masterpiece *Saving Private Ryan.* Everyone knows that it's a great film. Maybe it's the greatest. I would ask them to watch the movie and think about leadership. At the end of the movie, I would ask some questions to get the discussion rolling. "How many of LT Miller's guys got killed on the mission? What were their names? Anybody?" Eventually they would chime in with some feedback. "Why do you think those guys got killed? Anybody, Bueller, Bueller?"

"It was a war. That's what happens," chimed in OS3 Canga.

"Yes, that is right. Could Captain Miller have avoided any of those deaths?" I asked them.

"Yeah, all of them." It was Canga once again.

"Why is that, Petty Officer Canga?"

"Because every time he had them do something that they maybe didn't have to do, one of them got killed."

"Bingo, young man!" I was starting to think this lesson might be going somewhere. "So is that good leadership or bad leadership?"

"I don't know if it was good or bad." Now I had OSSN Trujillo engaged.

"Well, what is good and what is bad leadership, guys?"

"Not getting people killed for one?" That was OS2 Henard. This was turning in to a real discussion. These nuts were reluctantly getting involved.

It was getting close to chow time, so I had to wrap things up. I asked, "Who killed Captain Miller?"

"It was the German he let go at the RADAR sight, the one all of the guys wanted to shoot." That was from OS2 Van Horn.

I had to wrap things up. "Is anyone picking up what I'm putting down here?"

There was a pause as they all thought this over. "He made all the wrong decisions." It was OSSN Trujillo again. He said it as if it were a question.

"Yes, Seaman Trujillo. That is correct. But ask yourselves what would have been the right decisions? The word is leadership, fellas. Leadership is about making decisions. Sometimes any decision is the wrong decision. The higher up you go in rank, the harder and more important your decisions become. At some point, you must come to terms with the fact that all of your decisions will be wrong. It's called leadership. So think about that as you go through your careers. Someone's decision will affect you every day you are in the navy. Someday, you may be making those kinds of decisions. The important thing is to make a goddamn decision." The lesson was over. I was exhausted. "Get these guys out of here, OS1."

They all filed out for the chow line and were all still talking about my little leadership seminar. I thought about my father, who was a teacher in East Orange, New Jersey, a very rough town. He once told me that if he got through to just one student, then the school year was worth it. I understood what he meant.

Once the ship was out of the yards, it was time for underway operations and to prepare for the next deployment. This was the seemingly endless cycle of life in the surface navy. The ship's next deployment—and my last deployment on this ship, anyway—was to be a Combined Afloat Readiness and Training Exercise. The CARAT cruise is what is called a joint exercise because it involves forces from other nations. In the case of this CARAT, it would be the navies of the Philippines, Malaysia, Thailand, Singapore, Australia, New Zealand, and a few others. It wasn't what I would call high operational tempo (OPTEMPO) event. It was more of a port-hopping extravaganza.

The whole CARAT effort came about when the aforementioned foreign governments were clamoring for the US Navy to be more involved in joint training exercises in the Western Pacific. Much of this was brought on by the general North Korean madness and the Chinese shenanigans in the Spratly Islands near the Philippines and other imperialistic behavior in the region.

About halfway through the deployment, I was once again pleasantly surprised when I was selected for senior chief petty officer or E-8. I never thought I would make it to this level. I mean, I used to make fun of lifers like me. I was now the second highest ranking enlisted person on the ship. I was splitting my time between controlling aircraft, CIC watch officer, and running the operations and intelligence division of the ship.

I had a chief and three E-6s, a handful of second and third class petty officers, and a few unrated kids, E-3 and below. As on any ship, the division was a collection of comedians and knuckleheads. My favorites were the Ezes. I don't know why, but there were a large number of young Mexican American sailors in my division. I had a Gonzalez, a Martinez, a Gomez, and two Rodriguezes. Hence, they earned the moniker of the Ezes. They would crack me up on a daily basis and help me with my Spanish.

One day, I saw three of these potential criminals talking quietly in the corner of CIC. I knew trouble brewing when I saw it. Just like any parent could tell when a kid was up to no good, I could sniff these goofballs out pretty quick. I slowly closed the distance in the darkness of CIC between me and *los tres amigos*. I didn't quite hear the content of their up-to-no-goodness when one of them saw the "FIVE-OH"—AKA me, trying to listen in—and without missing a beat, he stepped back and stated rather loudly, "And that gentlemen is how a bill becomes a law." Maybe he got that from an old episode of *Friends*, but I had to laugh. I was impressed by how well he thought on his feet. It's a good trait for an OS.

Dealing or managing these young sailors wasn't all fun and games. Sailors would get themselves into trouble from time to time. There were some drug use violations and behavioral problems. The most common offense was unauthorized absence or UA. I didn't enjoy going to the captain's mast when one of my guys was on the pad. I would stick up for them as best I could, but I could only tell the truth.

There were many exercises and port visits in Manila and Subic Bay. It had been many years since I had been there, yet the place was the same but a little different. The Mt. Pinatubo eruption in 1991 did a lot of damage. But some of the bars survived. The US Navy had left, but it still smelled the same. Olfactory memories are the strongest. It looked a little different but smelled the same. We stopped in Brunei, Thailand, Singapore, and, of course, Pearl Harbor. It was a successful deployment.

The CARAT cruise, like all deployments, eventually ended, and so soon would my time on this ship. It was time to look at the next duty station. Of course, I wanted to stay in San Diego. I had actually purchased our condo from the owner who was in need of some capital. I got it for a good price at a very good time of the market cycle. My roots in San Diego were growing increasingly deeper. I was now a senior chief with enough time left in my career to pick up Master Chief or E-9. The conventional wisdom in terms of an upward career path was to go to the Senior Enlisted Academy and then go back to sea. I wasn't really digging that idea. If that meant I would never see E-9, I could live with that. There was an opportunity to snap up a neutral duty billet in San Diego with something called a Logistics Task Force. I'm an ops guy, not a supply or logistics guy, but this would buy me three years in San Diego. Then I could do five final years at sea in San Diego and call it a career. I was home, and everything was coming together; I actually had some money in the bank, a career, and the love of a great woman. If the powers that be decided to promote me, so be it. If not, I could very easily live with that too. That was the day I decided to ask if Andrea was interested in marrying me. I believe the year was 1999.

UNDERWAY 30

Logistics, Marriage, and Normandy

Logistics Task Force Pacific was perhaps the worst career choice and the most boring position for a senior chief operations specialist. But it was in San Diego, which was why I chose it. The unit was a resident command on Naval Air Station, North Island. We occupied a WWII-era building near the Commander, Naval Air Pacific Headquarters. The unit was commanded by a two-star admiral or rear admiral. The executive officer was a full navy captain or O-6. There was a smattering of senior officers, a few lieutenant commanders, and lieutenants. Nearly all these officers were from the US Navy Supply Corps. On the enlisted side, there was a command master chief who was a postal clerk. Then there was me and a handful of senior and junior enlisted. So I was in the middle of the pack. As a senior chief, that is unusual. Everything about this unit was unusual. I wasn't used to chatting with an admiral every day. We'd talk about the Padres and ball scores like we were in the corner gin mill shooting the shit with Joe Shit the Ragman. For me, the lack of responsibilities actually made me uncomfortable.

My official billet title was Operations Interface. To this day, I don't know what that means. What I do know is that I didn't do much operationally. I occupied what is called a "notional billet." That means that someday it may mean something. This was indeed a nail in the career coffin, but once again, it was my choice and decision. The good part was that I liked the folks I was working with. It was so relaxed; one might mistake it for an air force unit.

The first time one of the officers called me by my first name, I just about killed him with my eyes. *Nobody* called a chief by his name except another chief. Not the commanding officer, and not even the admiral—nobody. I got used to it after a while. But there was *no* way I would call an officer by name while in uniform. It's acceptable out in town but not on the job. This was one of those units where old supply officers went to get the awards they needed to either advance or retire. I tried to make the best of it.

One great thing was that there were no duty days. This was completely foreign to me. I embraced it. For one thing, it afforded me an unusual amount of time at home. This would be a good experiment or litmus test of the strength of my relationship with Andrea. I already thought it was pretty strong because she stuck with me through all my underway time away from our comfy little condo. We spent a lot of time together and were still actually getting along. We were still learning new things about each other and having fun. There was a lot of travel, many trips to Mexico on the weekends and trips up north to see her family. We traveled to the East Coast to visit my family and friends. Things were moving in a more permanent direction. It started to become the proverbial elephant in the room. I was very bad at discussing anything about marriage, commitment, or the future. She was very patient, and I appreciated this. I eventually realized that I needed to act like an actual grown-up, or I may fuck up a very good situation. We must've gone to a dozen weddings as an unmarried couple. I got so sick of fat aunties asking us, *So when is it your turn?* I wanted to say, *I don't know. When are you losing one hundred pounds?* These exchanges didn't affect any of our decision-making on the subject.

Our decision to get married was, by anyone's standard, unconventional. We were out to a lovely dinner at a local Mission Hills place called The Gathering. Wine was involved, and we ultimately addressed the five-hundred-pound gorilla in the room. We both agreed it was time to commit. I had a few issues. Number one was that I hated weddings. I thought weddings were the biggest and dumbest waste of money. I also thought it was rude to ask other people to make plans to travel and spend their money on a silly and out-dated ritual. The idea of buying a wedding dress and renting a bunch of tuxedos, throwing silly bachelor parties, and so many other ridiculous expenses made no sense to me. These were my wedding cynicisms. I am sure some of them are unreasonable. There are probably some diagnosable Freudian reasons behind these very strong feelings, but they are irreversible and deep-seeded. So the negotiation began.

To her endless credit, she gave me the whole no-wedding thing. She also agreed to keep the entire operation a secret. I did not want any other human meddling (that's code for her mother and family; my family could care less) in the logistics at all. So you're wondering about her terms. She wanted to go to Paris.

"Can we go to the Normandy battlefields?" I asked what I thought was a reasonable question. She agreed.

I had one more item of negotiation. It was something that I had actually contemplated. We needed to pick a date. I had one in mind. The year was 1999. I knew that February of 2000 was a leap year. The only reason I knew this was because I have two friends who were born on February 29. I thought it would be efficient and perhaps funny or quirky to get married on that date. That way, we only had to celebrate every four years. It was an asshole move, but you couldn't argue the financial logic!

A deal was about to be struck. She said that we should have a reception upon return of our secret mission. We were close to a handshake. After ironing out some minor details, the deal was inked.

We agreed upon a Las Vegas elopement. She impressed me with her ability to maintain secrecy. I know a lot of sailors who could learn a lesson from her. She planned the whole thing. She went to TJ Maxx and bought a thirty-five-dollar dress. We were to fly to Las Vegas. We had a room at the Monte Carlo. A limo would take us to the Clark County Courthouse. We waited in line and paid thirty-five dollars for a sixty-year-old lady with a cigarette dangling from her lips to type a marriage license.

You heard me right. She was sitting behind a genuine old-school writer of the typing type. She sounded like Lucille Ball. "What's your names honey?" I could have said, *Michael Gorbachev and Minnie Mouse.*

We heard a *Bing! Click, click, click, zzzzzzzzip.* "Here you are, kids," wheezed Cocktail Connie. She handed us our marriage license. We paid the fee and went across the street to the Little White Chapel. There was a short wait, but thirty minutes later, we were just as married as any other two idiots who rented out a hotel in Mackinaw Island, Michigan, and had a reception at the Russian Tea Room in New York City. We went out to the strip and gambled and partied. The next day, we flew back to San Diego to pack our bags for France.

We flew to Paris in Business Class and had a wonderful time. We did all the touristy stuff in the City of Lights. The weather was chilly, but nice. As per our deal, I rented a car, and we drove to the Normandy battlefields. We walked on Omaha and Utah beaches. We crawled through the bunkers, gun emplacements, and bomb craters of Ponte Du Hoc. I know that this was a bit of a concession on her part, but I could tell that she was almost as blown away by the historical significance and the beauty of the region as I was. The History Channel geek in me was subtly wearing off on her. Watching these things on TV was one thing, but being there put you in historical context. I could go on and on, but I will spare you.

We stayed at a forty-thousand-square-foot chateau and had dinner with the count. We spent a night at Mont-St-Michel. It was a fantastic trip. By this time, all the people at home, our families and friends, had received a card in the mail. We sent out a mass mailing on our way to the airport in San Diego disclosing the details of the operation. It was met with mixed reviews. I didn't care. We were very happy.

We made it back to San Diego, and I returned to shore duty with the LTF. One cool thing about the unit was the travel. Wherever there was a logistics exercise, a bunch of us would go. Unfortunately, some of these were in South Korea. Fortunately, a few were in Hawaii. Andrea tagged along on a couple of these boondoggles. It was a great, cheap vacation. My airfare was covered, and so was the hotel and rental car. I had to go to CINCPACFLT headquarters to stand watch every day. Oddly enough, I was usually one of the guys managing my old buddy the TPFDD during mobilization exercises. I learned more about this all-important living document. I experienced firsthand how the events unfolded that landed me in Saudi Arabia all those years ago. Captain Goodwin was exactly correct. I thought about Portman and just chuckled. I couldn't help but wonder where my one-time shipmate and nemesis was and what he was doing.

Once again, I tried to make the best of shore duty and finally got my college degree in aviation operations. I continued flying and training and added an instrument rating to my credentials. I was a qualified advanced ground instructor and an active member of the Armed Forces Flying Club at Montgomery Field in San Diego.

I enjoyed my time with the senior supply officers of the LTF, but it was soon time to go back to sea and be a real senior chief underway. This would most likely be the last command of my career unless I unexpectedly picked up E-9. There were a few career-enhancing teasers out there, but once again, I chose a reserve frigate out of San Diego, the USS *Curts* (FFG-38). I'm a sucker for the tin can. I checked aboard, and it looked very familiar. I was ready to get underway for a while. I'm not saying I missed being at sea. I'm just saying that I am much more comfortable doing what I do best.

Meanwhile, Andrea had gone from part-time receptionist to a licensed real estate agent and was the principal assistant to a very successful, talented, and over-the-top affable real estate broker. In short, she started making some very good money. Between the two of us on paper, we were a very good candidate to qualify for a mortgage that we couldn't afford. I was open to moving to a house if the price was right. I was picky about the location and pricing. I knew I would be underway a lot over the next few years, so she took control of the effort.

That was the day I realized that all plans for the future would be phrased, formed, stated, and written in the first person, plural.

UNDERWAY 31

The Last Sea Duty Tour

The USS *Curts* was just like any other fast frigate. She was a "pocket cruiser" or "figlet," as we would refer to the class of ship. There was a MK-13 missile launcher up forward capable of firing SM-1 and Harpoon. She had a 76-mm gun amidships and a CIWS mount aft right above the flight deck. There were torpedo launchers port and starboard. There were 30-mm cannon mounts on either side of the ship right next to the torpedo tubes. The ship was 443 feet long and forty-five feet abeam with a twenty-two-foot draft. This one was hull number 38. The 31st Oliver Hazard Perry off the assembly line. The first Perry Class was FFG-7, the Oliver Hazard Perry.

I did the normal check in. OI division was the regular collection of characters and knuckleheads from all over the place. I knew Chief Ron Kendall from the Tisdale. I also knew a couple of the guys in the CPO mess from various commands, schools, and training evolutions. I was on my fifth enlistment by now and knew a lot of people in the Canoe Club. The navy is not all that huge.

I liked the captain right away. CDR Railey was unusually brusque for a senior officer of the line. He cursed like, well, a sailor. He drank beer and smoked cigars. He loved the music of Van Morrison. He was about my age. He treated me with respect, as I did him. I knew we would get along just fine. We talked about the upcoming deployment. I shared my LEOPS experiences with him, and he assured me that this trip south would be different. I told him that I hoped so. He told me to be careful for what I hope for. We both laughed as we smoked cigars.

We were scheduled to get underway in a week. That gave me some time to complete checking in and get some gear onboard and my locker squared away. The command policy was that E-8 and above do not stand duty in port. I liked that very much. Of course, it would not be beneath me to stand in for a shipmate in a pinch, but it's still a nice perk.

The information technology on the ship and CIC had advanced significantly in the few short years since I had been underway. The ship had a high-speed LAN with email at all times. Even at sea! There was a telephone line available to the crew at all times. Even at sea! This was unheard of when I was growing up in the navy. I was beginning to feel like a fossil. It was bad enough that I was chronologically old enough to be a father to most of the crew, but their technological prowess was almost intimidating. I could always trump the intimidation factor with the fouled anchor and star on my collar.

One of the biggest tactical information advancements was the advent of chat. There are now various online secure chat rooms used for different levels of functions. In CIC, a link chat room had replaced the old Data Systems Administration (DSA) radio circuit. All the link management items were now handled over the internet. There were chat rooms for supply, logistics, operations, and all aspects of fleet activity. It was all very convenient, efficient, and productive until the internet went down. When that happened, there was panic. *I lost Third Fleet Chat!* is like screaming *We're all going to die!* That's what happened when you relied on one system with no backup. Technology is cool, but it can kick you in the ass and, as usual, at the worst possible time. We also had two beautiful 55-inch televisions to display tactical information and the chat traffic. They were also great in port to watch movies.

We were soon underway in SOCAL, completing all the requirements for deployment. There were lots of air operations. My quals had long since lapsed, but it didn't matter. There were young petty officers who were hungry for hours. It was time for me to step back. As an E-8, my focus was no longer a hands-on approach. I was now leadership, so my hands were in my pockets, and I would be standing behind the button pushers. I could always help out in a pinch, but it was their turn to learn and hopefully shine.

There was one time when I had to grab a console and take care of some old-school shit. I was crossing the brow early one morning prior to getting underway for a thousand different things, the most important of which seemed to be a maneuvering exercise with the four ships in our little squadron. The reason it was so important was because it was our commodore's last time underway with all of his ships. The plot thickened.

I was met on the quarterdeck by LCDR Schaeffer, the operations officer. "Good morning, Senior Chief."

"Good morning, Ops." If I liked and/or respected you as an officer, I would call you by your position; in this case he was "Ops," short for operations officer. Or I might refer to you as "Mister" followed by your last name. If I thought you were a dumb-shit, punk-ass, or shit-stain (excuse me, I mean defecation residue), I would refer to you by your rank such, as ensign, lieutenant, etc. I saved the word "sir" for special occasions. Except for the captain, of course; the captain was always sir or ma'am or just captain. The junior officers or JOs eventually picked up on this, and I could sense their nervousness and tepidity around me. I loved it. It was another subtle leadership nugget I had learned so many years ago from the master. The thin blue line was still in perpetual motion and pumping through my veins.

"You're a pilot, right? I mean, you can fly a plane?" Ops asked me.

"Yes, sir, I am, and I can. Why do you ask?"

I was intrigued. Especially because he had a strange look on his face as if he was searching for the right words. I smiled and half-chuckled and said, "What's up, Ops? What do you need, sir?" Those last five words were respectfully emphatic. I had a division to run, and of course, he knew this.

"Well, it's the commodore's last time underway with the squadron. And he knows that the Buick Open golf tournament is going on this weekend at Torrey Pines."

"I believe that is a correct statement, Commander. Is there something you need me to do?" For some reason, he looked sort of embarrassed. He was doing the Gary Cooper "aw shucks" thing and wagging his head from side to side. "Mr. Schaeffer, what the fuck are you trying to ask me, sir?"

"Well, the commodore was wondering if we, or you, could ask the blimp to get us on TV."

I let out a huge knee-jerk guffaw. Now I knew why he was so tentative. He was the errand boy with a crazy request and wasn't really sure how to make the request, but he had to at least make the effort and wasn't sure how. Now I was laughing. "No problem and no promises, Ops. Let me see what I can do." I rendered a smart hand salute and went to work. We were getting underway in an hour.

We got underway and made it out of the harbor. All units turned west and then north. The Torrey Pines golf courses (there are two) were atop the cliffs of La Jolla. It was a truly lovely spot. The weather was clear as a bell, and the ocean was flat. Once we secured from sea and anchor detail, I grabbed the air control console, where there was a dialable VHF radio remote unit. I happened to know the frequency for San Diego Departure in this sector due to my flight training and experience. The frequency is 199.6 Mhz. I dialed it in and gave them a call.

"San Diego Departure, this is the warship USS *Curts* with a request, over." I'm sure they weren't used to this type of request. They handled aircraft on their way to somewhere all day long, not some ship on the ocean. I'm sure they were wondering what the fuck.

Almost immediately a voice came in my left ear and the speaker above the console, and I heard, "Warship *Curts*, San Diego Departure. Say your request, over."

This was looking good so far. I keyed the mic with my right foot and said, "Departure from *Curts*, requesting the frequency that the golf tournament airship is operating on today, sir?"

"Roger that Curts, its 124.4, discreet."

Shit, that was easy! "Thank you, sir, Curts switching. Good day."

"Roger. G'day, Curts."

I'm sure they were all scratching their heads in the control room. I laughed to myself. Now it was time to have some fun. We were still very close to land, so the SPS-49 air search RADAR picture was shit. There was no way I could see a blimp on my scope. It didn't matter. I guess I was just looking out of habit. I dialed in 124.4. I noticed that Ops was standing over my shoulder and listening intently. I was still laughing to myself. I listened to the freq for a few seconds. It would be rude to just jump on a circuit and start transmitting. It's just good manners. I eventually hit the switch.

"To the Met Life blimp at Torrey Pines, this is the US Warship Curts on your frequency with a special request when you get a chance, Captain."

Less than two seconds later, a friendly and bubbly Australian voice lit up the radio. "Warship Curts, Snoopy Two with you. What can we do for you, mate?"

Holy shit, this was working! "Snoopy two from Curts. I know you're busy, Captain. On behalf of the commander of Surface Squadron One, we wanted to inform you that there are four US Navy warships directly west of your position. We are in combat formation and conducting maneuvering exercises. Your director may want to take a look." I thought for half a second and decided to depart from the professional military radio protocol and said, "It may look pretty cool on TV, sir."

"Roger that, Curts. Stay on frequency, and I'll get back to you in any case."

"Roger, sir, standing by." I glanced up at the operations officer and the door opened right behind me. In walked the beaming commodore. "Goddammit, Senior Chief, that was impressive!" Apparently, there was a speaker patched up on the bridge.

"We're not on TV yet, Commodore" The words were barely out of my mouth when the blimp called me back. "Curts, Snoop-Two, our cameraman has you. Is there any way you can come a little more east?" I looked over my left shoulder at the commodore, smiled, and raised my eyebrows as if to say *Well, Commodore, you asked for it.*

"Tell him hell yes! Ops, send an immediate execute, Corpen starboard 090!" He screamed in childish excitement. I heard this and said to the Met Life airship, "Roger that, Snoop-Doggie two [I couldn't resist it!], we're turning right now."

The blimp pilot said with a thick Australian accent, "That's great, mate. We come back from commercial in two minutes, the director is loving it!"

I thought the commodore was going to cream his khakis. Down in the ET shop, they were recording the CBS transmission of the golf tournament. We were getting dangerously close to land for a navy ship. Not to mention there were fishing and pleasure vessels nearby. We turned around and headed back to the east. The radio crackled again. CBS wanted more. Okay. That was enough for me. My job was done. "OS1, get over here and take over! All you're doing is talking to a blimp. There is no safety of flight issues. Just be the middleman between the commodore and Snoopy two, that's the blimp by the way."

He took over. I stepped back, put my hands in my pockets, and watched the action. It was funny. The word got out to the crew. They were showing the clips on the ship's TV, and the crew was eating it up. Needless to say, Ops, the captain, and especially the commodore were extremely satisfied.

I remember walking down the passageway shortly after I left CIC. I was on my way to chow. All the guys were smiling at me. One of them finally said, "Senior Chief, were you really controlling a blimp?"

"No, not really, son, I just talked to a blimp. Did you see us on TV?"

"Fuck yeah, it was awesome!"

That little episode bought me so much respect capital. I was forever known as the senior chief OS who controlled the blimp and got us on TV. I actually included a narrative of the event in my annual evaluation input. I did that kind of tongue-in-cheek, but it actually made it in to my final eval.

That was the day that I selfishly wished that my old chief, friend, hero, and mentor Doug Simons could have been there. He would've laughed his ass off. He may have even been proud. I was definitely a stain that day.

UNDERWAY 32

LEOPS Parte Deux

It was time to head down south again. Andrea dropped me off at the pier, and we said goodbye. I knew she would take care of business while I was gone. She was also actively looking for a house to buy. She would be joining me in Puerto Vallarta for a few days. I was looking forward to that.

We got underway like a thousand times before. It was summer, and the sea was calm, which meant that it was winter south of the equator. The message traffic said that the sea state would increase as we headed south. This was based on data received from the weather buoys positioned in various places in the ocean, which record and transmit the sea state conditions. Thanks to satellites and GPS, the buoys could now track the direction, height, frequency, and trend of the weather and waves/swells on the surface of the ocean, and they were amazingly accurate.

Sure enough, right on time and as predicted, and at the exact latitudinal position, the sea picked up. It wasn't rough. It was just really rolly. It was big and rolly. The sea was alive with large swells that started from a storm in the South Pacific. In this case, it was a typhoon near Australia. All that energy had made its way all the way across the gigantic Pacific Ocean and was now meeting up with shallower water near the coast and becoming very large and powerful swells. It was becoming very uncomfortable. The transition from big and rolly to uncomfortable and dangerous could take mere minutes. That was exactly what happened in this case.

My guys weren't digging it. I totally understood. Being seasick was a horrible and indescribable feeling. I have seen guys who would just as easily have died than have to try to function while being sick. It was the most debilitating feeling a person could experience. There was no pride. When a person was seasick, that person had forgotten who they were, where they came from, who their family was, and what was going on in the moment. It was a strange thing to witness.

The seas picked up. I could see the faces turning green. "Okay, guys, if you need to go out and get some fresh air, check with the watch supervisor. Nobody pukes in Combat, okay? I'm serious, if you're gonna puke, get the fuck out of my Combat!" I knew that if I smelled fresh barf, it just might push me over the edge.

Most of them heeded my direction. A few did not. I couldn't be upset. I knew that those poor knuckleheads tried their best to "nut it up." Meanwhile, the sea just got bigger, but it wasn't all that rough. The sky and sea were a nice friendly blue. It was just big. We were heading due south. The waves were coming at us from Australia, which meant from the south and the west. As a result, we weren't heading directly into the oncoming ocean. It was hitting us from the side and a little on the bow, which meant we were both bobbing up and down and getting hammered from side to side. It's a bad combination and very uncomfortable.

I wish I had me as a chief when I was a kid. I knew that a sick sailor was a worthless sailor. A good sailor would not admit to being sick until it was almost too late. I wasn't going to be that guy. "If you're sick, get the fuck out. I won't think any less of you," was my fatherly guidance.

One by one, they did just that. Uh-oh, the nice guy approach might just be biting me in the ass. One by one, the watch team begged me for their lives. In other words, "Please let me leave this dark, horrible place where the world is spinning and I am so uncomfortable and let me go to some space closer to the waterline where I can die in peace." Sure, if you're lucky enough to die.

I let them all leave. It got down to me and the OS1, the watch supervisor. He turned to me at one point and said, "Senior, I'm not feeling so good. I'm sorry but I may not make it."

"All right, get the fuck out of here. You did your best. I've got it."

He ran out of the space. I thanked him for not puking anywhere near me. Speaking of me, I looked around, and I was all alone in the Blue Light Lounge. The RADAR screens were spinning like they always did. Anything that could have flung off a horizontal surface had already been flung. The ship was really getting pounded hard. It seemed like we were getting thrown about from every direction.

At this point, the captain came into CIC. "What the fuck is going on here, Senior?" He was in sweatpants and a T-shirt.

"It's rough, and they were all sick and worthless, so I let them all go, sir."

I heard a voice chime in from the corner of CIC. It was OS3 Stover. "I'm here too, sir."

I felt like I just found a twenty in the laundry. "That's right sir, it's me and OS3. We've got it."

"Can I go to sleep, Senior Chief?" asked the skipper.

"You will be rocked like a baby, Captain."

"I will buy you several beers in Puerto Vallarta."

"That's nice, Captain, but my wife prefers margaritas!"

"Goddammit, are you trying to make me puke!"

"Never, sir."

"I'll get you whatever you want. Just keep my ship safe tonight."

"'I—I mean we, that is, me and OS3 Stover, will keep this this ship and crew safe, sir." I wanted to make sure OS3 got his props and credit.

"Very well, who's on the bridge? It's Forbes, right?"

"Yes, sir, Lieutenant Junior Grade Forbes has the deck. I will be in constant contact with him and personally visiting the bridge every fifteen minutes. He's doing fine. He's an Academy guy."

"Did I say I will buy you a beer?"

"Yes, sir, you did. You actually said several beers and a margarita for my wife. Let's make it two. I'm looking forward to it."

"Anything you want, thanks, Senior Chief. And thank you, OS3! I won't forget this." He shut the door to CIC and jumped in the captain's cabin face-first I'm sure.

I turned to OS3 Stover. "How are you feeling, young man?"

There was a time when I would revel in someone else's seasickness. It used to be fun to get a guy to blow lunch. We would rap about sardines and pork and beans. *I can tell by the look in your eyes you like to eat those big cow pies. Sardines (rest), pork and beans (rest). I can tell by the look on your face you got no disgrace.* We were merciless. I was not like that tonight. I had a job to do. I looked at Stover. He was hanging in there. He was a kid from Alabama. He had a baseball scholarship at Auburn, but he broke his leg. That voided the scholarship. His family didn't have any money, and there weren't many jobs in Alabama at the time, so he joined the navy. He was a good young man. He was very smart and a very capable OS. "It's just me and you, kid!" He was looking a little green. "Cover the radios. I'm going to the bridge to talk to the OOD. I'll be right back. Are you okay?" He nodded. I believed and trusted him.

When you stepped out of CIC on an FFG, there was a ladder that led directly to the pilot house or bridge. I climbed up the ladder, which was not easy. I saw Mr. Forbes hanging on to the steel cable that ran across the overhead. He looked a little scared.

"Okay, Mr. Forbes, OS3 Stover and I have the watch downstairs. Don't worry about a thing."

"But, Senior, I only have one guy up here. What the fuck am I going to do?"

"We, Mr. Forbes, *we*, will all get through the night. Tell you what. I will send Petty Officer Stover up here as another set of eyes, and he can spell the helmsman." I also thought that Stover could use a little fresh air. "Is that Okay with you, Boats?" I was talking to the young boatswain's mate who was driving the ship.

"That works for me, Senior."

"But he's not a qualified helmsman," Forbes countered; he wasn't quite getting it yet.

"He is now, Lieutenant. Listen, we are going in a straight line to the south. These two guys can trade off for the night. You keep them awake and alert, the RADAR is worthless, so keep all eyes open. Things will be better tomorrow. You're doing great. Just think of the great sea-story we have here. Let's just hope the ship makes it."

"Okay, Senior, but—"

"But what? We don't have a choice here, Lieutenant. I'll be downstairs handling the radio circuits and watching the OJ-197." That was the big command RADAR console. "You just talk to me on the bitch box every couple of minutes."

"Okay, Senior, we're gonna be okay, right?"

"You bet your ass, young man, we're killing it. You went to the Academy, right?"

"Yes, Senior Chief, that is correct. But they never taught us about this shit."

"This shit, sir, is what it is all about. Think about that." I really didn't know what that rhetorical spiel of bullshit meant myself, but I let it hang there. I wanted to see if he was still functioning in his frontal lobe memory center. I yelled, "Go NAVY!"

Mr. Forbes straightened up and yelled, "Beat Army!" I knew we would be okay.

"I'm going downstairs. As an Academy grad, ask yourself, What would John Paul Jones do?"

More senseless rhetoric as I made my way clumsily down the ladder. I could barely hear Mr. Forbes say, "But John Paul Jones didn't go to the Academy!"

Just as the buoys and technology had predicted, the sea mercifully calmed down as the sun was rising. LT Forbes, Stover, BM3 Overbeek, and I had driven the ship through the storm. The captain was the first one up, just before the sun rose in the east.

That morning at officer's call, the captain made a rare appearance on the fo'c'stle and was somewhat terse. Perhaps he was a little ashamed, nay, disappointed in himself for entrusting his ship to other people. He was a realist. He knew what happened last night. He was not one to bullshit.

"Mr. Forbes, Senior Chief Atwood, you are to strike below. You will stand no more watches from here to PV. I thank you both."

The other sailors were watching and listening with a bit of humility on their faces. I had to say, "Excuse me, sir, but we never would've made it without Stover and Overbeek."

"You're right, Senior. Those two are off the in-port watch-bill in PV. You got that, Chief?" He glanced at the ETC who was the watch-bill coordinator.

"Aye, Skipper, no problems with that, sir," he dutifully responded. I'm sure it was a big problem as the in-port duty sections were undermanned and overtasked, especially in a foreign country. We were all glad that the sun was shining and the sea was becoming a nice and smooth beautiful blue. I love it when the ocean is bright blue.

We would be in Puerto Vallarta in two days, and then Andrea would be there. We had a room. As an E-8, there was no in-port duty. This should be fun.

Fun it was. Andrea rented a Jeep and picked me up at the ship. The captain grabbed me on my way off the brow. "Hey, where are we having drinks and dinner tonight? I owe you, Senior, remember?"

Of course, I remembered, and I planned on taking him up on it. "Let me check with the boss." I did so, and we decided to go to a place called Su Casa. "See you at 1900."

"We will be there, Skipper."

"Get a table for six."

"Consider it done, sir."

Su Casa was just about the nicest restaurant in Puerto Vallarta. The captain and his wife were there. So were the command master chief and his wife. We never spoke a word about the storm or the trip south. True to his word, the skipper picked up the tab for all of us. I must've had ten beers, and Andrea had half a dozen margaritas. It was getting really drunk out when Andrea mentioned that there was a house in Point Loma that we may want to look at. "So buy it!" was my drunken financial advice. Brilliant! We all laughed.

We had a great time in Puerto Vallarta, but as always, it was time to leave. That is the recurring story of my navy life. I was always saying goodbye to somebody somewhere. Whether it was family or friends, I was always on my way to somewhere else.

Thankfully, the sea was calm on the way south. And it stayed that way. We made it to our patrol area with no problems. The ocean was flat. We relieved the USS *Jarrett* on station and settled in to our position. We received a secret turnover brief from FFG-33 full of hot areas and really good intel about where the drug-running bad guys might be doing business. The captain had an agenda, and he shared it with us. We were going to aggressively patrol our area and stop and board every contact and suspect vessel. This guy meant business.

I didn't know all that much about politics, but I knew that financing was very important. On this LEOPS deployment, things were different. If we encountered a target or vessel of interest, no matter what the origin, nationality, or statehood, it took mere minutes before we had state-sanctioned authorization to stop, board, inspect, seize, and, if necessary, sink that vessel. It was a lot of power. So what happened? I think it was something known as money. I'm sure that some folks down here in Central and South America received a very nice payday to allow us to prosecute these vessels on the high seas. It sounds downright pirate-like, but we now had a badge, so to speak, and we weren't afraid to use it.

On a typical day, we would send the helo out. Sometimes nothing would happen. And then nothing would happen again. Every tenth mission or so, we would get what looked like a dirty contact. When that happened, the game was on. Captain Railly could smell blood. We would recover the aircraft and chase down the vessel in question. The ship would "pour on the coal," so to speak. Our little frigate would cut through the water at thirty-plus knots on a calm day.

On this one particular day, and about ten or twelve other days, we came upon a vessel in question. The engineers were screaming that the system was being pushed too hard. It was like on *Star Trek* with Scotty yelling "Captain, I'm giving it all I can. She can't take much more!" We would run these guys down. Here's the best part. We'd close in on the suspected drug runner. The captain would order the gunners mate to fire a volley of 30-mm across the bow of the bad guys' boat. Here was this twenty-year-old kid standing on the deck with his fingers on the trigger of a very powerful and scary weapon. Every time we fired that thing, the suspect vessel would stop. The amazingly professional and proficient Coast Guard contingent would board, detain, and sometimes arrest the crew.

On one occasion, there was over one thousand pounds of pure cocaine stuffed all over the vessel. The crew was arrested. They were cuffed and stuffed in a pen in the helo hangar. The dope was seized and locked up. The vessel was sunk with a fusillade of brutal .50-caliber bullets and grenades. The vessel would have been a hazard to navigation. It had to be sunk. We did this about seven times. It was kind of fun, I must admit.

Of course, I realized that the cartel kingpins would provide us with an acceptable loss for them. They allow a certain amount of product to get seized in one place while ten times that amount was flowing someplace else. We made some headlines. The taxpayers thought that we were actually making a difference. It was a chess game. Despite the headlines, they were still winning.

We did this for six months. We would pull into Panama once a week or so. The captain would host "beer on the pier" in Panama. There would be coolers full of cold beer for fifty cents a can. This barely covered the cost; he subsidized the difference. The idea was to keep the guys close. Of course, we were all authorized and able to go into Panama City and hit the town. I did that a few times. It was pretty boring after a while. It seemed like there were about five songs that played in all the bars. I even started to recognize the girls who hung out or "worked" in the bars. We also went to Guatemala, Venezuela, and a few ports in Mexico on the way home.

It was the last night in Panama that I wish I could do over. We were heading home the next day. The captain had beer on the pier. I decided that I was going to stay on the pier and drink cheap beer, save some money, and get a good night's sleep. I saw Stover leaving the ship and asked him where he was going.

"Just out in town for some dinner and a few drinks."

"Okay, be careful, we're heading home tomorrow."

"Got it, Senior, I'll see you tomorrow."

I didn't think anything more about it. He made it to quarters the next day, although he looked a bit rough. As my good friend

Donald's dad would say, "His eyes looked like two pee holes in the snow." I was not one to cast stones. I'd shown up to quarters more than a shitload of times looking and feeling a bit rough, just like young Mr. Stover. As long as you were on time and could reasonably function, I had no problem with you.

We got underway without incident and started heading north. Wouldn't you know that the entire crew was ordered to submit a sample for urinalysis? That's what they call a "unit sweep." I didn't think twice about it. It meant nothing to me, until a week later, when the results came in. Stover had popped positive.

"Are you fucking kidding me?" I seemed to say that phrase a lot. "Did we have a little too much fun in Panama that last night?"

"It's bullshit, Senior. It's a false positive! I didn't do any drugs, I swear!" He swore up and down that he was innocent of any drug use. I had to back him up. He was my guy. I had no proof one way or another. The captain felt the same and was ready to stand behind this kid. Perhaps he remembered that rough night that we two kept the watch. "Petty Officer Stover, I will go to bat for you to the ends of the earth. The only thing I ask is that you submit to a polygraph or lie detector test. You do that, and I am in your corner, son."

He thought about that for a little and then broke down completely. He went to Panama City on our last night in port. He hooked up with a floozie and succumbed to the temptation of cocaine and sex. It could be a pretty fun combo, but not when you were in the US Navy. The captain's hands were tied. There is a zero-tolerance policy in the navy. He had to kick this kid out of the navy. This very capable, smart, and conscientious sailor would be an ex-sailor as soon as we pulled in to San Diego. It was such a shame. I knew it wouldn't be the end of the world for young Mr. Stover. He would land on his feet. I just wish he would have hung out with us and enjoyed some beer on the pier and stayed out of trouble. You just couldn't take care of everyone all the time. I thought of all the stupid shit I had done over the years and gotten away with. It didn't seem fair that this kid could fuck up once and that was it. Alas, that was it.

We pulled into San Diego on a beautiful Friday morning in early November. Andrea was on the pier like a good navy wife. It was so nice to be home. On the way to our condo, she blew right past the Washington Street exit and got on I-8 toward the beach.

"Where are we going?" I figured maybe a welcome home happy hour with some friends or something.

"I want to show you your new house."

"WHAT? Are you kidding me? What did you do? Holy shit. Where is it?"

"Relax, we haven't bought it yet. If you like what you see, I will need your signature to submit the offer."

"The offer? We made an offer?"

"Not yet, but tomorrow we will. That's if you like it, of course."

"Where is this so-called house?"

"The Wooded Area of Point Loma," she said slyly. She knew that was kryptonite to me.

"You found a house in Point Loma? One that we can afford? There's no way." My mind was racing. I had to ask the obvious question. "How much are we offering for this house in the Wooded Area of Point Loma?"

"499."

"As in thousands of dollars?" I asked stupidly. I knew it wasn't 499 beads or clam shells.

"Yes, that's right. That's what it costs."

I didn't know what to say. "Can we afford that?"

"Yes, I think we can. It needs a bit of work, so we can do a lot ourselves and save some money. I know it's where you always wanted to live."

I had nothing to say. I certainly couldn't argue. She was right. I would kill to live in that neighborhood, if it took all my meager E-8 salary, so be it. This would be a dream come true.

We stopped in front of the place. It was a dump. The roof was shot. The windows were old and crappy. The yard was a wreck. I loved it! "Are you sure we can do this?' I asked her.

"I know we can."

That was all I had to hear. I had learned to trust her business acumen over the years. I was prepared to be a slave to this house and make it our own.

Our offer was accepted, and we would spend the next few years fixing, improving, and renovating our humble little house in the Wooded Area. We soon had a great home in a fabulous neighborhood. Andrea was starting to make some serious cabbage in real estate. I was at the end of my navy career. I was also extremely happy.

I remember the day we moved into our house. The floors were torn apart. The kitchen was a mess. The whole house was a mess for that matter. I could see what it would look like. I had a vision. That was the day that I knew exactly where and with whom I would spend the rest of my life.

UNDERWAY 33

Portman's Return, Melanoma, and Utah

There was a lot of work to do on the house. We were still living in the condo and working on the house after work hours. It was exhausting. Meanwhile, I was still on sea duty, which meant lots of time underway, which was even more exhausting. We were making progress though. We got the roof done and painted the outside. I cleaned up the growth and overgrowth as much as I could with my limited time and tools in port. The whole house was gutted, and the hardwood floors were stripped. We ripped out the kitchen. It was a huge job. Eventually the house was livable, but certainly not cozy or comfortable. We moved out of the condo and rented it to a navy captain. I was now living in my house in Point Loma and the landlord to an O-6. Life was getting weird.

I was still spending weeks at a time underway. There was to be a short yard period followed by a spate of mostly local underway operations and then a deployment to the Persian Gulf. I had now been passed over for E-9 three times. It was not looking good career-wise. My twenty-six-year mark and the end was closing in. I knew it was my career decisions that have kept me at this level, but I honestly did not care. A fella could do a lot worse. I was a senior chief petty officer! I had a house in Point Loma and so much more. I was now over forty and thinking about life after the navy.

Alas, it was time to go out in SOCAL for the compulsory pre-deployment tasking, which meant more system checks and drills. There was firefighting training to be done and a thousand other things. I was underway when the northeast corner of our house had to be jacked up or raised three inches due to settlement. I was gone for about two weeks. It was nice to come home to a level house, but the ceilings were cracked and trashed. I had my work cut out for me. There was a ton of work waiting for me when I got home.

Andrea had a curious look on her face when she told me there was an odd message on the machine from none other than Willie Portman's brother. He said that Willie wanted to see me. "He'd like you to come to Salt Lake for a day," she said.

I had learned to respect her intuition. My own Spidey senses were tingling again like so many times before. I knew that there was something nonstandard going on here. Why would Portman want to see me? After all these years and all our ordeals, I thought we were done. And why didn't he call me himself? His brother left me a phone number. I called it. Curiosity got the better of me. Willie Portman answered on the first ring and sounded strange. He sounded tired and weak.

"Hey, it's Atwood."

"Senior Chief!" The exclamation was dripping with either sarcasm or respect. I'm thinking it was the former.

"What's up, redneck?" It was as if no time had passed. I heard him chuckle, but he still didn't sound good. He got right to business. There was no "How's it going? The wife? the house? The navy?" Nothing.

"I was wondering, no hoping, no insisting that you come to Salt Lake for a quick visit this weekend."

"Are you out of your fucking mind? I am balls deep in a house project that is just about kicking my ass. I've got a wife who will also kick my ass. That's a lot of ass-kicking! Why the fuck are you calling me?"

"Hey, you called me." It was a total kung-fu move, a redirection and brilliant. "It's important that I see you soon. Go to Delta tomorrow morning. There's a first-class ticket waiting for you to SLC. It leaves at noon."

"Wow! An hour and a half in the front of the bus. What the fuck do you want, Portman? I'm about to hang up."

"Atwood, please, just come out for a day. It won't cost you a cent. Come on, for old time's sakes. We were shipmates once, right?"

Goddammit! That's a hard one to argue with. Perhaps it was the Pavlovian training or the indelible shared experiences. I just couldn't say no to the man. The same man who actively tried to ruin me and my career at every juncture. The same man whose grave I was sworn to piss on. I heard weakness in his voice, and a part of me wanted to use that for something, but I didn't know what. Again, the curiosity was getting the better of me.

"Okay, Will. I'll see you tomorrow. I've got to be home on Sunday."

"I've got you on an early flight out to SD. You'll be home for Sunday morning coffee. See you tomorrow. And, hey, Atwood, thank you." He sounded more sad and humble than excited. I knew that this would be a strange trip.

"No problem, neck of the red type. Get some sleep. It sounds like you need it." We hung up.

Andrea was amazingly understanding under the circumstances. We had a lot of shit to do. I didn't have any illuminating, substantiating, or other type of information to support this type of last-minute operation other than an old shipmate wanted to see me and may need help. I had nothing! Maybe she understood that I was bound by some sort of unwritten and invisible duty or code. I think that she knew I would be mentally useless until I got to the bottom of this enigmatic situation. I left for SLC Saturday morning.

True to his word, there was a first-class ticket with my name on it waiting for me. It got better. For the first time in my life, there was a guy standing at the greeting area with a sign with my name on it. "That would be me." Out of habit, I immediately went for my military identification.

"That won't be necessary, sir. The car is this way." I dutifully followed as he grabbed my tiny backpack.

"Where are we going? And what's your name?" I asked. He was a big, strong, and somewhat scary-looking guy. I caught a glimpse of what appeared to be some "prison ink" on his arm.

"To Huntsman, sir. It's a very nice place. I am Curtis."

Well, it was also a very nice day. The sky was bright blue. The mountains could be seen from seemingly everywhere. They were in every direction. It almost felt that you could reach out and touch them. The air was so amazingly clear.

Salt Lake was a grid, like most modern western cities. We left the airport and headed toward downtown Salt Lake City. That was when I realized I had nothing to bring. "Hey, Curtis, can you stop so I can grab some beer and maybe a bottle of Jack?"

"This is Salt Lake. It's not that easy. I'll see what I can do. I should take you to Huntsman first. Tell me what you want, and I'll bring it to you."

"Okay, Curt, I'll chalk that one up to inexperience. How far away are we?"

"Less than ten minutes."

We drove on South Temple and E 100 S until we got to the entrance of the University of Utah campus. Holy shit, what a beautiful and picturesque place! Curtis turned the car past the main entrance and past the disk golf course. The street wound around a little to the west and then north. Just past the medical center, I saw the sign that read Huntsman Cancer Institute. I was starting to get an idea about what was happening here, and I didn't like it.

Curtis parked by the main entrance and opened the door for me. "C-Man, here's a fifty spot. Work your Utah magic and get me some Bud Light and a small bottle of Jack Daniel's. You can keep the change." I thought it wise to stay on this guy's good side. I gave him my cell phone number. "Text me, okay?"

"I'll see what I can do. Follow me. They're waiting for you."

They were indeed expecting me at the reception desk. "Hello, Mr. Atwood. Mr. Portman is on the third floor. Curtis will take you there."

I was kind of blown away and getting very nervous at this point. The place was as beautiful as a hospital could be. The staff couldn't be more pleasant. Wait. Hospital? This couldn't be good. This may have been a big mistake. Nasty little pieces of the puzzle were coming together, and I didn't like the picture that was forming. It was too late now. I was committed.

We got to room 321. Curtis handed me my bag, knocked on the door, opened it for me, and allowed me in. He stayed in the hall and closed the door behind me. I was not prepared for what I saw. The person on the bed did not look like Willie Portman. This was not the broth of a boy of my youthful memory. He looked horrible. Like Death eating a soda cracker, as my father would say. I couldn't help but gasp. The breath just left my body uncontrollably. None of my navy training could've prepared me for this. I almost screamed but managed to stifle the urge. I must've had a dazed, crazed, and amazed look on my face. I guess he was getting used to this reaction.

He managed a strained smile and said, "You look pretty good too." That broke the ice. I'm sure I still looked like a zombie. "Thanks for coming," he added.

"Why am I here? Why are you here? What the fuck is going on, Willie?" I was trying to get control. I had to take in the available information/data and assess the situation; the situation was not a good one. There were all kinds of tubes and electronic equipment attached to his now very frail-looking body.

"I'm dying." Ouch, that was a kick in the balls. I was starting to become situationally aware.

"Yeah? So am I!" I finally responded somewhat sarcastically.

"Hah! I guess we all are. But for once, I'm on the fast track and not you!" Bam! That one was a bit cutting, but he was so calm and matter-of-fact. He was laughing. In a strange way, it was good to hear his laugh. It took me back to a place and time when we were so young with very few pesos in our pockets. It was a moment of joint humanity, but it didn't last long.

"Why am I here, Willie?"

"You're here because I asked you to come, because you're an old friend and shipmate."

My eyes were now rolling back in my head. I was just about to give him the what-for. "Portman, you fuckin' dick!" Just then, he had some sort of seizure or episode. I don't know what it was called. All I know was equipment started making loud noises, and the hospital staff was there in less than five seconds to do what they did.

I just stepped back, and a few seconds later, Willie Portman was alive again and smiling. He stole an Alec Baldwin line from a David Mamet play *State and Main* and said, "So *that* happened." And then he added, "Where were we?"

"Should I go and come back later?" I was getting nervous now.

"Later is a luxury I can't count on anymore, Atwood. You're here now, so stay for a while. At least until they kick you out."

"So, what's wrong, Willie?"

"I have advanced and inoperable melanoma, stage four. They tried a bunch of procedures. They even put me in a coma so they could excise, that's a nice word for cut, chunks of my body out and hope they 'get it all.' Of course, it didn't work, but they had to try, I guess. Now I'm kind of just waiting it out in relative comfort. I'm getting my affairs in order, as they say."

I had to think. My mind was racing. "Wait a minute, melanoma is skin cancer! You grew up in a fucking igloo in Montana!"

"It was a tepee in Idaho, asshole," he dead-panned. Again, his sharp sense of humor under the circumstances caught me off guard.

"My point is, you weren't baked in the sun at the Jersey Shore when you were a kid like I was. Why the fuck do you have skin cancer?"

"That's the million-dollar question, and I'm done with asking it. Consider yourself lucky and check in with a dermatologist every once in a while."

"Jesus Christ, Willie, I don't know what to say. I don't know what to do. What can I do for you?"

"We'll get to that later. As for me, I am well cared for. I'm uncomfortable at times, but I'm not in pain. I'm over the anger. I'm working on closing out old business and making sure my family will be taken care of." I immediately thought that my visit here may somehow be a part of what he thought was "old business." Curtis knocked on the door and walked in with a paper bag with a six-pack of Bud Light and a half pint of Jack, handed it to me, and then walked out without saying a word.

"So how illegal is this, Portman?" I asked, showing him the contraband.

"I don't give a fuck. Crack me a beer and give me a swig of that hooch! I don't think I'll get expelled or sent to mast. We haven't shared a drink in many years, shipmate." He popped a beer, raised it in my direction and said, "To life."

"That was painfully ironic and asshole-like, Portman. Are you going to tell me why you really sent for me?" It was getting to be about four in the afternoon, or 1600.

"I'm not leaving this place, Atwood, not alive anyway. I've come to terms with that. My grandfather would say that I'm leaving feet first. My wife and kids are taken care of. The bills for this upholstered medical Marriott are handled. But that's all material bullshit. My last task is to deal with my past. My karma, if you will. I've been doing a lot of thinking. That's something I didn't do much of in my youth. I feel like I need to set some things straight in order to go in genuine peace."

I was speechless for a few seconds as my feeble little mind (now two beers and two large swigs of JD deep in to this strange situation) tried to process the data.

"Enough about me. Catch me up on you and the navy." He deftly sensed my discomfort and changed the subject. "What's it like to be a chief? Tell me about your ship and crew."

I spoke of Andrea and our house. I told the tale of CPO initiation and a hundred other sea stories. We laughed as hours passed. It had to be well past visiting hours. The nurse poked her head in a few times but never once said anything about me leaving. I got the feeling that he had some pull here. I didn't have time to start wondering why that was so. He dozed off, and I wasn't sure what to do. I decided to walk down the hall and find a bathroom. Curtis was sitting across the hall reading a book.

"Curtis, you're still here?" I was a bit surprised. There was more to this whole thing than I was aware of. I somehow felt that the pieces would be fitting together soon.

"Do you guys need anything?"

"I just need to take a leak, Curtis."

"There's a restroom in Mr. Portman's room or there is one right down the hall on the right."

"I'll go down the hall, Curt, thanks." My brain was running on overdrive as I emptied my bladder. The curiosity was also killing me. I had to see where this strange visit was going. I walked back down the hall, and Curtis opened the door for me. Willie Portman was awake and alert.

"I can't reach the beer. Hook a brother up, will ya?" he said with a laugh. I cracked two, noticing that we were running low. I thought that there had to be something wrong with this, but he was running the show, and no one interfered.

"This is driving you nuts, isn't it, Dan?" It was the first time in over twenty-five years that he called me by anything but my last name. "Thanks for coming all the way out here on such short notice. I think you may have added minutes to my life." We both laughed. "But seriously, I may ask you for a favor someday. It won't cost you anything. Can I rely on you, shipmate?" Things suddenly got serious.

"Will it be legal?" I thought it was a reasonable question. "Probably mostly legal, but promise me you will grant a dying man a last request."

"That's a low blow, Portman. That is an asshole move, even for you." I thought for a foggy second or two. "Playing the Death Card gives me no choice now. I'll do whatever you ask. I promise, shipmate." He had beaten me down. As usual, he played all of his cards perfectly. I promised to do something without any details or information. I was a bad poker player.

"I want you to piss on my grave." I waited for a laugh or a punch line or something, and then I realized he was serious. He asked if I heard him and then repeated his incomprehensible request.

I snapped out of it. "Are you out of your fucking mind, you fucking caveman? I'm not wrapping my head around this, Willie!"

"Yeah, I know, I get that. I want you to know that I am really sorry."

"Sorry about what?"

"I'm sorry for so many things. I want to mend our fences."

"Our fences are just fine, numb-nuts! You're fucking kidding, right? It's good to see you, but if you brought me all the way out here for a joke then you are way dumber than you look." My buzz was rapidly wearing off. Luckily, there was one more beer and a swig of whiskey left. I imbibed.

"I'm sorry for a lot of things I've done in my life, and I'm sorry for the things I have done to you over the years."

I stood up like a lawyer in a courtroom making a vehement objection. "You stop right now dumb-ass. You have done NOTHING to me. I am doing and have been doing just fine. You are being fucking crazy!"

"I deliberately didn't wake you up for watch."

"It all worked out." I felt strangely defensive. Once again, he was in control.

"I threw you under the bus when we got busted breaking in to the galley."

"We all enjoyed a fine breakfast. No harm, no foul.'" I thought to myself, *Bring it on beeyatch!*

"What about setting you up with the pregnant chick in Hong Kong?"

"It was one of the best nights of my life!"

There was a pause as he gathered his thoughts. I don't think he was expecting my parries to his thrusts. This gave me a strange confidence. As if this was some ridiculous argument or debate of some dysfunctional sort. There was a long silence as he mulled over what to say next.

"Did you know that I was the one who sent you to the Gulf in '90?"

"Of course, I did, you mouth-breathing moron! It was the most critical and pivotal point of my career. I wouldn't have made chief if I didn't go to the Gulf. I'm a senior chief now because you sent me to the Gulf!" My voice may have been elevated, but I didn't care. The hospital staff didn't seem to care either. "You don't get it, do you?" I said. He was listening. "Listen to me, you Pocatello-potato-eating punk-ass. Every time you tried to fuck me over, for whatever reason, it worked out in *my* favor. You screw me, and I win. That was the formula. You have nothing to apologize or atone for regarding me and my life and career. Don't you see that, you redneck elk-hunting hayseed?" I was angry and profoundly sad at the same time.

He paused for a few seconds and then smiled. "Okay, Atwood, we'll table it for now. How 'bout we play some cards?"

I knew that he never tabled anything. This issue was not resolved; it was merely deferred. So play cards we did. The game was cribbage. It was now close to midnight. We had played half a dozen games of cribbage. Of course, William J. Portman won all of them. I was dealing what turned out to be the last hand of the night. Curtis had magically showed up with an emergency delivery of beer. I think I drank most, if not all, of them. My brain was still processing the events of the day.

I was getting very tired. So was Portman. At one point, he nodded off. Who could blame the guy?

Okay, perhaps I would go straight to hell. When Willie Portman was sick and passed out on what he asserted to be his death bed, I looked at his cards. I woke him up, and it was the only time I ever beat him in a game of cards! Straight to hell indeed.

The nurses came in and said that it *really* was time for me to go. Portman was out. The poor guy was out like a light. I looked at him, and it was a profoundly sad moment for me. But what I felt or thought didn't matter right now. I wanted to play more cribbage. I wanted to talk more about our lives and a million other things. I was drunk. But he was done. I looked at him and said goodbye. His machinery was still beeping and doing what it was supposed to do. I was sufficiently intoxicated. I was dealing with a lot of shit.

And then I thought, *Poor me. Get over yourself! Your old friend is dying in front of your eyes.* I touched his hand and walked toward the hospital room door. It was after two in the morning.

Curtis opened the door, and I turned to leave when Willie stirred, opened his eyes, and looked at my direction. "I've got your promise right, Atwood?"

"Yes, you sick, insane son of a bitch." I wanted to say more, but I felt horribly inadequate. For a man accused of using too many words, I couldn't find one that was appropriate. What did I say? *Have a good one, dude Take it easy, man. I hope you get better, bro*? No, I just said, "Goodbye, Willie," and numbly walked out of the room.

"Thanks, Atwood." He always got the last word in.

Curtis was standing there. "I'll take you to your room, Mr. Atwood."

"Thank you, Curtis. I don't suppose there are any bars on the way to the room."

"No, sir, there is not. Again, this is Salt Lake. Don't worry, I've got you covered."

"You're a good man, Curtis. Why are you doing this?" I asked.

"Mr. Portman, that would be William's father, gave me a job when I got out of prison in 1980. I started by digging ditches by hand, and I slowly moved up the ranks. We did a lot of building here in Salt Lake."

"There are ranks? How does Willie fit in to all of this shit?"

"Mr. Atwood, you may not know this, but Portman Construction is very big here in Salt Lake."

"Would you please call me Dan, and please tell me how big?"

"Okay, Dan, Mr. Portman and William are the biggest construction and development operation in this valley. They are very well respected in the community. They are very successful, and they are very generous. They put a lot of money back into the community. They're like Salt Lake royalty."

Well, that made sense to me. What I didn't understand was why Portman wasn't bragging on it. The old Portman would've crowed about that all day long. But he was so uncharacteristically humble. I thought to myself, *Could this day get any weirder?*

There were a few minutes of awkward silence. Then Curtis chirped up.

"I feel like I know you, Dan. You know, he really appreciates and respects you. I must have heard the story of how you saved his ass in Korea a hundred times."

"I'm sorry, what happened in Korea?"

"C'mon, you know, he was in the losing side of a tussle and about to get his ass kicked. You came out of nowhere like a "white flash" and put a whoopin' on the dummy that was squared off with Willie. You knocked him out and then ran out the back door." Curtis was laughing. We were almost to the hotel entrance and close to the airport.

"I remember it a little differently, but it was a crazy night." I thought about setting Curtis straight by telling him the actual true story. It was Portman who saved the day, not me. I was baffled why he would change the story. He was such a braggart and bullshit artist. Again, the old Portman would never miss an opportunity to tell a self-important story. Instead he made me the good guy and the one who saved the day. "He is full of surprises, isn't he, Curtis?"

"He most certainly is. It was an honor to meet you, sir."

"You're a good man, Curtis. Thank you for everything." There was about fifteen seconds of silence. "I'm not gonna see him again, am I?"

"Probably not, Dan. I'm sorry."

"I'm sorry too, Curtis. I'm also very happy that I came out here today."

"Your flight leaves at six thirty. You should get to the airport no later than six."

"I can handle that, Curtis. Thank you for everything. Good night, buddy."

"Good night, Dan. Thanks for coming. I know it meant a lot to Willie."

I had nothing more to say. It was a strange and exhausting day. They had a room waiting for me. It was almost two thirty, or 0230. I pretty much figured that I wouldn't get any sleep. The events of the day were still pinging around in my head. I made it all the way to the room and flopped down on the bed before I started sobbing uncontrollably. It all came crashing down, and I lost it completely. It didn't help that I was overtired and half-drunk, but I had myself a full-blown gut-wrenching cry.

I grabbed my bag to retrieve my toothbrush. There was a sixteen-ounce beer and the fifty dollars that I gave to Curtis for drinks. He must have slyly put these items in my bag at some point when I wasn't looking. I thought that was a pretty classy move. He really was a good man.

I tossed and turned for a couple of hours. There was nothing good on HBO or any other channel. I decided to get up and shower and head to the airport. I went to check out at the front desk, and Curtis was in the hotel lobby drinking a coffee.

"Curtis, what the hell? Did you go home? Did you get any sleep? What are you doing here, you nut?"

"I was in the neighborhood. Come on, I'll take you to the airport. Delta right?"

"Yes, Curtis, Delta. Did I mention you are a good man and a bit of a nut?"

"Come on. We're five minutes away." He grabbed my bag, and we walked out to the car.

"I thought you might want some breakfast," he said coyly as I got in the back seat. There was an ice-cold sixteen-ounce Bud Light Lime on the seat.

"You know me too well, sir." I cracked the early morning beverage as we made our quick trip to the airport. I barely had it choked down as Curtis pulled in to the Delta terminal.

"Hey, Curtis, it was a real pleasure and honor meeting you. Thank you for all of your help. I wish you all of the best."

"The pleasure was all mine. I finally got to meet the legendary Dana Atwood." We shook hands. I thought he might break my knuckle bones with his powerful grip. I got through security and made it to the gate and plane. It was an uneventful flight to San Diego. I slept the whole way. Andrea picked me up, and I told her the whole story when we got home. She didn't know what to think, especially about the whole pissing on the grave thing. I think she just chalked it up to stupid-ass macho navy bullshit. I'm sure she was right. It was Sunday, and I was exhausted. Tomorrow, I would be underway again with many thoughts running through my head. It was good to be home. I was so lucky to have such an understanding wife.

That was the day I realized how fragile and fleeting life could be. I realized what we all should know to enjoy our health and our family and friends every day lest they be taken away from us.

UNDERWAY 34

The Last Dance

I had to get underway the day after I got back from Salt Lake City. It was more of the same shit. Flight operations, refueling, and constant drills and training were our mission. Fortunately, this was just a quick five-day shot. We would be pulling back into San Diego on Friday afternoon. I was actually starting to get sick of this shit. We pulled in, tied up, and I drove home. It felt so good to see and be in my house. It was even better when Andrea got home. I went through the pile of mail like I always did, like I had done a hundred times. I saw the dreaded USPS sticky note. What's worse was that the sender was the US Navy. "Oh shit, here we go again." It's never good news when you get a registered letter form the government. I know this from experience.

"What the fuck do they want from me now?" I actually said that out loud, in an empty room. I foolishly asked myself. There was no way in hell they were shipping me out again. That wouldn't make any sense. There were plenty of other swinging dicks out there. The navy did not need yours truly over in the Middle East.

Speaking of which, you may be wondering what impact the operations in Iraq and Afghanistan had on me or the other sailors. The answer is very little. As a blue-water sailor, I/we didn't get too involved with regional conflicts or issues. We still had our basic and fundamental job to do. It's the same job we had been doing since the days of sailing ships and John Paul Jones. We had to keep the sea lanes free and maintain a presence in the world. Secondly, we responded to humanitarian issues worldwide. Think about it. Whenever there was an earthquake, tsunami, or other disasters, the United States Navy was usually the first responder. We were there in Indonesia, in Japan, in India, Bangladesh, and countless other places. We were a rapid response force that was constantly reinventing ourselves as world events unfolded.

There were a few of us that volunteered to go over there. One guy in particular was a first-class electrician named Mac Donald. He was a single guy and was looking to make chief. He accepted 180-day orders to work in a customs unit in Kuwait. He returned with great fanfare from the unit and community. He told a funny story. I asked him a general question about how things went over there and what did he learn. He thought for a few seconds and said, "Yeah, I learned that you should be nice to the fat chicks at the beginning of deployment. Everybody loses weight over there, so when they thin down and start looking hot, they remember that you were nice to them when they were fat. So, when they slim down, you have a better chance of banging them."

I thought that was the most brilliant thing I ever heard, and it was spoken like a true-blue US Navy sailor. The thin blue line still ran through us all, whether we knew it or not.

Back to the mail. I went down to the post office on Canon Street to pick up my mystery letter from the government. I went home and cracked a beer wondering what Uncle Sam wanted from me this time. I can't say that I was surprised with what I read on the very thick stationary with the official letterhead. In short, I was being fired. I read the letter and laughed out loud. The letter basically said that I was creeping up on twenty-six years of service, and the fact that I was a mere E-8; twenty-six years was all I could do. *Thanks for playing. You can see yourself out.* It's called High Year Tenure. You have to move up or move out. So there it was. The end of my career was right there in black and white. I had to laugh again. In many ways, it was a relief. At least I knew exactly when and where my navy career would come to an end.

I went to work the next day and started turning things over to my underlings. It was much easier than I was expecting. These guys were so smart, competitive, and professional; they embraced the opportunity to assume more responsibility. I was very pleased and proud of these young people.

I still had one more very aggressive underway period ahead of me. We would be gone for almost three weeks. It was a trip that would take us north to San Francisco, California, Seattle, Washington, Anchorage, Alaska, and Vancouver and Victoria, British Columbia. There were a thousand evolutions in between. It was my last underway. It wasn't without humor.

We had a new skipper, a five-foot-three firebrand of a female navy commander. I liked her, and she trusted me. One night, she called down to CIC when I was on watch. She said that we needed to be in a certain position at a certain time. What course and speed did we need to go to get there on time? A simple time/distance problem; I could do it in my sleep. But that's too easy. I called one of the Ezes. It was Gonzalez.

"OS3, we need to be here at 0700 tomorrow, figure out a course and speed. We need to pass it up to the bridge." In my mind, I was busting out a chart and plotting the latitude and longitude, plotting the distance with a set of dividers and a ruler. This kid sidled up to one of our newer systems called Global Command and Control System, GCCS or "Geeks." He rolled the ball tab or cursor out to the position and dropped a symbol, or "pin" as we say today. Another simple click and drag gave him the distance. We knew the time factor, so it took about five seconds to calculate the speed. What would've taken me five minutes, he did in less than thirty seconds. I realized that it was indeed time for me to go. These kids were just too sharp.

"That looks good to me. Send it up to the captain."

A few minutes later, the captain came in and said, "That's exactly what the Navigator said, only it took them much longer to come up with a solution. You guys are good."

"It wasn't me, Skipper. OS3 Gonzalez just used the GCCS to figure it out. It was all him. These guys are good indeed!" It was a shameless effort to promote my guys.

"I agree, Senior Chief, but there is no I in team." It was a stale and tired old "leaderism." I let it slide.

OS3 Gonzalez then chimed in and said, "And there's no I in bukkake either, Captain!" (Go ahead, if you're over eighteen, google it, if you don't know what it is already. I will wait.) The captain walked out of combat. It was a good thing she was so short, because that bukkake missile flew right over her head.

"Holy shit, Gonzalez. Did you just say that to the captain? Are you a fucking retard?" Then I started laughing. That may have been the funniest thing I had heard. It was so out of left field, so obscure and actually correct. I couldn't be mad. It was a true statement. There *is* no *I* in *bukkake*!

I spoke of this last underway at the beginning of this journey. This would be it for me. I honestly felt that the navy was a better place now than when I had found it.

That was the day I abdicated all my power and turned my navy over to the next capable and more competent generation. I was done.

UNDERWAY 35

Retirement

Andrea picked me up when the ship pulled in. "This is the last time you'll be doing this, you know," I said to her.

"Are you sad?" she asked me.

"No, I'm not sad. I'm relieved. I've made it through twenty-six years of this insanity. Besides, I'm a sailor, I know how to say goodbye and move on."

She had a strange look on her face. It was a look of concern. "Okay, sailor, let's go home. I'm very proud of you." When we pulled in to the driveway, she started to get nervous.

"Hey, what's wrong? You look like you're upset. What is the problem?" She was never one to hide her feelings, and she had many of them. Not a poker player, this one. "Do you want to tell me something?" I asked her.

"Just listen to the answering machine when we get inside."

I pretty much had it figured out at this point. "It's Portman, isn't it?"

"Just listen. I'll get you a beer," she said sullenly. She brought the cold beer, and I inhaled it in about 12.256 seconds.

I threw my bag in the bedroom and hit the Play button. It was Portman's brother telling me that Willie had died. He thanked me for being a good friend and said that he mailed me a package as per his brother's instructions.

As the words were coming out of the machine, Andrea handed me a package that was postmarked in Salt Lake City, Utah. She had such a sad and caring look on her face, and she hugged me. "I'm so sorry about your friend, honey."

"It's okay, I've been expecting this. I'm prepared for it. It's just a shame. I think he had a lot more to do in his life. It's a bummer."

"I'll leave you alone. Do you want another beer?"

"That would be nice. Thank you."

I opened the package already knowing what it was going to say. I was surprised to see one thousand dollars in cash in an envelope. There was a short handwritten letter.

Dana, if you're reading this I am gone. I left on good terms. I'm glad you came out to see me. I'm glad you are doing well. I'm sure you are a good Chief. We both know how important that is. I will be at Mountain View Cemetery in Pocatello, Idaho. It's near Idaho State University and State Route 30 and I-15. I've got a great view of Putnam Mountain. You'll find it. Shit, you can navigate a ship across an ocean, you can find a grave in Idaho.

That line really hit me hard. I was reading this letter from the grave, and he was talking about his own grave site. A chill went down my spine.

You know why I am writing this. I'm sure you remember the promise you made. I expect you to make good. I'll see you in Hell, Jersey Boy!

And that was it. Portman was gone, and I had to fulfill the most unusual dying request in the history of mankind. If anyone knows of a crazier one, I am all ears. The most pressing issue ahead of me now was finalizing my twenty-six-year navy career. Mr. Portman could wait for now.

I had a month left in the navy. I started thinking about a retirement ceremony. It's what you did at this point. I wanted a very small gathering on the ship. Just some friends and family. I wanted my father there, but that was it.

That wasn't good enough for Andrea. As usual, she took it to the next level. She invited every old shipmate, my entire family, and her entire family. She arranged a big party room with a lawn at the Fleet ASW base for the reception. There would be heavy hors d'oeuvres and plenty of beer and wine. That was the reception. The ceremony would be on the flight deck of the ship.

My retirement ceremony was a lovely affair. It was February in San Diego, and the temperature was over 80 degrees. The East Coast people were loving it. My father, mother, and stepmother were all there. All my siblings were there with all of their kids. My old friends Achilles and Mark came all the way from New York. Good ole Hancock dragged his family from Arizona. People came from all over. My good friend from the MIUW, Chris Parker, came down from Seattle. He was now a PHD in political science and a professor at Washington University. (Go, Huskies!) Paulie and Brad the Nad flew out from Virginia. I couldn't believe the turnout. It was most humbling.

The captain said some very nice words. She was a little over-the-top in saying how wonderful I was. But then again, maybe not. My friend Master Chief Mike Karr did a great job roasting me and making everyone laugh. Then it was my turn. I really didn't know what I was going to say. I'd been to a thousand of these things, and I didn't want to be lame like some I had seen. My father taught me to always start with a joke. I thanked everyone for coming and then commented that my parents were sitting next to each other. "That is a testament to the strength of these ships. Master Chief, have a damage control team standing by just in case." Big laughs. Most people knew of the tempestuous relationship of my parents.

I mostly spoke of our navy and the fantastic young people who run it. I honestly don't remember much of the content of my speech. I know that I thanked my wife. There is a recording somewhere, but I refuse to watch it. I was in the moment, and the moment was over.

I gave my wife flowers, and I was piped over the side. That's a remnant rite from the British navy that we still adhere to today when someone is leaving the ship for the last time. Their peers—in this case, the chiefs—formed two opposing lines and saluted Andrea and me one last time. It was all I could do to keep it together. I wanted to crawl into a ball and cry. I couldn't do that in front of the guys and my dad. It was by all accounts a lovely affair.

The reception and after-party at the house was legendary. We raged like rock stars. I had so much fun with my family and old friends. I've got a stack of Polaroids somewhere documenting the debauchery. It was a fitting end to my life in the navy. Andrea set the whole thing up. It would've been lame without her.

So that was it. I had already packed up and removed most of my stuff from the ship. There were some uniform items, clothes, a couple of books, and my coffee cup that were retrieved by one of the chiefs and brought to my house. I was done. I had to go down to the Naval Station for some paperwork and a complete medical exam. I got a new retired ID card.

I had some connections and a line on a civilian job in Tactical Data Link software right here in Point Loma.

Eventually the family, friends and guests all went home. There were many trips to the airport. Things finally calmed down. Andrea and I were alone in a now quiet house. It was nice.

"So what now, Senior Chief?" she asked me. I think she knew where my head was at and what I was thinking.

"Well, I get a real job and hope that I live long enough to actually enjoy a real retirement. I've got a few irons in the fire. But there is one thing I have to do first."

I got online and booked a ticket to Pocatello, Idaho. There was a promise I made to an old friend and shipmate.

That was the day I embarked on the second part of my life.

EPILOGUE

I got a civilian job with the US Navy developing, testing, and integrating tactical data link software. I now work four minutes from home and travel quite a bit. I go wherever the US Navy and our allies are operating tactical data links. My territory is the planet Earth. When I am not traveling, I like to spend time at home.

I had a rare Saturday off to myself in March of 2012. I had finished all my weekly chores. I cracked a beer and sat on the couch to watch some college basketball with my dog. She's a big North Carolina Tarheel fan. I was just getting comfortable when my little white dachshund started barking wildly like she always does when a person is walking up the stairs toward the door. I didn't want to deal with a Jesus person or a salesperson, so my Op-Plan was to ignore. The dog then did something odd. She stopped barking like a rabid maniac and started whining and sniffing at the bottom of the door. This behavior piqued my interest. I looked through the peephole and saw a tall and slender Asian man. I opened the door. There was a handsome young man, maybe about twenty-five or thirty years old, unusually tall for an Asian. I guessed from experience that he was Japanese. He looked familiar. The dog was relentlessly sniffing his feet, ankles, and as far up this stranger's leg as her comically small body would take her. She was very excited about something, and I was curious.

"How can I help you, young man?" I felt as though we had met somewhere, but I couldn't put my finger on it, maybe on one of my business trips to Japan.

"Mr. Atwood?" he asked somewhat sheepishly.

"Yes, how can I help you?" I repeated myself. "There is a basket-ball game about to start, and I would like to watch it."

"North Carolina and Wake Forest?" he asked. "The Heels will spank them." There was just a hint of accent. Whoever this guy was, he had spent a lot of time in the States. It wasn't just the lack of accent; it was the use of slang and nuance. "Forgive me, sir, my name is Tatsuya, Tatsuya Imaichi." He offered his hand, and of course, I took it out of habit.

His name triggered a strange process in my brain. *Imaichi*. Did he say Imaichi? "Did you say Imaichi?" The pieces were falling in to place.

My head began to spin and then it flew out of control when he said, "Naoko was my mother."

It was supposed to be a simple afternoon on the couch watching TV, and it just got weird. It was about to get weirder. I was processing a lot of data. The dog's behavior, a tall Amerasian named Imaichi at my door. The fog cleared a little bit, but I was stuck on one word. "What do you mean Naoko *was* your mother?" I was still trying to make sense of things.

"She was lost at Fukushima after the earthquake and tsunami. She was on a business trip, and we never saw her again." He lowered his head and looked very sad. The door was still open as I was trying to gather my thoughts. I snapped out of it. I started to feel kind of sick.

"I'm so sorry, Tatsuya-San, please come in." I thought my lame attempt at trying to speak a little of his first language would help. I was at a loss. "Can I get you anything?"

At the same time, we both said, "I could use a beer." There was an uneasy but pleasant joint chuckle. I went into my garage "Man-Cave" and brought up two Bud Lights. I offered one to Tatsuya. There was an uncomfortable silence. I had some questions. I wanted to know everything about her, but I just asked why she was at Fukushima.

"She spoke Russian and was escorting and translating for a group of Russian scientists who were touring the facility."

There were a million more questions, but it was time for an important one. I had a good hunch what the answer would be. "So why are you here telling me this?"

"This very awkward for me, sir. I have practiced this in my mind many times." He took a deep breath. "Mr. Atwood, I am your son."

That was a bombshell. I was not expecting this. But on the other hand, I can't say that I was totally surprised. I had kind of figured it out. He is a stunningly handsome man! He has my eyes. Of course, the dog knew well before I did, but the words still hit me in the chest like a baseball bat. Again with the awkward silence.

"Let's go and sit down." It was almost tip-off time. "I'm trying to take it all in. First of all, I am just sick about Naoko, your mother. She was so lovely and smart, so pretty. Holy shit. Please realize that this is a lot for me to handle."

"Of course, here is my number in Los Angeles. This was rude of me. I apologize." He got up to leave.

"No! Please stay here. We need to talk." He sat down on the couch. The dog was whining and looking at him like she was in love. She could tell that this stranger was upset. It's amazing how intuitive their little brains can be.

"So you are my biological son." I must've sounded a bit incredulous. He nodded yes "So I'm guessing you're about twenty-five or so."

"I am twenty-seven, sir."

"Okay, enough of the sir shit! My name is Dana." He nodded again and remained silent. "Well, the math makes sense, born around 1984. It's just that I…I never knew about you. Why didn't she tell me? Why did you wait so long?" I had so many questions. I sat there for a minute and wondered if this day could get any stranger. Maybe if Seton Hall beat Duke. Then I realized that it could get stranger indeed. Andrea was not home yet. "I always thought that when I didn't go back to get her at the Naval Base gate in Yoko that day, she was probably so angry that she wisely wrote me off despite all of my written apologies and the begging for forgiveness. When I couldn't go and tell your mother in person, it drove me crazy! I felt horrible. She deserved so much better. I never heard from her again. Why?"

There was a tirade brewing in my little brain. Flood gates were opening up. Emotions I hadn't felt in almost thirty years were cresting. I was still trying to grasp the fact that Naoko was dead. And the way she died was so horrible, that poor, beautiful little girl. I bet her last thoughts were of her son. A son, who was also my son, who was now sitting in front of me for the first time after all these years.

"It's because of me, Dana. She found out she was pregnant and didn't want to burden you with responsibility. She always spoke very fondly of you. I know that she loved you at one time. So much so that she thought you were better off without her and a son. She always put other people's needs ahead of her own. She knew that you had no choice."

I had to think to myself that perhaps I should've been given a choice. Then I remembered the person I was when I was nineteen. That person was not capable of making a choice of this kind of importance. Even in our youth, she knew what was best for everyone.

I knew that in Japan, children of mixed race were looked down upon. In fact, if you were not 100 percent Japanese, you were "*Gaijin*." That meant you may be human, but you were not Japanese. It sounds very racist because it is.

That got me curious. "Tell me how you grew up. Was it hard being half-American? What about your schooling? How are your grandparents? What are you doing now? I have so many questions!"

"I grew up with my mother and my grandparents in their house in Kagashima." I thought back to that night so long ago when we met in Kagashima at the American Club. It was a special night. He continued, "I went to school and was subject to some racism, but that stopped when I got to be the biggest kid in the class."

We both chuckled. Then I got pissed. I thought, *Some punk-ass Jap kids are making fun and bullying my son!* I'd been a father for five minutes, and I was ready to fight. He told me that he had been speaking English his whole life. In fact, by the time he was ten, his English was better than his mother's.

"How did you know how to find me?"

"I always knew your name, so I googled you, of course. You're actually pretty easy to find. You might want to think about that."

I had plenty to think about right about now. "Why did you wait so long to contact me?"

He explained that his mother forbade him to contact me in any way, and being the good, loyal Japanese son, he obeyed. He told me that after Naoko died, his grandparents only lived another year and died within a month of each other. They were heartbroken. Naoko had a younger brother, but for whatever pigheaded, old-school reason, he resented Tatsuya and denied his existence. Perhaps the Japanese racist gene skipped a generation on the male side. By his account, his grandfather was a loving and fair father figure for him growing up.

"What do you do now?" I asked.

"I am a doctor. I went to UC Irvine undergrad and UCLA medical. I specialize in ocular surgery." Double holy shit! Maybe I did need Maury Povich to test some DNA here. *A doctor, are you kidding me!*

"What is ocular surgery?" I was such a dummy.

"When someone has severe blunt cranial trauma, I can rebuild their eye sockets and restore the eyes, hopefully with their sight, as well as cosmetically. There are also orbital surgeries and prosthetics involved." He said this to me very matter-of-factly, calm, and professionally.

He was looking at me like I knew what the hell he was talking about. "Are you sure you are my son?" That got a laugh out of him.

We watched TV a little as the Tar Heels put a holy whoopin' on the Demon Deacons. What a strange day. We watched the rest of the game and talked a lot over some more beers. He did most of the talking. He also had a lot of questions for me. He was understandably intrigued with my family history. I told him about my parents, their genealogy and lineage. He was very interested that my mother was a nurse and my grandfather was a dentist. He seemed to be reaching for some sort of familial connection.

I saw Andrea's car pull up, and the dog started barking at the familiar sound of it. Oh boy, here we go. She opened the door with her usual hand full of bags. The dog was freaking out as if she was telling her in dachshundese what was going on. It was all very exciting for the dog. Tatsuya and I stood up. I wasn't sure what to say. She intuitively picked up on the uneasy atmosphere.

I introduced her to Tatsuya. "Andrea, this is Tatsuya, he's, uh, from Japan. He's a doctor! He's uh…well, you see, it's kind of funny…" While I was falling all over my dick trying to find words, the look on her face told the whole story. She knew! How do women and dogs do that? Tatsuya was about to speak, and I finally nutted up and found the words. It was perhaps my first fatherly act. "It turns out that Tatsuya here is my son, Andrea. How 'bout that?" Okay, they were dumb words, but it was all I could come up with. I must've looked and sounded like the biggest dork!

"How do you do, Tatsuya? It is nice to meet you." I think she had the same dazed look that I must've had when the bomb was dropped on me. The girl was just coming home to her dog and husband (notice I put dog first). She looked at me with a look that I had never seen before. That made sense. It was a pretty fucked-up situation, and I was getting very nervous. This could get pretty ugly pretty fast.

"It's an honor to meet you, ma'am."

"Please call me Andrea. Would you like to stay for dinner tonight?" I don't think that she heard the words that she was saying. It seemed to be some sort of default response, a delay tactic, as another part of her brain was processing the situation.

I whispered in his ear, "You should do what she says. She's pretty bossy."

He stayed for dinner. We drank a ton and talked late into the night. He wisely spent the night in our guest room. We had imbibed quite a bit, and understandably so.

Our house is kind of small. The guest room is right across the hall from our bedroom. It's not very well insulated, so sound travels quite well from room to room. Andrea and I were lying in bed with the events of the day pinging around our brains like so many pinballs. Of course, we had to talk, but we had to do it in whispers. I told her the whole story from Blondi barking until she walked in the door.

"Andrea, I don't know what to say. I'd say I'm sorry, but I never knew anything. I can't be sorry about something I didn't do or something I didn't know about. Having said that, I'm sorry. You shouldn't have to deal with this. It's not fair to you."

"Emmitt Dana Atwood, being sorry doesn't help anything. We are grown-ups. All of us are, including your son." It was starting to get a little loud in our quiet house.

That was the first time I heard those two words spoken to me. *He is my son.* I shouldn't have drunk so much. "What do I do now? I don't know what to do."

"You will do what is right. *We* will do the right thing." We were still whispering. I wondered if he could hear us through the walls, probably.

"But why now all of a sudden out of nowhere?"

"Are you really that fucking stupid?" I knew she was serious with that language. She usually saved the salty stuff for when she was pissed off at me. I must have said something stupid.

"The boy lost his mother in the most horrible way possible. His grandparents are gone. He's got an uncle that won't talk to him. I don't know about his friends, but it sounds like he wasn't all that popular growing up. Dana, you dummy, you're the only family he has! He's reaching out to you. You can give the boy, I mean man, a grandfather! Can you imagine what he must be feeling? Accept him and embrace him. It's the right thing to do!" I don't think she was whispering very well anymore.

Of course, she was right as usual. I knew it the whole time, but I guess I needed to hear it for validation purposes. "Do you think I can do it?"

"Of course, you can do it! We can do it. I don't see a choice in the matter. I mean, it's not like he's a little boy in diapers. There's no child support. There's no risk of this situation winding up on day-time TV. He's a nice, smart, and very handsome guy."

"Of course, he is." I looked at her with my best love look and thanked her. I was so relieved that something that could've gone so horribly bad turned out to be a strangely positive and ultimately wonderful event. Andrea is truly magnificent. We were both a bit overcome with emotion. We hugged with a love that I had never experienced. We were both crying, but we weren't sad, far from it. It was a nonstandard but good day. It may have been the best day of my life.

That was the day I became a father in perhaps the most unconventional and unexpected way. It turned into a real George Baily or "butterfly effect" moment. When I had a moment alone with my brain, I did some thinking. I thought about the meaning of it all. That's always a mistake. I thought about all the what-ifs. That's a mistake too. What if I had just pulled out that one time in 1983 or, God forbid, used some sort of contraception? There would be no Tatsuya, and Naoko would probably still be alive. She would most likely be married to a Japanese businessman somewhere with five children. Maybe one of her children would rule the world someday. Maybe find a cure for cancer or male pattern baldness.

Tatsuya is a world-recognized ocular surgeon. He saves lives and improves the lives of people every day. I'm not saying that you can trade one outcome for another. Of course, we can't do that; it's impossible to rank the importance of life's events. There are too many things going on, too many twists and turns, moving parts. So many of these things are unknown and unseen. So many things that affect our lives are out of our control. That is why it is so important to try to control the things that you can as best you can and don't beat yourself up when something unexpected happens.

Tatsuya and I have become rather close. It's no longer awkward. Our family and friends have embraced him. His grandfather proudly introduced him to the gang at the VFW in Manasquan, New Jersey. He was a big hit. All the girls love him.

The two of us went to a San Diego Padres game against LA at Petco Park one Sunday afternoon. He had the nerve to root for the dreaded Dodgers. Since he went to college, medical school, and lives up there, I gave him a waiver.

He got up at one point after the third inning and got us a beer. He returned to the seats and handed one to me and said very casually, "Here you go, Dad."

My eyes welled up immediately and uncontrollably. I felt like I had swallowed a hockey puck. I couldn't speak to say *Thank you, son.* There would be time for that. Thankfully, the Padres turned an impressive double play, so I was able to disguise my emotions in the moment. I was a mess.

I don't know much, but I know that I have somehow escaped death and dismemberment. I have been to war. I made it through a gauntlet of unpredictable and hard-to-imagine madness. I also have a loving and understanding wife, great friends, and family. I have a grown son who is ten times better than me and the best dog in the world! I never would have had any of these experiences, I wouldn't be who or where I am today if I hadn't decided so long ago to spend a lifetime underway.

Printed in the USA
CPSIA information can be obtained
at www.ICGtesting.com
CBHW031459160224
4391CB00008BA/177

9 781684 561650